D0709192

THE
RECKONING

ALSO BY JEFF LONG

FICTION

Angels of Light

The Ascent

Empire of Bones

The Descent

Year Zero

NONFICTION

Outlaw: The Story of Claude Dallas

Duel of Eagles: The Mexican and U.S. Fight for the Alamo

THE RECKONING

JEFF LONG

POCKET BOOKS
New York • London • Toronto • Sydney

This book is a work of fiction. Names, characters, places and incidents are products of the author's imagination or are used fictitiously. Any resemblance to actual events or locales or persons, living or dead, is entirely coincidental.

 POCKET BOOKS, a division of Simon & Schuster, Inc.
1230 Avenue of the Americas, New York, NY 10020

Copyright © 2004 by Jeff Long

Originally published in hardcover in 2004 by Atria Books

All rights reserved, including the right to reproduce
this book or portions thereof in any form whatsoever.
For information address Atria Books, 1230 Avenue
of the Americas, New York, NY 10020

ISBN: 1-4165-1470-8

First Pocket Books trade paperback printing May 2005

10   9   8   7   6   5   4   3   2

POCKET and colophon are registered trademarks of Simon & Schuster, Inc.

Cover art and design by Tony Greco

For information regarding special discounts for bulk purchases,
please contact Simon & Schuster Special Sales at 1-800-456-6798
or business@simonandschuster.com

Manufactured in the United States of America

For Emma, my wild love went riding. . . .

THE
RECKONING

PROLOGUE

They fish him from the Mekong like a long, pale dragon, shouting and prodding him with bamboo poles, full of dread. He thinks his white skin scares them, or his loincloth made from the last strips of his American uniform.

Babies cry. A dog won't come close.

A village. He laughs at his good fortune. *Home free.*

"Food," he demands. "America."

They scatter at his voice. Their fear gives him heart.

He is mostly blind by now. His legs are too heavy to move. He can barely lift his head. He lies there like Gulliver in the gray rain.

After a while some brave soul sneaks close enough to tie his ankle with a vine. They leave him in the mud on the bank above the flood, tethered like an animal. This sobers him. He must appear very weak or they would bind him properly. But he seems to have some value or they would kill him or feed him back into the river.

As a Boy Scout, he was taught when lost to follow water downstream. And so for over a week he has been on the move, fording creeks that became muscular tributaries, climbing down around waterfalls and rapids, swimming, and finally drifting on a huge gnarled ship of a tree down the river. Evading and escaping, he'd thought.

He remembers emerging from the forest and its dark shadows, and working through seas of grass, following the water. He expected to descend into light. But as the waters mounted, so did his darkness. When it wasn't raining, monsoon clouds covered the sun. Day by day, his eyesight has decayed. He blames the water. The river is filled with parasites. Or the rain is driving him blind.

Before losing his compass, his course was reliably west by southwest, away from the savage borderlands. Away from the lotus-eating madness infecting his comrades. Deeper into Cambodia.

But the farther he traveled, the more things seemed to melt from him. His paper map dissolved the first day. His clothing flowered with fungus and blue moss and fell apart. His web gear and rucksack vanished. Possibly animals stole his boots in his sleep. Thinking it was his rifle, he carried a tree limb for miles. The illusions nibbled him away. Now they have him.

The men sit at a distance, out of the rain, watching him. He can hear their whispers and smell their tobacco pipes. Raindrops patter on his eyeballs. He can't shut his lids anymore. It should hurt, but it doesn't. He stares into the rain drumming on the bones of his head.

Like every prisoner in a foreign land, he clings to his exceptional circumstances, his singularity. He is young, just nineteen. If he could stand, he would tower over his captors. He has a girlfriend waiting for him. He can throw a football, do algebra in his head, and play "House of the Rising Sun" on the guitar. His folks have the Chevy he rebuilt parked in their garage. If only he could explain. Coming here was not his doing. Somehow the currents brought him to this point in time. The war was somebody else's idea.

At last his captors feed him. Out of caution or because of the rain, they don't light a fire, so there is no rice or cooked food. They give him a little fruit, plus insects and water creatures. By this time, after so many weeks subsisting in the forest, he knows some of the tastes and textures. Crickets have a nutty flavor. The beetles crunch more. The shrimp still wiggle. He is so hungry.

They can't bring enough over the coming days. As his sight fails, he grows more ravenous. He chews grass, tree buds, even clay, anything to slake the hunger. While he can still crawl, they let him forage, moving his tether when he has consumed everything in a circle.

Floating on the great tree in the river, he dreamed of being carried out to sea. Peasant fishermen would find him, or sailors or pirates who would ransom him. Or the U.S. Navy would gather him in. He would be saved.

On the third day, guerrillas arrive. With the last of his vision, he realizes that he has traded one set of shadows for another, the shapes in the forest for these gray phantoms. The world has blurred, but he can still see that they wear black. He recognizes the banana clips in their rifles. The only mystery is their red-checkered scarves. They are a whole new species of enemy to him.

They speak in whispers above him. He can't understand a word. They seem afraid and uncertain of what to do with him. He lies among their legs, stranded in the tonnage of his body. He despises them. He despises himself. In their place, he'd waste him. But all they do is wait.

The men in black pants and red scarves are the last sight he sees. Soon after their arrival, his blindness completes itself. He can't tell day from night anymore. Time slows. The rain comes and goes, thick and warm as piss.

Maybe two more days go by. His limbs grow heavier, heavy like the earth. He listens to the river. Occasionally someone touches his eyes with a twig. That and the rain, like flies he can't kill. He is losing his mind.

Then one day, or night, a man speaks to him in English. "Are you awake or asleep?" he says. His voice is close to the soldier's ear.

The soldier thinks it must be a dream. He hears men murmuring nearby. "Hello?" he calls.

"Look at you," the voice says, clearly shocked. "How has this happened?"

The young soldier fills with hope. "Thank God," he says. He would reach for the man's hand, but can't lift his arms. "I prayed. Who are you?"

"A passenger, like you. They sent for me. I came to help." He sounds like a Frenchman. He could be a colonial, maybe a doctor or a priest.

"Can you save me?"

"I will do what is possible. But time is short. You must tell me everything."

Like holy confession. A priest, he decides. The soldier calms himself. He has to play this right. "Whatever you want, Father. I'm blind. My arms are like stone. I'm eating dirt. What's happening to me?"

There is a pause. "Let us talk."

"Something's wrong with my eyes, Father."

"Yes, your eyes. Can you see?"

"Not really."

"Something, surely."

"Nothing real. Only a dream, the same one. I'm in the forest again. There are giant heads, and spires with monkeys. I need medicine, Father. Can you get me to the Americans? They'll pay you."

The stranger evades his plea. Not good. Whose side is he on? "Where did you come from?" the stranger asks.

"Chicago, Father. America."

"Yes." The man is patient with him. His voice is kind. "You mentioned a city, where this curse began."

A curse, exactly. That's what this was. "You mean the ruins?"

A silence, then, "You found the city?" The ruins excite him. He seems to know them, or of them.

"On a mountain, Father. Right when we needed it. An old place surrounded by walls. Wild, you know, unreal."

"The wars have not injured it?"

"It's untouched, like a thousand years ago. There was no sign of anybody. It was empty."

More silence. The man asks, "Do you remember the way?"

What way? Water flowing into water? But this could be his ticket home. "Absolutely. I can show you once I'm better."

"And the rest of your men?"

The soldier could deny their existence. He could hide them. But now he has mentioned "we," and he is desperate. "They're still there, all of them. I told them to come with me. But they chose a fool over me. We followed him onto the mountain. He led us wrong, then told us to stay. So he died for his sins. And the rest of them will, too."

His interrogator is quiet a minute. He doesn't ask how many Americans are left, nor their unit or any military information. His only interest seems to be the ruins.

"*Âme damnée,*" the man finally murmurs.

The American has no idea what that means. "Yeah," he says, "like that."

"Fallen angels," the priest says. "And yet you escaped."

The soldier grows wary. "I warned them. We were coming apart at the seams. Everyone was afraid. We were lost. There were voices at night. No one knew who to trust or what to do. It was every man for himself. Finally, I left to get help. They won't last long up there. I followed the water. The water brought me here."

"Are they fossilizing as well?"

The young soldier can't cut through the accent. "What?"

"Your eyes," the priest says.

The soldier grows quiet. "What about them?"

"You have not touched them?"

A hand hoists his heavy wrist and guides his fingers to his face. He feels the familiar shape of his cheekbones and forehead, but avoids his eyes. He doesn't want to know.

"Touch them," the voice says.

"My eyes?"

"I, too, am maimed," the priest tells him. *Mayhem-ed,* it sounds. "There was a bomb. This was a year ago. For a time, I could not bear to see what was left of my body. But at last it was necessary. I had to touch the wounds. Do you understand? We must accept our fate."

The soldier feels his dead eyes. "Oh lord, help me." The lids are peeled back in wide round circles. His eyes are as hard as polished jade. He knows from the ruins what they look like, the green jade eyes. They don't belong in his face.

His hand is returned to his side. It settles upon the mud, like an anchor. His fingers sink into the earth.

"Father? Don't leave me."

"I'm here."

"What will happen to me?"

"The people are afraid. They want you to go away."

"Put me on the river. I'll go. Far away."

"I will put you on the river," the man promises.

Relief floods the soldier. Even blind, he has a chance. "Thank you, Father. Tell them thank you."

"Don't come back to their village, that's all they want. Put this place out of your mind."

"I swear."

"But remember the city. It is punishing you. I think you must return to there someday."

Not in a million years. "Yes, Father."

Then the soldier hears a sound he knows too well, the drawing of a knife. It is done softly, but there is no mistaking the linear hiss. The murmurs stop in the distance. "What are you doing, Father?" he whispers.

"Releasing you," the voice answers, "so that you can finish your journey."

The soldier's heart thunders in his chest. He waits for a tug at his ankle, for the vine tether to be cut. Instead a hand grips his forehead. His throat is bared.

From the start, he knew this was no priest. But he couldn't help but hope. He still can't. "Forgive me, Father," he says. "I was only trying to go home."

"Be brave." The voice is kind. "The dream goes on."

1.

She arrived on the remains of a big American deuce-and-a-half left over from the Vietnam War, its black and olive camouflage peeling. Rust gored its flanks. The beast had no brakes, or if it did, the driver—plastered with burn scars and missing three fingers—had some superstition against touching them. They began their halt a mile out, a matter of patient downshifting and calculation.

"Here?" Molly had to shout her disbelief over the engine noise.

The driver shook his head, not here. He gestured farther ahead.

Through the cracked windshield, the land lay flat and checkered with rice paddies. The mop-topped sugar palms bent at wacky angles and the far-off villages perched on tall, skinny stilts reminded her of the illustrations in a Dr. Seuss book. In every direction, the horizon melted into haze and heat mirages.

Molly thought there must be some mistake. There was no sign of a dig or a camp. And it was so hot. The heat drove at her. It disowned her. She shoved back at it, trying to belong.

The New American West was her gig, not Asia, especially not the part with dead souls from the baby boomers' war. Her writer friends were baffled. They already thought she was made in the shade. She was the get-girl for photo features about ski country plutocrats, gang bangers on the rez in Navajo country, crop circles in Nebraska, and psychotherapy for brain-damaged Everesters who would be king. She had a regional following and a cute Victorian town house in Boulder.

Why risk her place in the universe? To them, Cambodia was like some weird fit of hubris. Molly could barely explain it to herself.

She had first learned of the existence of an official grail quest for soldiers' bones at a gallery opening in Taos. The artist's brother was a navy kid full of tales. Something in his mention of a circular, never-ending bone hunt funded by taxpayer dollars had triggered her instincts. The *New York Times* had gone for it. Now she was here.

A white rag hung from a bamboo pole, and she decided that was their landmark. Her sense of relief as well as her misgivings welled up all over again. She wanted the forensics team to see in her a kindred spirit. Like them, her job was to lay bare old secrets. And she was jet-lagged and Cambodia's furnace heat had sapped her pluck.

Let them be kind, she thought, *or at least not hostile. Let me get a foothold.* They were U.S. military. They were their tribe. She was hers, a professional outsider forever working her way in. She knew better than to count on the kindness of strangers, yet found herself praying for it anyway.

It shouldn't have mattered. The story was her mission. She'd moved heaven and earth to land this assignment with the *Times* Sunday magazine, and she meant to make it work. She could freelance for the Rocky Mountain region until doomsday. Or she could make her grab at the brass ring. The same week she turned thirty, Molly had cropped her black hair and gotten the last of her hep-A shots and flown off to the dark side of the moon.

The truck finished its long drift, coming to rest precisely beside the white rag. They sat idling. The driver stared ahead with both hands on the wheel. Molly squinted into the white light, searching for some sign of Recovery Element 1, or RE-1, as this particular recovery team was designated. Their concealment aggravated her. She did not want to take them on blind faith.

Finally, she reached for the rope that served as a door handle. Climbing down, she hurried to the back to drag her big black mule bag from between stacks of wooden Coca-Cola boxes. The truck departed with an intricate clattering of gears.

She was a week late, a matter of finishing other assignments, and of course no one was waiting to greet her. By now they had probably given up on her. Molly turned in a slow circle, one hand shading her eyes. The sun was high and her shadow was barely a splash underfoot.

She felt tiny and vulnerable standing there in her mountain-biker T-shirt. "Vicious Cycles," the slogan said. She'd saved it for this very moment, to make a macho debut with the GI Joes, to show she had some pedigree. *Some pedigree,* she thought, panting for air. Heat rash bubbled on her bare arms.

She unlocked her mule bag and rummaged for a loose white shirt with long sleeves. She had Irish skin that instantly freckled and burned. Vampire skin, a boyfriend had once called it, the ruin of a body built for the thong. Naturally, she'd forgotten a hat. But she was sure the soldiers would swap or sell her something, if she could only find them.

She walked to the far side of the road, hoping to find them toiling away in a large hidden pit. Instead, to her dismay, she looked out upon a labyrinth of emptied paddies, and heaps of dirt, and footpaths branching off this way and that into mirages.

She refused to call out. She couldn't possibly be lost. It was broad daylight and the immense floodplain lay flat in every direction. An orange pin flag marked one of the paths. The flies flocked to her sunscreen, and they had a bite like bees. Cursing in whispers, she set off along the path with her camera bag swinging.

At the end of ten minutes, she spotted a figure quivering in and out of sight on the far side of a drained lake. Molly wiped the sweat from her eyes. Through her longest lens she decided that with his blond hair and long jaw he had to be one of the American soldiers. He seemed to be looking right at her, but didn't return her wave.

Take the bull by the horns, she thought, descending from the footpath. By the time she unraveled their trail system, he might be long gone. She was about to start directly across the dried lake bed when a man spoke behind her. "I wouldn't go out there," he said, "not if it was me."

Molly turned. The man was tall and thin and tidy, with a red-and-white-checkered Khmer scarf hooded over his head. Dirt smudged the knees of his baggy Levi's. He was clean shaven and wore a T-shirt emblazoned with the movie-star face of Che Guevara. A mason's trowel hung from one hand. On the ground behind him, a dented and scratched steel briefcase sat neatly upright on top of two sticks, obviously his work kit. And something else, she noticed. He was not sweating. In every way, he seemed to govern himself, even in this climate.

"I didn't see you," she said.

"The place is littered with leftovers. War junk. Nightmares," he said.

UXO, he meant. Unexploded ordnance from thirty years of killing. Ordinarily she would have rolled with the sermon; it was gentle enough. She was new to the territory, and as a journalist she valued the early guide. But she was tired and pissed off by the heat and this strange flat maze, and was in no mood for wisdom.

"I've had the lecture," she said. "The orange flags mean the area's cleared. Red means stop. But the lake bed is empty." It was a silly thing to say. Just because you couldn't see the danger didn't mean it wasn't there.

"Ever seen them fish?" he said. "Take one grenade, any vintage. Remove pin. Throw in water. It's easier than a net. The problem is, the stuff is old. Half the time it just sinks into the mud and waits." He paused. "What I'm saying is, Molly, let it not be you. You're much too pretty."

He knew her name. And he was hitting on her? *In this heat?* She fanned furiously at the flies.

He leaned down to offer his hand, and reading her race, affected a brogue. "Duncan," he said, "Duncan O'Brian, descended from kings. As for you, Miss Drake, there's no mystery. Everyone's known you were coming."

She thought he only meant to shake, but he took a good grip and lifted her from the lake bed. He was simply not going to allow her to be stupid. She desperately wanted to sit, but it was too soon to show weakness. It showed just the same.

Before she knew what he was doing, his scarf was draped over her head like a veil. "There, that should help," he said. "It gets brutal out here."

The scarf was a marvel. Immediately the air felt cooler. The blinding sun became bearable. The flies disappeared, and with them the feeling of assault. To her surprise, the cloth smelled clean, like rain, not sweat. The small bit of shade heartened her. She had a place to hide. All of that in a stranger's gift.

"I'm fine, thanks." She started to lift away the scarf.

He brushed aside her pride. His hair came to his shoulders, streaked with gray at the temples. She could not tell his age. A very weathered mid-thirties, or a young fifty.

"It's called a *kroma*," he said. "The Khmers use it for everything you can imagine, a hat, a shawl, a fashion statement, an umbrella, handcuffs, a basket for fruit, a sling to carry their babies. The checkered pattern represents the cosmic tension between life and death. Or knowledge and ignorance. Your pick." There was a touch of the hermit to him. He loved to talk.

The strength was coming back into her. "I only wanted directions," she said. She pointed at the man across the lake bed.

"From our gypsy child?" He had a farm-boy smile. "Not a chance. He never comes close, and you can't get within two hundred yards of him. We've put food out for him, in case he's American. But he leaves it for the dogs. We're not sure who he is or why he's like that. He just showed up one day. The first time I saw him I thought, Ah, boy, you've reached the end of your magical mystery tour. Look at him, all borrowed together. Peasant pants and Vietcong sandals made of old tires. We know the sandals, we've found his tracks, tire tracks. Probably Michelin rubber, from the old Michelin plantations to the east. And no hat, you notice?"

It took Molly a moment to catch his teasing, the "no hat." "I thought he was one of you."

"One of us?"

"A soldier."

Duncan smiled. "In that case, I'm not one of us either."

"Come again?"

"I'm just a visitor like you. One more civilian."

"You're not a soldier?" Her eyes flicked down at the Che shirt.

He flashed her a peace sign. "Ever heard of Kent State?"

She connected the dots. He was talking about the event, not the place. "You were there?" she said. It dated him, though she couldn't remember the date. Before her time.

"On the grassy hill, on the very day," he said. "May 4, 1970. I heard the bullets cut the air. I saw the blood on the lawn. It took me all the rest of the spring and summer to come out of hiding."

Some other time. "But I thought they only used their own people for recoveries," she said.

According to the information officer, Joint Task Force-Full Accounting and the Central Identification Lab based in Hawaii deployed their own military investigators, linguists, anthropologists, and assorted other experts. At a cost of tens of millions of dollars per year, JTF-FA and CILHI were the official forensic archangels of Vietnam and other foreign wars. They were very territorial about it, she had come to learn. The bones were holy relics. "Sacred Ground" was her working title for the piece.

"They have their rules," Duncan said. "They make their exceptions. I'm not the only one. You'll meet the other soon enough, John Kleat. The captain took us in. We like to think we're of some small use."

"You came together?"

"Kleat and me? Nope. I just happened to be in the neighborhood, an archaeologist down from the jungles. My specialty is temple restorations. But I know my way around grid strings and a hole. I help where I can. And I try to keep my place."

"And Mr. Kleat?"

"Kleat," said Duncan, "has come searching for his brother."

Molly pricked her ears up at that. "His brother was the pilot?"

"No, we know that much. But Kleat, he's philosophical about it. The digging season is like an annual pilgrimage for him. He believes one of these years his brother's bones are bound to surface."

"Have you done this before, gone digging for them . . . the others?" She fumbled, unsure of what to call them. The dead? The fallen heroes? They would have their own lingo.

"The boys, you mean?"

"The boys," she repeated.

"Oh, I keep my eyes open when I'm out with my temples. Sort of a professional courtesy, don't you think?" Duncan looked off across the labyrinth, then back at her. "And what about you, miss?"

"Me?"

"Camp is on the far side of the road. I can take you there. Or if you like, we can go on to the dig site."

She told him the dig site. They started walking. He carried his steel briefcase in one hand, the trowel in his other.

"They're all waiting for their fifteen minutes, you know," he said. "They think you're going to make them immortal."

2.

Duncan led her along a succession of paths toward a surf roar of men's voices and clattering tools and the drumbeat of earth being chopped and a generator snarling to pump away water. They arrived at a small army of locals pick-and-shoveling through more paddy walls, raising a cloud of orange dust. Molly curbed the impulse to reach for her camera, waiting to meet the head honcho and get the inevitable ground rules.

Duncan called "Captain" at two Americans on a dike above the toil, but neither heard. They were busy consulting a map with a wiry village elder, or a Cambodian liaison officer. The old man had a dark brown moon of a face with burr-cut white hair and one pink plastic leg. Somehow he heard Duncan over the din. He lifted his head abruptly and looked at Molly as if he'd been waiting for her.

"Old Samnang," Duncan told her, walking closer. "He's the work boss. In the old days, before Pol Pot, before Nixon, he studied at the Sorbonne and taught music and math at the Royal Academy in Phnom Penh. That was then."

The two Americans noticed her now. Molly figured the taller one to be the mission leader. He looked commanding with his sun-bronzed skull, photogenic as hell, a seamed scar looping across his throat. He wore black cargo pants bloused in his boot tops, a close second to the American uniforms that were forbidden on these military excavations.

But it was the squat younger man dressed in a Hawaiian-print shirt, Gargoyle sunglasses, and a baseball cap who descended to them. Molly took in the cap, the veins, and the wedding band. The captain was an Orioles fan, a gym rat, and married. And a hopeless legs man. Even the Gargoyles could not disguise his stare.

"Welcome to the kingdom, Ms. Drake." The young captain didn't mention that she was badly overdue. He didn't try to own her. She liked that. His eyes flickered at Duncan's *kroma* on her head, and he did not begrudge Duncan's first contact with his guest of honor. "You plunge right in," he said to her. "Already out meeting the natives."

"Mr. O'Brian saved me. I was about to go off chasing phantoms."

"The gypsy kid," said Duncan.

"Some poor mother's son," the captain said.

She had not meant to apologize, but since all seemed forgiven she saw only merit to be gained by it. "The week got away from me," she offered.

"No problem."

She looked around at the mounds of dirt. "I was praying I wouldn't be too late."

"If you mean have we found the pilot, we have not."

She tried to read his tone. Was he optimistic? Discouraged? They had been here for nearly three weeks. Generally their digs didn't go longer than a month, which was a blink of the eye compared to other digs she'd covered. At Canyon de Chelly, Yellowjacket, Little Big Horn, and elsewhere, it took years and even decades to lay bare the past. Coming over on the plane, she had worried about their quickness. She had sold her editor on a find, not a hit-or-miss process. She needed bones for her story. But she could not say so, not to these bone hunters.

Duncan seemed to read her mind. "We'll find him," he said.

"If he's here," the captain qualified, "we'll find him."

"He's waited long enough," Duncan said. She sensed a subtle tug of war between the captain, under deadline, and this long-haired middle-aged archaeologist who did not even wear a wristwatch.

The captain didn't take it personally. He clapped Duncan on the shoulder. "A true believer," he said.

"They're talking about the July Fourth issue," Molly said. She offered it as information, but also motivation. The captain needed to understand she was under deadline, too. She didn't volunteer that the next big patriot slot wouldn't come until Thanksgiving, and no one at the magazine wanted to wait that long. This was just another Vietnam rehash with a short shelf life, less a war story than a nostalgic nod to the Rolling Stone generation. And she needed bones. It came down to that.

The captain said, "We'll be long gone by July. Once the wet season starts, we close shop."

"When does the monsoon come?"

"Every year's different. Sometimes May, usually mid to late June. The meteorologists are forecasting a late arrival this year. That gives us a little more wiggle room if we need it. But there's time for all that later. First let's see to you. We've got another three hours left to the workday here, but let me suggest you get squared away at camp. Rest up this afternoon. Drink lots of water. Wash the dust off. I should warn you, the shower sees a lot of action around seventeen hundred hours. I'll make the introductions at dinner."

She was more grateful than she allowed herself to show. Her body was still operating on mountain standard time, as in 2:00 A.M. And this heat. Three mornings ago, she'd scraped frost off her windshield. Now she couldn't seem to take a whole breath. It felt like slow suffocation.

"Just point the way," she said. "I'll find it."

"You're new to the territory. I'll get someone to run you through mine awareness tonight, and assign you an escort."

It was exactly what she didn't want, a keeper hemming her in. But she smiled gracefully. "I'll learn my way around," she told him.

"Until then," the captain said, "I think Mr. Kleat was on his way back to camp." He waved at the big American.

"I'll see you later," Duncan said.

"Your scarf," she said.

"My gift, Molly." He touched his trowel to his forehead and walked off into the dust.

Kleat came down the slope of the dike in big, clod-busting strides. Molly took in his details. Here might be her centerpiece, this brother of a missing soldier searching through the years. He was not so tall as he had seemed up there. His head was large and his neck surprisingly thick, as if it carried a great weight of ideas. His steel-rimmed glasses flashed in the white sun. He did not cover his baldness. He looked ambitious.

"We were starting to think you'd given up on us," he said to her.

"You said you were heading back to camp," the captain said to Kleat.

"Sure," Kleat said, taking his cue. "I'll show her in."

The captain started back up the dike, then turned to Molly. "One other thing," he said. "When we find him, no photographs. Don't shoot the remains."

They'd told her already. "Absolutely," she said.

Kleat led the way. Molly followed him away from the noise. After a few minutes' walking, he said, "Boulder."

She heard the scorn. You got it all the time. "The People's Republic," she confessed. "What about you?"

"Angeles City."

"L.A.?"

"Christ, no. The Philippines. There's a nice colony of vets live there. We live like princes. Beers cost twelve cents. Like that."

"What do you do?"

"When I'm not here? I'm a contractor." He didn't volunteer what kind of contractor.

"They say you come to Cambodia every year."

He didn't answer. "I thought there'd be more of you," he said. "A crew of assistants. Helpers."

"I like working alone."

"I've read some of your articles on the internet. That fisherman who cut off his own leg. The Columbine murders. Those peace-scam artists. And your piece on the Super Max inmates, 'A Season in Stainless-Steel Hell.' "

Molly didn't know if he was trying to flatter or control her. They knew her better than she knew them—where she lived, what she wrote, her photos. She noted that he didn't say if he approved of her work or not. "It's a job," she said.

"Why give them personalities, though?" he asked.

"The inmates?"

"Just kill them, I say."

"It's a matter of what we do with evil," she said. "That was my point."

"And now you're working for the big dog. The *Times,* right? Moving up in the world." He was testing her, she realized. Deciding if she was good enough.

Humility. "They're trying me out. I'm a very little fish in a very big pond."

He gave a small grunt, but still had reservations. "Cambodia, though. Why chase the dead?" He gestured at the trenches and square holes along the trail. "Why come after these guys?"

"Memory," she said. "Memory is flesh. As long as we remember, they're still alive, don't you think?"

He didn't answer. She followed the sleek, gleaming prow of his head as they zigzagged along the maze of footpaths above paddies and between heaps of red dirt. Finally Kleat began to open up.

"It looks like a jumble," he said of the dig. "But this is how it's done. There's a method to the madness. Our metal detectors have found pieces of the plane scattered to kingdom come. But you can see the general east-west line of our digging." He showed her his topo map with colored-pencil markings. "Here's the crash trajectory."

The site was vast and complicated. He described how the dying warplane had ricocheted across two linear miles of rice fields, disintegrating in leaps and bounds. Afterward, local peasants had patiently rebuilt their paddies over the gouged earth. Then the Khmer Rouge had come, erasing whole villages, and, along with them, all memory of the buried plane. Later the Vietnamese army swept through on their "liberation" of Cambodia. Then the United Nations entered, determined to jump-start the devastation known as year zero. Not far behind them came the men and women of U.S. military forensics teams. Ever since, they had been resurrecting American warriors from the Cambodian hinterlands.

"Sometimes the locals show up with a bone that has no story. In this case, we have a story but no bone, not yet," Kleat said. "We know exactly who we're searching for and when he disappeared. All we need to do is find him."

The "we" jarred her. According to Duncan, he and Kleat were outsiders. But to hear Kleat, he was a full-fledged member of the recovery team. She glanced at him. Was he out to steal the captain's thunder?

He stopped by a trench surrounded by torn sheets of metal lying across the mounded earth. Some had been fitted together in puzzle pieces. Red and black and green cable and wire stretched like bunches of fried snakes. A collection of digging tools was stacked in the trench below.

"It's weird in a way," he said. "When the refugees got relocated to this area twelve years ago, they inherited the tools left behind by dead villagers. Talk about memory, there was no memory here, just the land and a bunch of strangers. But then it turns out the tools had a memory of what happened in this place."

He bent and pulled up several of the shovels and examined them. He found what he was looking for and handed it to Molly. The head was wider and blunter than on an American shovel, and the metal was brighter and silvery. The edges looked crudely cut and you could see where a local blacksmith had hammered it to fit the wooden shaft.

Kleat scratched away some of the dirt. "Can you see it?"

There was a number stamped in the metal, and beneath that the inscription "Made in the USA." She took out her camera and started getting shots.

"It comes from a section of the stabilizer flap of a Cessna O2 Sky-master," Kleat said. "It was a slow, twin-prop airplane used for forward air control. The pilot would mark targets with white phosphorous rockets, then the bombers would come. This one left from Ubon Airfield in Thailand on January 3, 1969, to scout the Ho Chi Minh Trail, but he never came home. After the plane crashed, the peasants beat the sword into the plowshare, literally."

He explained how military investigators had found plow blades made of cut-up propellers, wooden ox bells with bullet shells for clappers, and handmade sickles and pots and pans still bearing telltale serial numbers. The recovery teams always deployed with a database called Brite Lite.

"The pilot and his plane just vanished into the abyss. All signs of the plane, even the crash scar, disappeared. Thirty years of farming devoured every trace. Even the satellite photos showed nothing. We knew the plane was out here somewhere. We've known for years. We just didn't know enough." *We.*

"So you've got farm tools left by ghosts, and a plane without a pilot," she said.

Kleat cut a look at her full of suspicion. "There's nothing supernatural about this," he snapped.

Molly was taken off guard. "Of course not," she said.

"I've done this before," he declared. "An air crash isn't rocket science. The physics are simple. The path of impact is known. We have his trajectory. We're unearthing his wings. It's a matter of time. He'll answer to us."

That was a curious way to put it, even imperious, as if the dead pilot were a fugitive or a truant. Molly gently slid the shovel back among its brothers.

They continued along the path. It was past noon, but the sun only seemed to reach higher in the sky. The light would have been painful if not for the checkered shawl draped across her head and shoulders. They walked in silence for another half mile or so, the straps of her camera bag creaking. The air smelled of water and sewage. The trail seemed to go on forever.

Then, far off in the sheets of heat, Molly caught sight of the gypsy man. By now she had no sense of direction, no idea where the road was or—looking back—where the excavators were harrowing the earth. She fastened on the gypsy as if he were a magnetic north. It felt like she was traveling in circles around him.

"There he is again," she said, pointing.

Kleat squinted across the fields. "Him," he said.

"Who do you think he is?"

"There are always stray dogs around the bones. I told the captain it was a mistake encouraging him. This is a recovery, not a lonely-hearts club."

"Duncan said he might be a drug addict or the son of a missing soldier."

An expression came onto Kleat's face, as if she were joking. "But that *is* Duncan," he said quietly.

She brought her camera up and telescoped the figure through her lens. There was the mane of brown hair and the sparkle of his steel briefcase. Duncan was walking along the top of a paddy wall with a long stick in one hand, poking at random.

She lowered her camera. "I didn't know." She couldn't think what else to say.

A stray dog? Kleat didn't make any attempt to apologize. She didn't say anything. Suddenly she didn't know whom to trust. In this flat land that seemed incapable of hiding anything, everything seemed concealed.

3.

It was a story to sweat and bleed for, and she did both over the coming weeks, down in the trenches, under the sun, earning her way into the family of them.

She was a photographer first, a writer second. The lens was her habitat. It was her sanctuary. Prose came more slowly. It always came after the picture.

The afternoon the *Times* editor called to assign her the story, Molly had gone straight to Mike's Camera and maxed out her credit card on a digital Nikon with all the bells and whistles. She had wanted it forever, but could never justify the sticker shock, over $10,000. Now that she was going national, though, she figured the camera would pay for itself.

With digital you could edit the image and change the look, even turn color into grainy black and white, as she'd contemplated, to evoke a '60s 'Nam-scape. It would give her the ability to mimic the great war photographers, Henri Huet and Tim Page and Larry Burrows and Kyochi Sawada and Robert Capa, all without lugging blocks of Velvia and Kodak through the tropical heat.

The camera was unlike any she'd ever owned. It was more than the usual sum of lenses, filters, and film, more than a boxful of memories. Its instant recall made it both a tool and a communal event.

On a hunch, she had brought a pair of five-inch barber's scissors. Her dad—her stepfather—had been a barber. *Never underestimate the value of a free haircut.* The scissors paid in aces with the recovery team. People flocked to her tent in the evenings. While she trimmed their hair, they talked about music, sports, movies, and home. She shared anything they wanted to know about photography, from the rule of thirds to underexposing one f-stop for the midday glare. Also she showed them her camera, and that was the real icebreaker.

With a flip of a switch, they could see themselves the way she saw them. She flipped the switch. The display lit up.

Here was their dig, and in the distance nut-brown children wrestling on water buffalo, *National Geographic* country as far as the eye could see.

Here were the faces of RE-1, black, white, and brown, all rendered one color, the color of Cambodia's dirt, the color of blood oranges. Here they mined the earth, here they shook it through screens with quarter-inch mesh.

Here was the captain in repose, toasting her with a bottle of warm grape Gatorade while he smoked his evening Havana and read one of her *Vogue* magazines. He was smart and freethinking, a postmodern soldier who reveled in not carrying a weapon, and lived to raise the lost souls from the dirt.

There was Kleat, a dead end. The brother angle would have been so sweet. But after the first week of him, she knew there was no way around his hatred of the people and the land. Kleat treated Cambodia like a curse or a disease. There was no way she could turn his bile into nobility, and so Molly had dropped him from her story and started framing her shots to exclude him.

And here was Duncan, who was not part of her story either. But she could not keep her camera off him; there was something she liked. Here he stared into a dark square hole covered with grid strings, like a scout about to leap into the underworld. Here he stood among the laborers, head and shoulders above them, spinning some hilarious joke in fluent Khmer. Here he sat on his briefcase with his sketchbook on one knee, drawing faces and scenes and artifacts that no one was allowed to see because of his shyness.

She peeked into his tent one afternoon, and was startled by its austerity. It was bare except for a black Ace comb and a toothbrush tucked in the wall pocket. He slept on the ground without sheets or a sleeping pad or a mosquito net. He owned nothing but the clothes on his back and whatever he carried in that briefcase.

Here was their base camp, a hodgepodge of wall tents, pup tents, and her North Face dome. They had pitched their camp where a village once stood, not knowing that for some reason the locals thought it haunted.

They used a clothesline strung between trees for their occasional volleyball games. Barbecue ball, she called it. Roasting the weenies. Almost six feet tall, she played like a gladiator, six-packing the ball into the faces of husky trash talkers. She bloodied noses, made kills, tooled them mercilessly . . . and they loved her for it.

Not unnaturally, so far from home, they began to court her. It was nothing personal. After she sliced herself on a piece of the wreckage, the special forces medic who stitched her thigh proposed marriage. Another Romeo braved the mosquitoes and recited Shakespeare to the wall of her tent at night. One morning, Kleat caught her shooting him. He rose up from his washbasin, the water dripping from his salt-and-pepper chest hair, and opened his arms to her.

She felt like a hypocrite, keeping them at bay. After all, day after day, she stalked them intimately. But that was the way it was. Molly didn't tell them about one bad night in Oklahoma long ago. She just gave them her policy: no hookups on a shoot. And went on seducing them for her camera.

Each night, she downloaded her day's harvest into a digital wallet, a portable hard drive, and cataloged her shots and watched her story grow. While the soldiers listened to Dr. Dre or Beethoven, read paperbacks, or played Game Boys, she lay on her back in the dark of her tent and the images lit her face. The wallet became her dream box. Some nights she couldn't tell if she was awake or dreaming with the crickets going wild outside under the Cambodian stars.

Among professionals, the purists argued that digital wasn't pure. The geeks argued that there were still bugs in the machine, and there were, in hers at any rate, some serious gremlins in some of the shots. She became aware of them gradually.

Within a week of arriving, Molly had gotten their labyrinth memorized, and made a habit of waking first each morning, before dawn, to visit the dig site. Every day the site grew longer. There was nothing much to do at this hour. Night still pooled in the holes. It was too early for the teams to work and too dark for her to shoot. But it was cooler then, and she had her best privacy. She wandered along the cut-open earth, alone with her thoughts in the gray mist. But not quite alone, she began to realize.

Ghostly figures ambled across the fields, distant and only half visible above the ground fog. She supposed they were villagers. Some wore *kromas* over their heads or around their necks. Some carried mute babies.

By five the sky would start to gain color. Roosters crowed far away. She could practically taste the wood smoke of breakfast fires in invisible villages. Then, just as the sun broke the horizon, a faraway temple bell would ring once, just once. Each dawn broke that way, with the bell's single gong. The early morning wanderers would fade off and she would return to make her breakfast.

On a whim one morning, Molly lugged along her tripod and snapped a shot of the villagers in the dim light. She didn't expect much, and when she downloaded the camera into her wallet at the end of the day, there was next to nothing. The camera had captured the fields and haze, though none of the wanderers.

But a few days later, in scrolling through the JPEG files, she discovered that her morning shot was populated. The wanderers had been buried in the pixels somehow, and the camera was finally letting them rise to the surface. Not only that, every time she turned the display on again, the image changed. Like spirits, the villagers came and went. There might be five people when she turned the device off, and ten or dozens when she turned it on again.

The photo became something of a freak show, attracting a small audience of soldiers who would drop by to see if the digital figures had moved around or vanished back into the mist. Duncan joked that her camera was possessed.

A navy explosives specialist diagnosed the ghosts as faulty software. Digital noise, he called it. In getting compressed and decompressed, the image apparently altered itself, as if peeling away layers of reality.

One morning she noticed one of the hooded figures trailing her in the muggy gloom. She stopped. He stopped. "Hello?" she said, approaching him.

It was old Samnang, wearing a blue-and-white *kroma* like a shawl, and under that a headset for his tape recorder. All but buried in the mist, his prosthesis had a blue sandal glued to the pink foot.

"Ah, *bonjour,* Molly," he said. *Maw-lee.* His accent, so beautiful.

"Samnang, what a surprise," she said without surprise. It was so clear. "Did the captain tell you to follow me?"

"The captain? Not at all."

"This was your idea," she said.

Samnang sniffed at the air. "The hour is so fresh, don't you agree?"

She could have been rude and insisted on her privacy, but she liked Samnang. He was as honest as a monk, and the American recovery teams hired him year after year to run their crews. He jokingly compared himself to a chicken scratching in the dirt for a living. She had never heard him speak about his past. He never mentioned the loss of his leg, never said a word about any family. Following Duncan's example, she made a point of calling him by his full name, not Sam like the others did.

Finally she said, "So what are you listening to?"

During the wet season, when excavation was pointless, Samnang used his U.S. dollars to go around the countryside collecting folk songs. *Before the water washes them away.*

He laid the *kroma* along his neck and handed Molly his headset. He pressed the button. Expecting folk music, she was amazed to hear Margo Timmins singing on *The Trinity Sessions.* "The Cowboy Junkies?" she said.

He smiled sheepishly. "An old vice of mine."

After that there was no way she could refuse his company. They started walking together.

"Duncan told me about your photograph of the morning people," Samnang said. "I thought to see them for myself."

It occurred to her that he had come to protect her. Did he fear they might resent her presence? But they seemed unaware of her. For that matter, they seemed unaware of one another.

"They're harmless," she said. "They never look at me. They never come close."

"Are there any out there now?"

She counted a woman with two children in the fog, and a man standing in place, looking off. "Just three," she told him.

"But some mornings, more?"

"Many more. I wonder if they're studying the damage. You know, figuring out how to repair the paddy walls before the rains come."

"What are they doing now?"

She glanced at Samnang and his black eyes glistened inside the lips of his shawl. He was watching her face, not even trying to look for them. Was he testing her, or were his eyes too old? She turned her head. Several more had appeared a hundred yards to the side, motionless or nearly so. One drifted along some hidden dike path. "Nothing," she told him. "They're just standing out there, like they're waiting for a train or something."

Samnang nodded his head slowly, intent on her face.

"My other thought was that they might be foraging," she said.

" 'Foraging,' " he repeated.

"Like a cargo cult or something. Salvaging the plane's wire and metal. Getting a little treasure before the day starts and the Americans show up. This is their backyard, after all."

"Have you seen them taking anything? Reaching into the ground? Digging?"

"Never. They never do anything. They don't even talk to each other."

He had risen early for her. He could still be sleeping. She felt responsible. "You shouldn't worry about me," she said. "I can take care of myself."

"The villagers are quite frightened by them," Samnang said.

She frowned. These *were* the villagers. "I don't understand."

"They complain to the government. They want them gone."

She was trying to keep up with him. "So these people come from another region," she tried. "They're poaching the metal."

"No, it's not that."

"Then what?"

"It is a local matter."

What a strange battle. A trespass each morning before dawn, and with babies and children, too. But never a confrontation.

"You said the villagers complained. Why don't the soldiers make them leave then?" she asked. The Cambodian government had posted a dozen troops to guard—or contain—the American forensics expedition. They did little except lie in hammocks, or squat above the dig and gossip in the sun.

"They are just as brave as the villagers at this hour," Samnang said. "No one comes, except you."

"And you," she said.

He smiled. "Anyway, it wouldn't help. You find these morning people all through the country."

That was the second time he had said it that way. "Morning people?"

"Now you have made me one, too," he joked, growing even more elliptical. She decided to drop it. A local matter.

Just then the sun cracked the night. The haze lit like fire. In the sudden flare of color, it was hard to see. The figures began to dissipate. That distant bell rang across the fields. Its single note vibrated in the air.

Molly felt the heat against her face. "I have to see that bell someday," she said.

Next morning, he was waiting for her again. It was clear. Since she was going to persist in these morning walks, he would accompany her. Their walks became for her the high point of every day.

When Kleat heard about her new friend, he advised her to dump Samnang. "Ditch him," he said. "The old man's KR. Or was."

KR was a universal phrase, part of every language spoken in Cambodia. Khmer Rouge, a French label, the Red Khmers, red for Communist, red for blood. "That's crazy," she said. "He was a professor at the university. How could he be KR? They killed people like him."

"Open your eyes. You haven't seen him with the men? He never raises his voice, and he's a cripple. But they always do what he tells them. One word and it's done."

"That's how it's supposed to work, Kleat."

"But they're *afraid* of him."

It made no sense to a guy like Kleat how this gentlest of men was able to control the pent-up tempest of the workers. Born and raised in violent refugee camps, many of the local Khmer men were semi-wild. At night some got drunk in their villages, gambled, beat their women, and bloodied each other with knives and axes. Molly had pictures of that, too.

But even the worst toughs obeyed Samnang without question. "They respect him," she said.

"He has a power over them," Kleat argued.

"Like voodoo?"

"Laugh. He's KR, I tell you."

"The KR don't exist anymore."

"Tell that to the workers. They have their memories."

"If he was KR, what's he doing here?"

"The same thing you're doing," Kleat said to her. "Making a buck. Doing penance. I don't know."

Duncan was sitting there. He said it was none of Kleat's business, even if Samnang had been KR. "Everyone has secrets they'd rather forget."

"Not secrets like that," Kleat said.

"Let up," Duncan said. "Survival always has a price tag."

4.

At the end of her third week, Samnang approached Molly. "I have something to show you."

They rode in a Land Cruiser hired from three brothers who lived in Samnang's hometown, Kampong Cham. The driver, a heavily tattooed boy, drove them to a nearby village. The village was built on stilts for the rainy season. There were even bridges between some of the huts, and a dock with canoes lying on the dirt. It seemed inconceivable the land could ever be flooded. Water was their faith, a phantom thing, nothing Molly could believe in. All she'd seen since arriving was dry, cracked earth.

On a slight hill beyond the village there was a shack with a corrugated tin roof and no walls. Inside sat a cheap cement Buddha, like a garden gnome. To one side, hanging from the rafters, was the bell.

Samnang took a small hammer and rang it for her. The pitch was perfect.

She was delighted, and went closer. "But it's made from an old bomb shell," she said.

"Yes." Samnang was pleased by her surprise. "It is inescapable, don't you think? That the rubble should be turned into order. Even into beauty."

"No," she answered. "I would think it was the other way around. Beauty fades. Civilizations grind to dust. I would say loss is the norm. Chaos. Noise. Not music."

Samnang touched the bell with his fingertips. "But you see?" he said. "They have restored themselves from the horror."

On May 29, a dog brought a human femur to the site.

Molly got a picture of the dog just before one of the Cambodian soldiers shot it, the bone still in its mouth. The Americans rushed over, excited that this might be evidence of their missing pilot. But one glance told them it was another false lead. The thighbone didn't come close to matching a six-foot Caucasian's. It could not belong to their pilot.

Very possibly the bone had come from a mass grave somewhere in the region. Killing fields hid everywhere, even around here. After every rainy season, bones cropped up, often no more than tiny white fragments. In the beginning, Molly had mistaken the crushed bits along the outer paths for bleached seashells. Then she'd spied checkered fragments of disintegrating scarves mixed among them and realized she was walking on the dead.

Curious to see what would happen, Molly followed the bone. The forensic anthropologist with RE-1 judged the femur to be Southeast Asian Mongoloid. He wrapped it in bubble wrap and turned it over to their Cambodian liaison officer. The liaison officer kept the bubble wrap and gave the bone to a soldier, who tossed it into a distant ditch, dog food again.

She watched it all through her telephoto lens. Then she saw Samnang go over. Looking around to make sure no one saw him, he took the bone and buried it by a tree. He lit a stick of incense, and she realized that Kleat was right.

Samnang was guilty. He probably had been KR. Finding the dead was his way of doing penance.

One of the Cambodian soldiers, or a villager, perhaps, must have seen Samnang ministering to the bone and drew the same conclusion. There were eyes everywhere, factions and subfactions and jealousies. For one reason or another, KR or not, Samnang was dismissed from the dig that evening.

The purge was swift. Molly heard about it at the last minute. She rushed to the road to say good-bye, but the truck carrying him away was already leaving. She caught his face in her camera, and he turned his eyes away from her. She figured that was the last she'd ever see of him.

As the red dust settled, Molly saw a figure watching the departure from out in the fields. At first she thought it was the gypsy kid standing in the ball of the sinking sun. But when she shaded her eyes, he turned into Kleat, and she realized who had gotten rid of old Samnang.

5.

By then the dig was nearly done. Their dead reckoning had failed. The crash site looked like a carcass—rice paddies breached, dirt piled by the sifting screens, holes collapsing, and grid strings let loose—and still the pilot eluded them. After a month of brute labor, RE-1 had pulled up hundreds of pieces of the cockpit and fuselage and wings, seemingly everything but the bones that were their quest.

As they reached the end of the crash trajectory, the Americans sensed their failure. They took it personally. Their high hopes came tumbling down. One night, at the beginning of June, two of the youngest marines got into a fistfight over a stolen *Hustler* magazine. They fought like jealous teenagers, and everyone was embarrassed by the display.

After the captain got the two fighters separated, it turned out that others, including Molly, had suffered petty thefts, too, mostly letters and snapshots from home. Whoever it was had snitched her barber's scissors. The culprit, probably some desperately poor Khmer—though Kleat made sure to accuse the roaming gypsy—never was caught.

The stealing was almost beside the point. What mattered about the fight and the thefts was that it suddenly became clear their losses outweighed their gains. Their daily miseries—the spiraling heat, the snakes and bugs, the dust of dried paddy sewage that festered in their sinuses, and a hundred other small things—could no longer be sustained with hope. Whether the pilot had ejected or been cast loose of the jet or dragged away, it was plain they were not going to find him.

As if to hasten their departure, they received news that a typhoon was building to super class in the South China Sea. With winds in excess of 150 miles per hour, it already equaled a class 4 Atlantic hurricane. The navy meteorologists could not say when and where it might strike land, in four days or six or ten, in Malaysia, Thailand, or Cambodia. But it was sure to usher in the mother of all monsoons. The rains would come. The roads would turn to grease and the paddies would fill. Rivers would run backward. The villages would turn into islands.

On the evening of June 7, the captain invited Molly, Kleat, and Duncan to a private gathering inside his wall tent. He had lawn chairs for them and coffee mugs for the last of his Johnnie Walker Black.

"We're terminating the recovery," he told them. The search was over. He had already broken the news to his team. "I wanted to tell you separately. To thank each of you for your hard work."

Molly sat back, stunned. Her shock was a curiosity to her. For at least a week now, she had been trying to invent a story that glossed over the fact that she was essentially writing about empty holes. "It's over?" she said.

"Can't you hear?" said Kleat. "It's done."

Duncan tried to rally the captain. "You don't give up on the good ones," he said.

"We're not, Duncan," the captain said. "But at a certain point you say, enough."

"A few days more," said Duncan. "Where else could he be?"

For Molly's sake, the captain said, "I'm disappointed, too."

"There will be other seasons, other excavations," Kleat said. He was adamant.

Other chances, she thought, but not for her. The *Times* had not sent her to write about barren dirt, not after a pitch entitled "Sacred Ground." The bottom line was that without the bones for a climax, her story was not a *Times* story at all.

"We start redeploying tomorrow," the captain said. "I'll arrange transportation for you."

Molly went through the motions of the captain's farewell celebration. Afterward, she meandered through camp, dealing with the letdown. She could hear soldiers through their tent walls. They were excited to be going back home.

The paper was covering her travel expenses, and she'd get a kill fee for her trouble. Maybe one of the airline magazines would take a condensed version, and she could spin off a travel piece for the *Denver Post*. She'd never recoup the cost of the camera, though. Ten grand. She'd gambled big, and lost.

On a whim, she took a few pickup shots of the camp. Wasting battery juice just to waste it, she paused by a hole that had once been the village well and fired her flash into the darkness, not even aiming. There was nothing to see with the naked eye. The hole was deep and the flash too quick, and when she kicked a pebble, it plunked on water so stagnant it smelled gray.

She didn't bother looking at the image on her camera display, just turned it off and returned to her tent. She began packing some of her things, but that only made her feel worse. Lying down, she held the camera overhead and flipped on the display.

The bones were waiting for her.

She gaped at the illuminated image. How could a camera see through water? Actually it was possible with a long enough time lapse. But she'd used a flash. The light would have bounced off the water.

There was a hint of poorly focused white sticks beneath the water. Garbage, she decided. Twigs tossed in by children or the wind. More digital noise. She turned the camera off, then on, to see if the image corrected itself. This time, there was a rib cage and a long tail-like spine.

An animal, she thought. Then saw the skull.

6.

First thing the next morning, filled with excitement and disbelief, they lowered one of the marines on a rope, by his ankles, headfirst. He took a deep breath. They dunked him into the water, gave him sixty seconds, and then hauled him, soaking wet, back up the shaft and into the sunlight. He held a handful of human vertebrae. There was more, he said, much more.

Things got noisy fast. They snaked hoses down the well shaft and the pumps roared. They rigged a klieg light over the hole, and fired up another generator. As the water drained off and small glittering shrimp writhed in the mud and water weeds, the brown tips of bones jutted up like driftwood.

They lowered a man again. This time he brought up two skulls.

"What in God's name," a soldier muttered.

Their forensic anthropologist examined the skulls. Neither was Caucasian. One belonged to a child. The nuchal crest at the base of the skull was rounded, the forehead smooth, the wisdom teeth not yet descended, the whole aspect gracile. Probably female, he said, probably eight to ten years old. He laid it on the ground and went to join the others peering into the hole.

"The fucking KR," Kleat said.

It was a mass grave, not fifty feet from their camp.

Duncan knelt down and took the skull. "Look at you, poor bug," he whispered.

"What?" said Molly, not sure she'd heard.

He looked up at her, and there was a streak down his mask of red dust. Through her lens, at first she thought it was sweat. But it was a tear for the nameless girl. She got the picture.

The find staggered them, the enormity of the murders. They were familiar with the killing fields. All had seen the displays of bones in places like Phnom Penh. But this was slick and shiny. The event of death seemed unfiltered, unprocessed. It could have been yesterday.

Just the same, it was not their pilot. They switched off the pumps and cut the light. Their eleventh-hour hope went as dark as midnight.

The captain turned away. "That's that," he said. "Let the Cambodians have it. This isn't ours."

But Duncan would not give up. "He's down there," he told them. "I'd stake my life on it."

The captain turned to him. "Duncan," he said softly, "the cockpit is two miles away."

"The well was used for burial once, why not before?" Duncan said. "Think about it, the morning after the plane crashed. There's metal and wire lying everywhere, a windfall of riches. But also there's this body of a stranger, and not just a body. A ghost."

"Ghosts," Kleat scoffed.

"A serious liability in these parts," said Duncan. "These are peasants straight out of the tenth century. I've spent time among them. They see spirits everywhere. Tiger spirits. Forest spirits. Witches flying in the night, drinking people's blood. They've already got their hands full with ancestors. Now suddenly a body falls from the sky. What would you do? Conduct a respectful Buddhist cremation? For a stranger? Waste a week going off to find the authorities? Authorities, by the way, who might try to lay claim to your plane parts. The body was a nuisance. A pollution. So they dumped him here."

"Into their drinking water?" said the captain.

"It's an old well in an abandoned village. And the tradition could have carried over. Years later, when the Khmer Rouge needed a dumping ground, some villager might have led them to the same well."

"There's no way to be sure the pilot is underneath the rest of them."

"There's only one way to be sure he's not," Duncan answered.

"We've never encountered a situation like this," said the captain. "Never."

And yet Duncan had planted the possibility among them. Suddenly it seemed that week after week, they might have been digging farther away from what they were looking for. And now the dead from one era could be hiding the dead from another.

But they could not simply dredge up the bones to see what lay at the bottom. The Cambodian liaisons suddenly became officious and prickly. There were problems, it developed, diplomatic, jurisdictional, archaeological, and cultural. Molly loved it. With a single, giant twist, her story had not only been saved, but was taking on dimensions she'd never dreamed of.

Among other things, as a matter of policy, American bones were supposed to be separated from Southeast Asian Mongoloid remains at the site of excavation rather than at the central lab in Hawaii. The Department of Defense had learned the hard way how difficult it was to repatriate Asiatic remains. The Vietnamese government, especially, regarded any bones found in the proximity of American remains as those of *ling nguy,* or South Vietnamese puppet soldiers.

There were also issues of territorial authority. This might be a shared underworld, but it happened to lie within Cambodian soil. Who owned the dead? Should the Cambodian authorities be the ones to oversee the excavation of the well? Did that place American soldiers in the role of undertakers for Cambodian citizens? What if there was no American pilot beneath the layer of Khmer Rouge victims? Did the Cambodians even want the mass grave to be exhumed? The competing interests created a tension that made her story at once international, delicate, and highly emotional.

The captain ordered the area around the well ringed off. There was a process to be observed, channels to go through. Cambodian soldiers were posted around the camp to keep away the locals. The men on the labor crew were told to return to their villages. The captain, the forensic anthropologist, and their Cambodian counterparts all retired to a tent and began placing satellite calls to their headquarters. Instructed to stay away from the site, Molly and the others waited in whatever shade they could find. Hours went by.

The team members couldn't get over it. They treated Molly like a seer, as if she had a gift for this. "How did you know to look down there?" one asked.

"I didn't," she said.

"But you went right to it."

"Yeah, after four weeks, right to it."

As the day dragged on and they still sat idle, Kleat stewed. "What are they doing in there? We could be down clearing the hole."

"It's not that easy," Duncan said. "They're on to us by now."

"Who?" said Molly.

"The locals. These are the dead they inherited their earth from, literally, the original owners of the land they're farming. The villagers could demand to cover the bones over or burn them to ash. One way or another, they'll have to exorcise the spirits."

"Screw their boogeymen," Kleat said.

Molly began to worry. The captain emerged from the tent with a frown on his face, took a long breath, and returned inside. Plainly, he was getting nowhere fast. Once more she felt her story slipping away. They needed proof.

While the rest of the team nodded off in the heat or waved away flies, she got to her feet, ducked under the tape, and stood beside the well. It was darker than ever down there. Expecting nothing, she snapped another blind shot of the depths, then pulled up the image on her display.

"What you got this time, Molly?" someone called to her.

She looked up from her camera display. "You need to see this," she said.

They stirred and came out into the high sun and crowded around. The display was full of muddled bones . . . and something else. They all saw it. Mixed among the skulls was a flight helmet. "You've done it again," Duncan whispered.

At 1700 hours—Molly had acquired military time—an American helicopter landed on the road, bearing a colonel and two Cambodian government officials wearing sunglasses. Molly went out with the others to photograph them, and was surprised to see how many villagers had flocked to the area. The Cambodian soldiers were keeping them at a distance from the camp.

The colonel was not pleased. "Quite the circus," he shouted to the captain as the rotors wound down. Dust flew everywhere. He gestured at Molly. "Who's this?"

"She's the *Times* journalist I told you about," the captain said.

The colonel did not shake her hand or thank her. "You were shooting the bones," he said.

"I didn't know what was down there," Molly told him. His unfriendliness confused her. Hadn't she just provided them with proof?

The colonel looked away from her. He noticed Duncan and his long hair and Che shirt. "And him?"

Molly saw the captain's throat tighten. "A local archaeologist," he said.

"All right," the colonel declared, "let's get this thing under control." The captain led him and the officials to the mess tent. An hour later the colonel and the officials departed on the helicopter.

The captain announced that the excavation would resume in the morning. They had been granted a week—seven days—no more. After that the site would be returned to the kingdom of Cambodia. "We've got our work cut out for us," he said. "If he's down there, we'll find him."

There were high fives, and Duncan whistled through his fingers. The captain did not smile. He asked Molly and Duncan and Kleat to join him.

There was no Johnnie Walker Black this evening. The meeting was brief. He was grim. "Due to the sensitive nature of the mission," he informed them, "your presence is no longer expedient."

Molly's mouth fell open.

" 'Expedient,' " said Kleat. "What the hell does that mean?"

The captain's lips pressed thin. Clearly he had argued. Clearly he had lost. "I have been advised to compress the operation to essential personnel only. We're letting go of the work crew." He added, "And you."

"You can't do that to us," Kleat said. "I've paid my dues. Year after year—"

"Be ready to leave at 0700 tomorrow morning," the captain said.

Duncan appealed, not for himself, but for Molly. "Without her, you'd have nothing," he said.

The captain looked ill. He lowered his eyes. "That will be all," he said.

7.

"Like outcasts."

The words poured with smoke from Kleat's mouth.

Molly was sitting with him and Duncan at a window table over-looking the Mekong River. It was a brand-new restaurant to go with the brand-new Japanese bridge leading east. Sunset lit the water red. Fans spun overhead, politely, enough to eddy Kleat's cigar smoke but not rustle the pages of Duncan's *World Tribune.* The starched white tablecloth was immaculate.

None of it seemed real.

"We find their pilot for them," Kleat said, "and like that, *adios, pendejos.*"

"For the record, he's not found yet, only his helmet," said Duncan. "And one other thing, it was Molly who found him. Not us." He raised a toast to her.

Molly gamely lifted her glass. Kleat passed.

The ice-cold Heineken was like culture shock. She sat there. Her farmer tan torpedoed the dandelion-yellow sundress she had been saving for just such an evening. It jumped up at her, the sunburn and freckles to her upper arms, then the shoulders as white as moons. She looked half naked to herself. And her hair, like something chopped to Goth with surgical scissors, which was what she'd resorted to. She lifted her chin. Nothing to do about it tonight. Beauty, skin deep, all that.

The sun went on sinking. Only this morning, the sun had seemed like a peasant disease, breaking them down all day, leaving them sore and weary by night. Now, with a drink in hand and the fans cooling the air, she did her best to see the sunset as a thing of great beauty. She tried to savor her postexpedition daze, to relinquish the heat and dust and insects. She put off thoughts of whatever came next. The day was ending. The month. A full month she had spent grubbing after the dead.

Kleat started in on her. This last supper was his idea. Molly had actually hoped they could part friends. Dumb.

"You were told," he said. "Day one. Their first commandment. I heard the captain tell you. No shooting the dead. Anything but them. So what do you do?"

The scar at his throat turned purple. He never talked about the scar. He seemed to think it spoke for him. Most of the people on the dig thought it came from a sloppy thyroid surgery.

"We've been through this," Duncan said quietly. "The camera was just their excuse." He was still holding his *World Tribune,* five days out of date, devouring every word.

"We got pulled down with her," Kleat said.

Molly sighed. He couldn't help himself. She only wished he could have waited until after dessert. The waiters hadn't even arrived with her salad. The restaurant was known for its salad Niçoise. For a month, she had been waiting for it.

"A deal was struck," said Duncan. "They were given a week to recover the pilot. However they're getting through those bones, it's not for public consumption, American or Cambodian. They don't want outsiders to see it."

"Get this straight," Kleat said. "I'm not one of you."

"I don't mean this harshly, John," Duncan said, "but that's all you are. One of us."

The veins stood out on Kleat's burnished skull. He leaned in. "I belonged."

"I'll say it again," Molly said. "I thought the well was empty."

"You knew. Somehow you knew."

"She has a gift," Duncan said. "Leave it at that."

It was useless talking about it. The captain had been ordered to make a clean sweep. His three guests had been loaded into a Land Cruiser and sent away.

She looked from one man to the other, each freshly showered, their whiskers scraped off. The dig had thinned them. Their clean shirts hung on their shoulders like stolen laundry. They looked like sticks of hard driftwood among the last of the Europeans at the tables around them. The package tours had all but shut down. The monsoon season was almost here, and the typhoon was circling in the South China Sea.

"It was never your brother down there anyway," said Duncan. "We knew that from the start. You said he went missing along the border. That's a hundred miles to the east. And this was a crash site. We were looking for a pilot, not a soldier on foot."

"You don't get it." Kleat was plaintive. "They'll never have me back again."

The sunset trembled. Thunder, too low to hear, vibrated the window in the frame. The glass buzzed like locusts.

The typhoon qualified for a name, an Asian name for a change, Mekkhala, Thai for Angel of Thunder. It was only the coming monsoon's daily grumble, but everyone tied to it the angel's thunder. The restaurant owner had sheets of wood ready to protect his expensive windows. The glass vibrated again. It would come soon.

"I'm sorry," Molly said.

Kleat wasn't prepared for that. His eyes seemed to crouch. "Tell it to the captain."

"I mean about your brother," she said.

The stub of cigar flared.

"I hope you find him someday."

"Because you know how it feels?"

"Yes."

"Not your orphan story," he said. "Again."

This was a mistake. "Forget it," she said.

"No, really. Sharing losses while you gave them haircuts? You think that made you part of the team? We came to locate soldiers."

"I know."

"Molly," he said. "Your mother was just some hippie chick."

"Enough," Duncan muttered.

"Why?" said Kleat. "I'm curious. You make me wonder, both of you. We didn't come together by accident. We draw up the dead for a reason. It was a rough, dirty, hot toilet of a month. You suffered for this."

"We all suffered," said Duncan.

"But the thing is, you didn't have to. I need to be here. And the captain and his team, we have a duty to perform. Not you, though."

Duncan shrugged. "Just lending a hand."

"The boys have waited long enough."

"Something like that."

"You talk like it was your war."

"Wrong address, friend." Duncan flashed a peace sign.

"Tell me, sitting on your campus back then, were they all just fools to you?"

"Not a single one of them. I'm only saying that it wasn't my war. I wasn't here."

"And yet here you are," said Kleat.

"In the flesh."

"Of all places."

Duncan gestured at the glorious river. He took a deep lungful of the air, and Molly smelled it, too, the scent of bougainvillea as thick as hash smoke. "It grows on you," he said.

"I didn't mean the territory in general. I was talking about our little dig. Where you had no real business. Professionally speaking."

"Professionally speaking," Duncan agreed, "no business at all."

"Getting right with God? The old pacifist burying old warriors?"

"That must be it," said Duncan.

"And you?" Kleat said, turning to Molly. Duncan wouldn't fight him, maybe she would. "Do you mind me asking?"

How could she mind? She was an inquisitor herself. "Go ahead."

"Just to connect the dots, you know. We've got a soldier, my brother," he opened one hand, then the other, "and your mother. A suicide."

She blinked at his malice. "I never used that word."

Kleat considered his cigar, one of the captain's Havanas. "She parks her baby with a friend, leaves twelve bucks and a week's worth of cat food. Then takes a hit of LSD and wanders off into a blizzard. That is what you told us."

"Not like that, I didn't."

Not until it came time to fill out her college application forms had Molly learned that she was adopted. She had taken it hard. She'd actually made her parents—her stepparents—apologize. Then she'd run off to hunt for her birth mother. Over the coming years, she had changed to her mother's maiden name, and her sleuthing skills led to journalism. That was her point in telling the soldiers on the recovery team, to identify where she came from, not to infiltrate them with a sob story.

"So you found her, and it made you whole," Kleat said. He wanted blood.

"It took me three years to find a picture of her," Molly said. She had it now, in her passport wallet, a Texas driver's license issued in 1967. But no way was she going to share that with them, at least not with Kleat. "It took another two years to find her grave." She did not describe the miner's cemetery in Breckenridge, altitude 9,600 feet, wildflowers everywhere.

"At least she got a grave."

Molly stared at him. From the start, he had treated her like treason waiting to happen. She'd thought it had to do with her occupation, but it was both more and less personal than that. He was one of those troubled souls in constant need of a scapegoat, and for some reason, she'd been filling the role for a month. Going along to get along, maybe. Not anymore. The story was stone cold. Let the bastard go find another punching bag.

Molly looked out the window. The river was on fire with red. Small boats ferried back and forth, the far shore going dark.

The cocktail hour was dying. Soon the waiters would bring their dinner. The evening could end.

A tiny desperation crept in. Tomorrow was almost here, and her future was in tatters. She'd banked everything on the *Times*. From this piece others would flow, then book deals, and film options. But the world was no longer her oyster.

Kleat was making a quick escape, back to his twelve-cent beers and five-dollar wives. He'd already booked a flight out of Phnom Penh, two hours to the south, for tomorrow afternoon.

Duncan had decided his restoration work in the north could wait until the rainy season passed. He was going to the big city. Though he must have resupplied in Phnom Penh countless times over the years, he acted like Marco Polo about to enter the marvels of Xanadu. He couldn't wait to investigate its streets and markets and temples.

In short, one of them was going, one was staying, and Molly was torn. Nothing waited for her at home, no obligations, no cat, no boyfriend, and no deadline. It had been too early to plant her herb garden on her little deck before leaving, and it would be too late by the time she returned. There was a friend's wedding in July, a half marathon for breast cancer in August, her yoga classes at the Y, and an astronomy class up at the university. And bills to pay and work to scare up.

But she was here. Asia no longer intimidated her. After a month in the field, she was toughened and road ready, and Duncan had caught her eye. He was an islander, of sorts, solitary and curious and uncomplicated.

She was going to ask him to guide her through Angkor Wat. Not tonight, but once Kleat left, she meant to propose a short adventure before the storm. It was a whim, one that hadn't occurred to her before an hour ago. She suspected it might lead to other things between them, other cities, maybe another life, a bend in the road.

She wasn't quite sure how to handle their age gap. Kent State was ancient history, though Duncan didn't seem old enough for it by a decade. She had tried to imagine him thirty years ago. He would have had a little more meat on him, and fewer creases around the eyes. But he would have had the same sweet calm. A keeper. Thirty years ago.

She'd never tried a winter-summer relationship, never even thought about it. On the other hand, he wasn't exactly winter and she wasn't exactly summer. She told herself it shouldn't matter. If things didn't work out, the typhoon was all the excuse she'd need to flee.

The glass trembled again.

8.

The restaurant grew quiet.

Kleat looked at his watch. "Six sharp," he said. "Send in the clowns."

Molly turned as the entrance lit with the color of tangerines. Three old monks filed in, led by a child. Bits of the sunset seemed caught in their saffron robes.

She had heard of them. They were blind. The owner let them in each evening.

All around, tourists hushed reverently, even the Germans at the bar. Chairs creaked as people twisted to see. A woman started to applaud, and stopped herself. This was not like on the sidewalks where the amputees and widows leaped out at you. The monks were well washed and stately, a taste of Cambodia to go with your umbrella drinks. The waiters backed against the wall and bowed, theatrical with their white gloves pressed together at their foreheads.

"*Tanto quiso el diablo a sus hijos que les sacó los ojos.*" Duncan said.

"What?" said Molly.

"It's an old saying. 'The devil loved his children so much that he poked out their eyes.' "

"Only it was the KR, not the devil," said Kleat. "And they used spoons."

She was reminded of Brueghel's painting, the blind leading the blind, stumbling among the rabble. No rabble here, though. Nor stumbling. The young boy's head was shaved to the skin, a novitiate. They wove among the tables with serpent grace, gathering their alms, American dollars mostly. Molly saw one couple sign over a traveler's check. The man and woman pressed their palms together in an awkward *sampeah,* but of course the monks could not see them.

"The waiters will be taking a cut," Kleat observed.

As the monks approached, Molly saw old scars glistening at the center of their wrinkled foreheads. Their third eyes had been ritually mutilated. They held their heads high, each connected by a few fingertips to the shoulder ahead of him.

"What, no sins to pay for?" Duncan asked Kleat. He was opening his steel briefcase to get his wallet.

"At these prices, I'd say it's already built into the menu," Kleat said.

Molly stood to get a dollar bill from her pocket.

That was when she noticed the gypsy from their dig. He was standing in the doorway staring straight at them. She jerked with surprise.

"What's he doing here?" she said. The two men looked up at her. "There," she pointed.

Just then the line of monks passed in front of the doorway, blocking her view. When they had moved on to the next table, the opening stood empty.

"Never mind," she said.

He'd never come within two hundred yards of them, so why would he be here? His place was in the mirages, along the horizon, in the ball of the rising or setting sun.

She started to sit down, but he had moved, and was watching them.

"There," she said, startled all over again.

He had maneuvered across the room and was standing by a table with a French couple. He had gray peasant pants and a green and black camouflage T-shirt with ragged holes. He was barefoot. The French pair was not pleased by his presence.

They all saw him now. It was as if he'd stepped out of her camera.

"Incredible," said Kleat.

The baggy gray pants had once been black. The cuffs stood at his knees, shredded by dogs. His shins were crisscrossed with bite wounds.

Some of the soldiers back at the dig had thought he might be a freelance journalist down on his luck, way down. Or, as Kleat had suggested, a heroin addict lost in inner space. Duncan wondered if he might be the son of an MIA, shipwrecked by a lifetime of hope. There was even the possibility that he could be an actual, living MIA, though no one on the dig really believed that. It was a powerful piece of MIA mythology, the POW who was still out there, or the defector who'd decided to stay into infinity. One such man, a marine named Garwood, had in fact surfaced in Vietnam years after the war. Ever since, Molly learned, the Garwood factor had become red meat for the MIA movement. They fed on it endlessly. The official military forensics teams viewed themselves as an antidote to such wishful thinking. Their only prey was the bones, though they tipped their hat to the MIA movement.

The stranger didn't nod at them. He was gaunt. A hundred twenty pounds, Molly guessed, no more. Duncan had said he must eat weeds and insects, like John the Baptist. "He must have followed us from the dig," she said.

"Impossible," said Kleat. "It took us five hours by car to get down here. We would have seen him behind us."

"One way or another, here he is."

"He's stalking us," Kleat said.

It did feel like that. But which of them was he after?

The man began walking toward them. The boy. He was much younger than she'd thought. His blond hair was almost white from the undiluted sun. He had a cowlick and reminded her of Dennis the Menace, on smack. All he lacked was a slingshot in his back pocket.

Kleat placed one hand on the table. Molly looked twice. His hand was covering his dinner knife.

"Relax," said Duncan. "He probably just wants some of our peanuts and beer."

The fans loosened the countryside from creases in his clothing and his hair. The sunset lit the fine dust into a fiery nimbus. The French couple covered their food.

Molly expected bad smells, the reek of old urine and feces and sweat, but he only smelled like dust. He came to a halt behind the fourth chair at their table, with the window—and the sunset—behind him. It was hard to see his eyes. A thin corona of red dust wafted from his shoulders.

"What are you doing here?" Kleat demanded.

"I see you out there," the man said. "Going through the motions. Wasting away."

"Is that so?"

"Like starved hogs. All that dust for nothing, Jesus."

For all his raw bearing, he had a voice like the breeze. Molly had to strain for it. He was American, no faking the West Texas accent. Twenty years old probably, going on a thousand, one of those kids. He'd seen it all.

"It don't work," he said. "You can't hide."

"It worked. It took a while. But we found our man," Duncan said. "Molly did."

"Who?"

"The young lady," said Duncan.

The stranger didn't waste a glance at her. "What man?" he said.

Kleat lifted his chin. It showed his scar like a second smile. "A pilot. He's found. It's done."

The stranger stretched his fist to the middle of the table and opened his fingers. Molly looked for track marks on his forearm, but there were none. Then she remembered that the poppy was so cheap here, people just toked it. A clot of hard black dirt, as hard as cement, fell from his hand onto the tablecloth.

"Quit pretending," the man said.

The thing looked worthless, an animal turd, nothing. A chain protruded from one end.

Kleat lifted the chain with his dinner knife. "Jewelry?"

"You could say that."

It was a fistful of mud grabbed from the earth and dried in the sun. Molly saw his finger imprints. Then she saw an edge of flat metal at one corner. With that and the chain she could guess what it was. She took it from Kleat and scratched at the crust with her fingernail, but it was baked on hard.

"Here," said Duncan. Without ceremony, he sank it in his water glass. He stirred with his spoon and the water clouded dark gray, then black.

While the clot dissolved, Molly spoke. "We left food for you. You never ate it."

The man didn't say a word to her. He just stood waiting, infinitely tolerant. Flying on junk, she thought. But his eyes were too bright, too present in the shadow face.

"We know what it is," said Kleat, "if it's even real."

"Real as you or me," the man answered. "Real as anything."

"Three possibilities then." Kleat issued a thick stream of smoke. "You bought it. It's your own. Or you looted it. Is that what you did?"

Duncan scooped out what was left of the clot and crumbled it over his dish. What emerged was a small, flat metal plate, a dog tag, just as she'd suspected. Her heartbeat quickened.

If this really had been stolen from the well, then it was a possible proof of identity, perhaps their only one. She'd learned that the forensic labs wanted teeth, preferably an entire mandible, to match to dental charts. In addition, DNA testing could work, though only if a maternal relative had stepped forward over the past thirty years to offer blood. Without the benefit of primary, organic identifiers, the agencies had to rely on circumstantial evidence: a wedding band, a class ring, an engraved pocketknife. Or a dog tag.

"It's a message," the gypsy said. Deep gone, that face. *Lost in the arms of Asia,* thought Molly.

"Excellent," said Kleat. "What's it say?"

"Quit your pissing around."

Kleat, the searcher, flushed. "That's the message?"

"I'm still waiting," the boy spoke.

"What it says," said Duncan, washing the tag in his water and wiping the embossed letters, "is Samuels, Jefferson S. There's a birth date. His blood type. Protestant. And a serial number."

Molly knew everything about the pilot RE-1 had been searching for, from the date of his shoot down to the root canal in his left molar. And his name had not been Jefferson Samuels.

"Nothing," Kleat said to the man. "You have nothing."

The man dropped two more clots on the white tablecloth, two more tags.

Duncan cracked them open like eggs, black dirt all over the white tablecloth. He read the second tag, and the third. "Sanchez, Thomas A. Bellwether, Edward P."

"Who the hell are you?" Kleat demanded.

Molly tried, more gently. She pointed at his arm, at the tattoo like a ghost beneath the dust. "Is that your name? Lucas Yale?"

"Luke," he said.

Molly looked at Duncan and Kleat, and the name meant nothing to them. It defeated her, the uselessness of the name. She had nothing more to ask.

"Where did you find these?" Kleat said.

Luke looked at Molly for the first time. "I come to show you. Let's go."

"Just tell us," said Kleat.

"It's not so easy," the boy said. The red sky bulged behind him, a great final burst of coloration. Night was falling.

"You're playing a dangerous game," Kleat said, "kidnapping the dead."

In fact, the practice was as common as despair in this fertile green country. Peasants trafficked in human bones all the time, trying to prize money from the Americans even when the bones weren't American.

"How much do you want?" said Molly.

The stranger smiled at her suddenly, and he was missing significant teeth on the right side, upper and lower. What teeth still remained lay green in there. Duncan was right, the boy must have been eating grass and weeds, rifling the land. But then Molly saw that it was moss, actual moss, growing between his teeth, like something out of a movie. The tropics had taken root in this young ancient. It showed in the leather of his face. It peeked from his mouth.

"No charge," he said, "not for you-all."

"Show us on a map," said Duncan. He took a map from his brief-case. He suspected the stranger even more than Kleat did, and that put Molly on alert. His instincts were telling him something.

"Never mind that," Luke said. "It's off the map."

"Come on, this is the twenty-first century. There's no such thing as off the map. They have satellites."

"Well, if it was on a map, they wouldn't have ended where they are," said Luke.

"How far away is this place?" Molly asked, trying to cut through the mystery. The key was to get your source talking.

"It's a ride. We need to leave."

"A ride. Does that mean an hour? A day? Two days?"

"One night's ride. Tonight."

It sank in.

"You're joking," Kleat said. "Leave tonight? We've been on the road all day. I have a flight to reschedule. We need to rest. Prepare."

"There's six more," Luke told them.

That shut Kleat up.

"Six more dog tags?" Molly was incredulous.

"Bones, weapons, whatever it is you need." Molly could see his tongue in the gap of missing teeth. "It's all there. All yours."

They were quiet for a minute. Nine soldiers? Molly felt something like rapture. She was saved. Here was her *Times* story, minus the scolds at the Pentagon.

"And all we have to do is follow you?" said Duncan.

"I can't make you do a thing."

"They don't belong to you," Kleat said. "These tags, the bones, the relics, whatever you found."

"What more do you want? I'm saying come on. They're all yours."

"Sit down," Molly said. He could walk out as easily as he had walked in, and then where would they be? "Eat with us. We've ordered our supper. We can talk things through."

Luke stayed on his feet.

"There are proper channels for this kind of thing," Duncan said. Molly could hear his turmoil. The boy confused him. Molly had never seen this side of him. Things were moving too fast for him. "You could have told the captain at camp. You could go to the embassy. Why here? Why tonight? Why us?"

Luke said, "Because you want it so bad."

It was true. He had them cold. Week after week, he'd been watching them. He couldn't know their individual appetites, but he'd seen their hunger.

The possibility grew on her. An American drifter circling through his own tropical dream world, stumbling upon relics from the war, why not? And it was perfectly conceivable that a drug addict, or schizophrenic, whatever he was, would trust three civilians over the captain and his soldiers. Uniformed or not, the military would represent an authority that might take him away. An authority that had rejected her and Duncan and Kleat.

Luke pointed at the new bridge. "I'll wait on the far side there. You have two hours."

"Two hours?" Kleat snapped.

Molly spoke to Luke. "It's just so unexpected. There may be a serious storm coming. We can't afford to be stranded in some godforsaken place. Is there a village nearby? How many days will we be gone?"

He was backing away from the table.

"You've waited this long, and there's so much to be done," she said. Slow him down. Keep him here. But he was leaving. "We have to arrange transportation, find food, get our gear."

"I told you," Luke said, "I can't force a thing. You have to make up your own minds." Then he turned and walked off. The doorway swallowed him.

Duncan was the first to speak after the boy left. "The poor kid belongs in an asylum," he said. "Or in Cambodia."

"You don't think it's real then?" said Molly. *But we can make it real.* The story held that kind of childlike potential. You just had to believe in it.

"We'll know soon enough," Kleat said. He stabbed his glasses tighter against the bridge of his nose and produced a small dog-eared notebook. It was his bible, an index of all the American soldiers who had never returned from Cambodia, including his brother. He had copied it from Brite Lite, the team's database of the missing. He leaned over the first dog tag and thumbed through the pages.

Just then the waiters arrived with dinner. Seeing the dirt and mud, they wanted to change the tablecloth and bring clean napkins and silverware. Duncan instructed them to set the various plates wherever there was room. Determined to have their ceremony, the waiters lifted the lids from the dishes with a flourish. Molly's Australian lobster steamed. Kleat's steak ran bloody, the way he'd ordered it. A hamburger sat in a croissant—a makeshift bun—for Duncan. No salads.

Kleat grunted at his index and picked up the second tag.

"Even if he was telling the truth," said Duncan, "he's withholding information. And if he isn't telling the truth, we'd be fools to rush off into the night with him. They have gangs out there. He could be part of them. This is a desolate country."

"You think he might be bait?" said Molly.

"I don't know. There's something about him. He's too much in love with his own mystery."

"How's that make him different from any of us?" said Kleat. "We're creatures of our fictions, every one of us."

His mood had shifted. He was suddenly in high spirits. And Molly noticed that he was speaking once again in the plural, "us," not "me." It was no accident. He was, she realized, team building. He needed them. Not an hour before, he'd been ready to damn them for spoiling his place with the captain. Now he was trying to recruit them.

"I've had enough make-believe in my life," Molly said. "I agree with Duncan. The boy is up to something. But what if he's also telling the truth?"

"It would be a coup," said Kleat. "The search-and-recovery agencies average twenty finds per year, at a cost of close to a hundred million dollars. Per year. Here's our chance to take home nine sets of remains, paid for with the spare change in our pockets. Imagine that, three civilians, on their own."

His excitement verged on lust, and Molly felt it, too. For Kleat it would mean sweet revenge for his eviction from the dig. It wasn't in her nature to live for payback. The story was its own reward. This could translate into a book deal, maybe even Hollywood.

She started constructing it in her mind, a brief history of the misbegotten war and then the tale of discovering nine of its lost children. She would keep herself out of the story, but at the same time make it deeply personal. Once she had names for the whole bunch of them, she would dive into the soldiers' pasts and weave the story of their nexus in the jungle.

The sunset died. Its vast light winked out. Kleat finished by candlelight, grinning, knowing.

"What?" said Molly.

"Private First Class Edward Bellwether," he read to them. "Master Sergeant Jefferson Samuels. Private First Class Thomas Anthony Sanchez. They're real, or were. All three of them are listed as unaccounted for. And get this. They were part of the same platoon, an armored cavalry unit with the Blackhorse Regiment. All three were last seen embarking on a reconnaissance along the Ho Chi Minh Trail inside Cambodia on June 23, 1970." He paused. "I'd say we have ourselves a mission."

Molly drew in a breath, all the aromas mingling, firing her hunger. She looked out the window, but darkness had turned it into a mirror and she saw only herself. Her world felt reversed. On the verge of leaving, they were returning. Instead of being driven out, they could go back in, deeper, to greater reward, all on their own terms.

"What about the other six men?" asked Duncan. "What does it say about them?"

"There's no way to cross-reference names and events. We could try calling the Department of Defense; it's seven in the morning in

Washington. But that might only tip off the captain, and we already know what he thinks of us. No, we have to go with what we have."

"I still don't like it," Duncan said.

"We're talking about just a few days more."

"You don't know that. And if the typhoon makes landfall . . ."

Kleat bent to his steak. "We can do this thing."

"In the middle of the night, though," Duncan pondered. "What's his game?"

"The kid's full of demons. A psycho. So what. He's found something."

"He wants a sense of control," said Molly. "I say let him have it. Let him run the show his way. Soon enough we'll have what we want."

"And then he can go back to prowling around the moon," said Kleat.

"I was going to say, then maybe we can take him home, where he belongs."

Kleat's jaw muscles bunched. He was ravenous. "That's your business."

"Your mind is made up then," Duncan said to Molly. It was a question.

She looked at him. "I want this," she said.

He looked at the window turned to mirror. "Then I'll go, too," he said.

9.

The idea of the journey hijacked them. This was a quest of their own making. It had the effect of making the last month with RE-1 nothing more than preparation for a much larger voyage.

Mindful of Luke's petulant deadline, driven by it, they nevertheless forced themselves to stay at the table for fifteen precious minutes. They devoured their meal with the haste of thieves stealing someone else's dinner, knifing the meat to pieces, tearing open the lobster, going for protein. Between bites, they made lists, compiled a budget, created a treasury of $458 American, and assigned each other tasks. Then they cast off through the town.

It was simple, really. Having just come off one expedition, they knew exactly what was needed for their next. Also, they didn't require so very much. They agreed that the search would last no more than one week, round-trip. The remains were either real or they were not. A quick look, a quick retrieval, then they would race back to the city. At the first raindrop, whether it fell from the monsoon winds or was driven by the typhoon Mekkhala, they would all obey reason.

Kleat was sent back to their hotel to collect their clothes and other possessions, while Duncan took a taxi with Molly to try and find old Samnang.

Kampong Cham was not a large city. A few inquiries led them to Samnang, getting ready for bed in his cement-floored apartment. He graciously invited them in. His plastic leg was propped to one side. Incense was inking up from a little shrine in the corner.

Like Duncan, Samnang questioned the midnight ride. But like Duncan, when he saw Molly's resolve, he agreed to join them. They were doing this, she understood, to protect her.

With Samnang's involvement, the expedition metamorphosed from an idea into reality. He immediately knew where to obtain everything they required. He gravely fitted on his leg, then locked his door, leaving the incense to burn itself out.

By taxi they drove along the river to a small, walled compound, the home of the three Heng brothers. Molly knew them, or at least their faces, from the dig. One had driven her, Duncan, and Kleat from the dig that very morning, which gave a promising symmetry to tonight's venture. It was almost as if she were being delivered to her proper destination.

The brothers owned a white Land Cruiser from the UN days, along with an antique Mercedes truck dating back to the French colonial period. Once the expedition was presented to them, they pounced at the chance for more work. Driving into the night didn't bother them at all.

It now unfolded that the Heng brothers owed their relative wealth to the black market. Molly marveled at their hoard of military rations, fuel, tents, medicines, weapons, and digging tools stolen from various UN armies, USAID, the Red Cross, and, she recognized, the RE-1 dig. There were enough provisions here for five expeditions.

With Samnang's help, Duncan bargained the brothers down to what he called their "all-inclusive rate." With fuel, the week of driving, supplies, and "equipment rental," their fee came to four hundred and twenty dollars. Shouting back and forth, the brothers dashed around the courtyard with boxes and bags and jerry cans of fuel, loading the truck and wiping the dust from the seats for their passengers.

It was not quite eight-thirty as their little convoy crossed the bridge leading north.

Luke was waiting for them where he'd said, sitting on his

haunches at the far side of the bridge in a globe of yellowing electric light. The bats were rampant here. Molly had seen them before, hanging from the highest branches like leathery fruit, but now they dove from the shadows, cutting swaths through the clouds of huge moths drawn to the lamp.

As they approached, he stood in their headlights and Molly noticed the dogs. There were twenty or thirty of them, skeletal orange and tan things, circling Luke, keeping their distance. Until Cambodia, she had never given two thoughts to the expression "dog eat dog." Hungry enough, they really did. She had pictures of puppies being carried away in the jaws of mongrels, of a dog gnawing at a dog skull. Her shock had amused Kleat.

He stood without a wave or a greeting, holding not one thing in his hands, not even a cigarette. Under the road dirt, his skin gleamed in the headlights. The dog bites and thorn cuts on his shins had the plastic gloss of old scars.

For a moment, a terrible moment, Molly saw her mother in him, crazy as hell, ricocheting from the kindness and torment of strangers, lost to the world, surrounded by dogs. A chill shot through her. For all the smothering wet heat, goose bumps flared along her arms and legs.

The sight of him made Molly fear for herself as she had been long ago, for the half-forgotten infant in her mother's arms. How many animals had circled them, too, waiting for a meal? How many lamplights had her mother sheltered beneath? The miracle of that baby's survival flooded Molly, not with awe, but with terror.

Had flies billowed around the smell of breast milk on her mother's blouse? Had truckers ejected the roadside Madonna and child when they caught a whiff of unchanged diapers? Molly had floated through a gauntlet of loathing and dangers that she could never precisely know. But the sight of this stranger, this walking suicide, threw her into a panic.

Molly's hands went to her stomach, her womb, as it were, and felt the passport wallet hidden under her sundress. Inside it were her passport and money and one other thing, perhaps her most valuable possession, the driver's license issued in 1967 to a teenage girl named

Jane Drake. The image came to her, Molly's same black hair, Molly's same green eyes. Molly had three inches on her, and outweighed her by ten pounds, but they were still the same woman. She closed her eyes and drew up the sweet optimism on that face, and it was nothing like the harrowed madman in their headlights. Her alarm subsided.

She snapped a picture of Luke through the cracked windshield, mostly to return to herself. The big Mercedes pulled alongside. Kleat looked down from the cab. "What are we waiting for?" he said.

Molly was sitting in the front seat of the Land Cruiser. Luke took the backseat, next to Duncan. He was thin as a willow wand, but when he climbed in, the vehicle sagged under his weight. She thought the shocks must be worn out.

"Please fasten your seat belts and place your trays in an upright position," Molly said to him. She was excited. A great discovery was about to unfold. Then she glanced back, and Luke's face was joyless.

10.

Highway 7 lunged at them. No neat white lines. No mile markers. No speed limit. No warning signs. Speed was their only safe conduct, or so she gathered from the way their driver drove. They didn't slow even when they passed through darkened villages or swerved for pot-holes Molly could not see.

She had never ridden at night in Cambodia, and so help her God never would again. To conserve their headlights, everyone drove with their lights off. Trucks, cars, buses, all hurtled at them from the darkness. Only at the very last instant would their lights spring on, then off, blowing her night vision, leaving her—and presumably their driver—more sightless than before.

The boy hunched in the darkness, like a reptile, his chest to the steering wheel, his forehead pressed to the glass. He was the youngest of the brothers, maybe nineteen or twenty, with wrists little thicker than the plastic steering wheel. Born and raised in refugee camps, they had come up through misery she could only imagine. He was wearing a blue-checkered *kroma,* and his arms and neck were cross-hatched with tattoos. He kept humming Smashing Pumpkins tunes learned from the RE-1 soldiers.

She wished Duncan would tell some of his jokes and stories, but he was mostly silent beside the stone lump of their guide. The boys weren't having fun. It was a road trip, not a funeral. She tried to prime the pump. She handed out little Jolly Rancher cinnamon candies from her bag, offering one to the driver.

"His name is Vin," said Duncan.

"Vin," she said. The boy smiled.

"Heng Putheathvin," Duncan amplified. "Among Khmers, the surname goes first, though it varies from child to child depending on the parents' whim. It can get confusing. They might use the mother's surname for one child, and the father's for another. It's like a gift they decide upon at birth. Sometimes the father will give his surname to a favorite child. Sometimes he gives it to a bad luck child just in order to protect him. Or her."

"A bad luck child?"

"It's a curious custom, a kind of fetal scapegoat. While the baby is still in the womb, he or she bears responsibility for any bad luck that lands on the family. Say a mother goes into labor and sends her son for the midwife, and along the way a dog bites the boy. The infant is held responsible. From then on, you're marked. Everyone around knows you brought bad luck from the womb. But the father can help deflect it by giving you his family name."

"That's so unfair," said Molly. "To blame an unborn child."

"It's that destiny thing," Duncan said. He spoke to Vin in Khmer. The boy responded shyly. Duncan laughed. "I asked him, and Heng is their father's name. He said he and his brothers are all bad luck children."

"Ask him about his tattoos."

Duncan and Vin went back and forth. Vin seemed quite proud.

"They're called *sak*," said Duncan. "It's warrior magic. The tattoos protect him from knives and bullets. He has them on his arms, legs, and chest, even a little one in the part of his hair. He got them because his brothers have them. His oldest brother has the most elaborate ones. That's because he was actually a soldier with the government. His brother has killed men. Rebels. Vin wants to get a tiger done on his legs, the tail down one leg, the head down the other. That way he'll be safe from the land mines."

"Jesus, man." It was Luke, staring at Duncan in dismay. "You talk like a believer."

"We're not in Kansas anymore," Duncan said to him.

"And what's this?" Molly asked, pointing at the most unusual marking. She'd seen it earlier. Duncan shined his light on Vin's neck. At the upper tip of a series of welts lay a reddish image of George Washington.

"That," said Duncan, "is an American quarter. In reverse."

"He had a quarter tattooed on his neck?"

"Not tattooed. It's folk medicine. *Koh khchal,* 'coining,' in English. It's not so different from medical philosophy in medieval Europe, the idea of ridding yourself of bad humors. A healer, or it can be a parent or a friend, dips a coin in kerosene to get a good grip, then they rub like hell, usually on your back or chest or arms."

Duncan asked Vin a question. "He has a headache. One of his brothers gave him a good, hard session. The coin can get pretty hot. His brother pressed it on his neck, like a signature. George Washington was here."

"Tell him I have a tattoo," Molly said, "a butterfly."

Duncan told Vin. "He said he'd like to see it someday."

"Oh, it's in kind of a private place."

"In that case, I'd like to see it someday."

Molly's eyes flicked up at the mirror, but she could see only Luke's dark face. Duncan laughed and told the boy. Vin tucked his head, mortified.

"You didn't have to embarrass him," said Molly.

"He'll survive."

"Listen to you." It was Luke, his voice hard.

"Yeah?" asked Duncan.

"You're losing yourself."

"No harm in connecting with the culture. It is their country."

"Maybe," Luke said, "you should stick with your own kind."

"And why is that?" said Duncan.

"It's all tricks, you know," Luke said. "You're only fooling yourself."

Duncan's smile faded.

Molly turned to Luke. Talk about bad luck children. "What about you?" she tried. "Where do you come from?"

It was like talking into an empty pipe. He said nothing more. The Jolly Rancher candy sat in his hand. After that the talk died. The miles went by.

A small light flipped on and off as Duncan periodically marked their position on a map spread across his legs. She guessed they must have covered two hundred miles, though it was impossible to know with the gauges broken or unhooked and the dash light dead.

For years the American embassy had been warning against travel into the distant provinces, especially at night. Rogue soldiers and war cripples were epidemic, with a nasty habit of highway robbery. The wars were over, she told herself. Those days were done. But she knew they were not really. Violence lay just beneath the skin here. Rebels still came together for various causes, and the countryside held more land mines per square mile than even Afghanistan or Bosnia.

But mile after mile there were no roadblocks, no highwaymen, and Molly tried to relax. Apparently the bandits had exploited the road too efficiently. It seemed they'd driven themselves right out of business.

During one stop to put more oil in the smoking truck, Kleat came up to them.

Molly made some remark about the wild night driving.

"You're afraid? Good," said Kleat. "Fear is a gift. It purifies us. Listen to it and you can see right through the night." He was exultant. "And how's our guide? How are you doing, Slick?" he said to Luke.

Luke looked at him. "Johnny Hollywood," he said, like he knew him.

It startled Kleat. He flinched, almost as if it meant something. He spit on the road. "Do we have some problem?"

"Are you really sure you want to be here?" Luke asked him.

Kleat glanced suspiciously at Molly and Duncan to see if they'd been talking among themselves. Molly shook her head at him and frowned. She didn't know what this was about.

"I'm helping pay for your ride, aren't I?" Kleat said to Luke.

"That don't make it your party. Slick."

"How's that?" Kleat said.

But Luke only trained his eyes back on the road. He had nothing more to add. Molly couldn't make sense of it. Neither one of them played well with others. But hell if she was going to be the mommy. Let them sort it out.

Kleat let loose his grip on. He returned to the truck and climbed up into the cab. The convoy started off again, back into the flash of metal giants roaring by in the night.

The moon broke from the clouds, and the paddies bracketing the road jumped to life. The highway became a dark strip sandwiched between hundreds of reflected moons. The land turned dreamlike, a world of harbored water arranged in honeycombs. The clouds sailed over, returning them to darkness.

Molly checked her watch. Barely eleven. A long night of the soul still ahead. Thankfully, whether because of the deepening night or their growing remoteness, the traffic grew sparse. They passed more villages, more paddy fields with their thousand moons.

"Mamot," Duncan noted. The map rustled. A little later, he said, "Snuol, is that where we're going?"

Molly could see Luke in the rearview mirror, his face yellow in the penlight. He tapped his dusty head. "I haven't forgot. It's all up here."

"Up there," said Duncan. "Is that like a state of mind or something?"

Molly listened. It wasn't like Duncan to taunt.

"What's to worry?" said Luke.

"It's just that you seem to be making it up as we go along."

"And you're not?"

Molly wanted Duncan to leave it alone. If the night was a bust, it was their own fault. Luke wasn't duping them. They were duping themselves. He had whispered to their expectations, and they had run with it. The man wasn't about to give up his secret, and that was that. Their destination, real or not, was the only currency he had. She wished Duncan would quit worrying with the maps and turn off his light. It glared on the windshield and made the road that much harder to read.

"Run it past me again," Duncan said, "how you found this place."

"It seemed like the place to go," said Luke.

Duncan persisted. "You were just out knocking around? Slumming in the provinces?"

"Like that."

"Except you don't have the look of a tourist. More like a runaway."

That had been another conjecture among RE-1, that the gypsy had escaped from some Asian jail. It would explain why he stayed at a distance, but always stayed. According to the theory, he was scared and homesick and needed their proximity. He didn't sound scared or homesick tonight.

"There's things you can't run from," Luke said. "You're here, aren't you?"

"Not really. You can thank Mr. Kleat for our presence. He's the one so hungry for it." Duncan didn't mention Molly, even though she was his real reason for coming along.

"The big appetite." Luke seemed amused. "What's he think is up there?"

Up where? Along the road or higher? Molly was listening intently.

For a month, Kleat had been slandering Duncan behind his back, calling him a liar, a sad sack, a fraud, laboring to get him tossed from the dig. Duncan wasn't stupid. Molly knew he knew. Now was his chance to strike back.

Instead, Duncan said only, "Redemption."

It was gracefully said, and Molly was glad for it. Somewhere in the complicated knot that was John Kleat was a human thread. It would take a good heart to see it so cleanly, and Duncan was saying he'd seen it. She was glad, not because she cared about Kleat, but because Duncan was a rock. Maybe she could trust him.

"Redemption?" said Luke.

"He's been looking for his brother for years."

A noise came from the backseat, startling Molly. It sounded like an animal—a monkey, a jackal, something with sharp teeth—a single, feral bark. A hoot. Vin jerked his head to see in the mirror.

It was a laugh, but not like anything Molly had ever heard. "He says that?" said Luke. "He says his brother?"

"I'm missing the joke," said Molly.

"What brother?" said Luke.

"He went missing in the war. It's unfinished business."

"You sure you want to be sticking up for him?"

"I'm just telling you."

"He wants back in," Luke told her. "That's how come he tracked you down. He thinks he found a ride. He thinks he's going home."

Molly had no idea what he was talking about. "He didn't track me down. He was there at the dig when I arrived."

"Waiting for you," Luke said. "We knew you were coming."

We?

"Sometimes there's no second chances," Luke said. "He wants to belong so bad. He won't ever belong."

"Belong to what?" Duncan said. "Who's this 'we' you're talking about?"

"The boys," Luke interrupted. Molly frowned. That was Duncan's term. Had the man sneaked up one night and overheard them? It wasn't impossible.

"Whatever," said Duncan. "I take it you belong."

"Same as you."

"And me?" said Molly. He was like Job, this raving prophet, but without a god to blame for his misery and ugliness. She wanted to hear what he would say.

He looked at her. "Who else do you think we come for?"

A huge dark shape—a truck—thundered past, lights out. The Land Cruiser rocked in its wake. Her thoughts scattered. It was a relief, she decided, to quit the conversation.

11.

They came to a town, or what was left of it. The moon made a brief appearance, and the destruction leaped out at Molly, the dirt as red as Mars. Here and there lone walls stood scored by thousands of bullet holes, the rest of the houses chopped away. Otherwise the place was a shantytown floating on stilts between the rubble.

"Snuol," Duncan read from his map.

"What happened here?" Molly asked.

"I'd say the United States Army paid a visit," Duncan said. He had taken the red and white *kroma* from around his neck and draped it over his head, like blinders almost.

"Birth is death, brother," Luke said. "Somebody has to feed the machine. This was their turn."

The destruction fascinated Molly. The war had erected an architecture so grotesque, it verged on beauty. And the people let it stand, that was the strangest thing. They chose to live among the ruins.

"We're getting there now," said Luke.

"North to Kratie," Duncan guessed. "From there, it's not so far to Sambor."

"You know the country?" Luke was amused.

"I came this way years ago," Duncan said. "I was retracing the footsteps of the great Dutch explorer Van Wusthoff. He was making his way to Vientiane. This was back in 1642. He was the first Westerner to set eyes on the supposed ruins of Sambupura, the capital of a pre-Angkor civilization in the sixth century. Sambor, it's called now. The locals stripped it clean centuries ago. They took away the building-stones to make dikes. There are a few foundation stones left in the ground. Some scholars doubt the Sambor stones mark the real Sambupura. They think the stones are just traces of a satellite city, that the capital must have been somewhere else. Skeptics say Sambupura never existed, it's just the local version of Shangri-la."

"More tricks," Luke said. "You and your folklore and history."

Duncan was quiet for a moment. "It's what I do. Temple restorations. My specialty is the pre-Angkor period."

"Let's say that's so," said Luke. "What's that change?"

Duncan looked stricken. His little light hovered above the map. Molly didn't know why he let the crazy gypsy get to him.

The road forked ahead. "Tell the boy to go right here," Luke said.

They exited Highway 7 onto a side road that actually improved. The ripped asphalt of Snuol smoothed into compacted dirt. Duncan's map rustled. "East to Mondulkiri," he said. "This is an old logging road. The Ho Chi Minh Trail branched all through these parts."

"History," Luke said.

Night spilled over the windshield. Molly felt vaguely seasick. Since leaving the dig site at seven that morning, she had been on one road or another for over sixteen hours. She was tired. Her head ached. She was thirsty from the lobster, and her mouth tasted sour. She prayed Kleat had grabbed her toiletries kit when he'd gone to the hotel. She was going to want a toothbrush, a T-shirt, and a tent, in that order.

The moon came and went. Molly found herself nodding off in short bursts.

A hand slapped the top of her seat. Molly started.

"It's coming," Luke said. "Tell him."

"We're there?" She peered out the window. "How can you see anything?"

"Are you going to tell him or not?" Luke reached over the front seat and stabbed at Vin's ribs. It hurt, Molly could tell. Vin bared his gold teeth and stepped on the brakes. A swirl of dust enveloped them.

"Did I say stop?" said Luke. "Go off up there."

"Sit back," Duncan said to him.

Luke's arm withdrew. The backseat creaked under his weight. Vin gripped the steering wheel, angry at being prodded. At last he flipped on his one good headlight.

There was only the red dirt of the highway and high, green grasses. The grass enclosed them. Slowly Molly made out a dark mass in the distance, the sloping hip of a mountain, or an upward march of trees. In either case, nothing but wilderness.

"We keep going," said Luke.

"Going where?" said Duncan.

The truck arrived behind them in the moonlight. It approached with the immensity of a shipwreck, its tattered canopy flailing like a torn sail. Bald car tires wired to the prow served as a bumper.

Vin went on sucking his golden front teeth, making up his own mind.

A fingernail tapped at her window. Molly cranked the handle, and her reflection became Kleat. "Lost?" he said.

Samnang's round face appeared behind Kleat, a creased brown melon with white hair.

"There's a road," said Luke. "It goes through the grass."

"An invisible road," scoffed Duncan.

"What are you saying?" Kleat asked.

"Turn around now," said Duncan, "we can be back in Phnom Penh for breakfast."

"Turn around?" said Molly.

"Look for yourself, there's nothing out there." He wiped his hand across the map.

Luke didn't argue. He had switched off, tuned out. It was their decision.

Kleat fumed. "If it was in plain sight, they would have been found already. Sometimes you have to dig a little further, that's all."

Molly didn't see Samnang slide away. He simply appeared in the light beam, moving up the road, hitching his false leg ahead. One by one they all quit talking.

His shadow reached in front of him, long black lines like puppet strings tied to each limb. He followed the edge of the highway, peering into the overgrown ditch. Fifty yards ahead he stopped and began parting the grasses.

Everyone got out and went up the road, all except Luke. He sat in the car, knowing whatever he knew.

Samnang was working deeper into the tall grasses, feeling along with his one good foot. "A track for oxcarts," he announced to them. "It hasn't been used for many years."

The three brothers descended from the highway and joined Samnang, chattering away, eager to continue. They wanted a week of wages, not taxi fare for a night ride. They churned through the grass, trampling it flat and tying bunches at their tops as landmarks.

Abruptly the night detonated around them. A clamor filled the air. It sizzled and crackled like wild voltage, loud, almost tangible.

The suddenness and volume startled Molly. She whirled around, searching for a source, but the noise pressed in from every direction. Cicadas, she realized, thousands of them.

She'd never heard such a massed voice of insects. She registered it as anger, but that was only because it was so alien to her. She stepped back from the grass.

That suddenly the noise stopped.

The silence had a slight sucking vacuum to it. Molly felt pulled by it. "What was that?" she said.

The men had frozen. They were staring at the grass on all sides of them.

Then Kleat waved at the night. "Bugs. Nothing."

The clouds opened to the moon, and the distant mountain revealed itself as a pile of low hills crowned with dense forest.

"Okay?" Kleat said. "It's there. The man said it was there. There it is."

Molly gazed up at the mountain.

"An oxcart path," Duncan said, dismissing it. "A mountain."

Kleat was having none of it. He grabbed a handful of grass and gave a fierce yank. It was a foolish gesture. The roots were deep and this was saw grass, with firm, sharp blades. His fist slid up and came away empty. Kleat snapped his teeth in pain and opened his cut palm. When he shook his hand, drops of his blood spattered into the dust like petite explosions.

They followed the oxcart path. The convoy climbed through grass growing higher than the doors. The grass stroked the windows like fingers of seaweed. Behind them, the truck's headlights swam through an ocean of brilliant green lines.

Their pell-mell highway dash slowed to a crawl. The path was rutted and winding and hard to see, but it rose gently. The shovels and jerry cans piled in the rear quit clattering. They merely rustled at the curves. Molly could practically feel the grass slithering along the undercarriage.

She relaxed, grateful for the quiet and the sinuous path. With each looping turn, the moon shifted in the sky. It seemed to have grown to twice its normal size, as if they were rising off the planet.

"We're farther north than I thought," said Duncan. "We're reaching into the Annamite range. The mountains run all the way to China. It's wild country. The lowlanders stay clear of it. The hill tribes live up here pretty much the way they have for ten thousand years, taking animals, throwing down a little corn between the trees."

"History," whispered Luke.

At three-thirty they crested a ridgetop and stopped. Ahead stood all that remained of a bridge, a single stone pillar rising from the wide riverbed. Beyond that, higher up, a tall forest took over the grassland.

"Now where?" said Duncan.

They got out, except for Luke, who once again left them to their own conclusions. Molly faced back the way they had come, expecting their path to be flattened by the tires. But the grass had folded shut behind them. They would have to hunt their way down just as carefully.

To her surprise, the logging road lay far below them. Winding back and forth, they'd ascended hundreds of vertical feet. From this height, you could see moonlit paddy fields far to the west, and curious rows of ponds. They were not ponds, she realized, but bomb craters.

Kleat paced along the riverbed rim like a trapped tiger. "We're close," he said. "It's right there in front of us."

"It's just a forest," said Duncan.

"It's cover," said Kleat. "It makes sense. We're looking for the remains of an armored cavalry unit."

"How do you know that?" asked Molly.

"Who do you think the Blackhorse Regiment was? The Eleventh Armored Cavalry. They were famous, George Patton's men. 'Find the bastards and pile on,' his orders. Nine men, Luke said. That would have been enough to crew two tanks or armored personnel carriers. That's what we're looking for. Anything that large, left in the open, would have been spotted by plane or satellite years ago. I don't know how these guys got lost. But those trees are where they went."

"Not across that bridge, they didn't," Duncan said.

"Why not? Bombs were falling like rain all through this area. Our pilot was returning from a run along this very borderland. Sometime after the Blackhorse soldiers crossed over, the bridge must have caught a bomb. That would explain why they never got out."

"Except the bridge is too primitive," Duncan said. "See these stones? It was a cantilever design. That dates it to a thousand years ago, or earlier. A bridge like that couldn't have taken the weight of a tank. And look at how the building stones have been shoved downriver over time. Some of them are huge. No, this fell to pieces centuries ago."

"The closer we get, the less you care," Kleat said. "Or are you afraid of something?"

Molly stood away from them. The night air was a joy to breathe. She actually felt cold in her sundress.

"Even if they got across thirty years ago, it doesn't mean we should follow them," Duncan said. "Look at the width of that riverbed. It carries some major water. Once the rains begin, we'll never be able to cross back. We'd be stuck over there for the next six months. And that, not a bombed bridge, would explain why they were never seen again."

"I don't see any rain."

"It's coming."

"June 23, 1970," Kleat said to him. "That's the day they went missing. They were part of the Cambodian incursion. Nixon sent them. That's what Kent State was all about."

"I remember."

"Somehow these nine soldiers got separated from the main body. Maybe night was coming on. The enemy was out there. They couldn't stay in the open."

"And you think they drove this far north? We're halfway to Laos."

"Maybe they were going for the high ground. Maybe they saw the trees. Maybe they were being pursued."

Molly left them arguing. The night, the dark morning, was too fine to spoil. Venus stood bright. The constellations beckoned. For a month, swamped by haze on the plains, she had missed the stars. Down there, in another couple of hours, the dawn people would be plundering the site, dodging through the mist. Up here, she felt free. She clutched her arms across her chest and meandered along the broad rim.

At first she didn't notice the strange ribbing under her shoes. It rose out of the ground only gradually. At last the notches threatened to trip her. She bent to run her fingers across the imprints and they were as hard as ceramic.

"Duncan," she called. "Kleat."

They were arguing. She called louder.

"What?" said Kleat.

She showed them the marks on the ground.

Kleat had a six-battery bludgeon of a flashlight. He shined it on the rows of corrugated imprints, each the same fourteen or fifteen inches wide, leading off like dinosaur footprints. The track marks ran a hundred yards before sinking back into the earth. The clay had captured the passage of vehicles. The sun had baked it and made it impervious to three decades of weather.

"Blackhorse," Kleat said. He identified the prints as the marks of two armored cavalry assault vehicles, ACAVs, both the same size, one following the other.

"They came this way, up the hill, along the river, chasing a way to cross without the bridge. What more do you need?" he said to Duncan. "They're over there. They're waiting."

12.

They came to the pass where the stream spread across the wide riverbed, and the Eleventh Cavalry strays had left more prints in the clay. The water, at the deepest point, came axle high to the Land Cruiser, though it built against Molly's door on the upstream side, slapping and gurgling. The moon made a skin of silver on it. Dangling her hand out the window, she found the water had the temperature of blood or bathwater.

"It's got to be one of these drainages," Duncan muttered at his map. She could hear him back there, twisting the paper to try to fit it to the terrain. Couldn't he see the handle of the Big Dipper, the stars skipping up to the North Star? They weren't lost, only in motion.

She closed her eyes and, midstream, they seemed adrift on a raft. Her feet were wet, and she saw an inch of water on the floor. She laughed.

"You're happy," said Duncan.

She didn't turn. "Yes," she said.

It pleased him. That pleased her.

She didn't try to explain her joy. After all these weeks, she felt released. The tension of searching for the pilot, the pushing and pulling of tool against earth, of man against man, civilian against soldier, of Kleat against Duncan, all of it seemed left behind. Her trespass upon the pilot, with her camera, was a thing of the past. The highway and its dark menace were forgotten.

The sun would find them somewhere. That was the heart of it. The farther they got from the main road, the more it felt like she was finally reaching a center. When the time came, one way or another they could always retrace their journey, and eventually she could return to writing her words, publishing her photos, and promoting her name, the maiden name—the only name she knew—of a woman who had forsaken her. For now, she just wanted to keep going.

The river—or her happiness—changed Duncan, too. His anxieties fell away. He put aside his map, and she thought that now they could cast themselves into the journey. They had made their crossing. Their hell-bent midnight ride could slow. She could start to know Duncan without the background noise and her urgency to catch the recovery team's story. They were on their own now, threading up a path across a river that was just a stream upon a mountain that was just a hill, wandering off the maps. Two searchers, that's who they were.

The bones were an excuse. That divorced her and him from Kleat, who was so bound to his dead and his duty. She hadn't come to resurrect soldiers any more than Duncan had. The missing pilot had drawn them as a novelty, an opportunity, nothing more. Now they could enter a territory of the heart.

They had never talked about what preceded Cambodia for him. For a month, they had worked and lived within inches of each other, but she still didn't have a real handle on him. For all his tales of high school football and a dog named Bandit and his summer-long Harley solo to Anchorage and special barbecue recipes and favorite old movies, she had no idea why he'd landed here, or even when. The one time she'd asked, he'd dodged. *Sometimes it feels like I was born here,* he'd said. *Like I'm like some dusty thing out of a Kipling novel, just one more relic of the empire.*

Not Kipling, she thought. Conrad. And not Kurtz, not *Heart of Darkness,* but *Lord Jim.* Duncan had secrets, maybe dark secrets or sad secrets or old guilt. One does not go to the jungle out of innocence. He never talked about a wife or children or another woman, never crouched over snapshots of a lost family or a lover who had chosen a different man or died a tragic death. He never mentioned where that part of his life had gone. Survivor guilt, she guessed. Maybe that was what attracted her to him. He seemed to carry her same sense of a past best unrepeated, of a voyage without anchors. Like an orphan, he acted never quite worthy of love. They were perfect fodder for a grail quest, the two of them.

They passed worn blocks of stone in the river wall, evidence of ancient channels. That perked him up.

"Incredible," he said. "We're looking at water control that predates the Angkor kingdom by centuries, and on the opposite side of the country. A massive hydraulics system in the mountains, for Pete's sake. You need to understand, water is everything here. There's not another country like this on earth. For the Khmers, the world is water. When the monsoon comes, almost half the country vanishes under water. The Tonle Sap River reverses course. Great battles were fought on inland boats. Their civilization was founded on wet rice cultivation. The Angkor empire rose and fell based on their ability to control water. The Angkor kings captured the rain in huge pools and would dole it out in drought years or choke their enemies with thirst. But where did the Angkor genius come from? What sparked their greatness? Who passed to them the divine mandate? Who came before them?"

Luke would have muttered "history" had he been conscious. But he had gone to sleep or was traveling in his head. His eyes were shut. Perhaps his delirium had cycles, or the loss of his secret had emptied him. Hibernation suited him, Molly decided. He looked younger without the junkie eyes. Asleep, he looked resigned to himself.

Trailed by the hulking Mercedes, they wound higher along the contour lines. The moon spun left to right across the windshield, a moving target. Molly let go of the urge to orient herself. There was no longer any question of where they were headed.

The prow of the forest seemed to descend to them. White mist leaked from the throat of the trees. Early morning fog was part of the Cambodian clockwork. But tonight it looked to Molly like a word exhaled, like a syllable spilling downhill to greet her.

To the right and left, creeper vines stitched shut the forest wall. The only possible entry was directly through a break in the screen of trees. She wanted to ask Vin to stop for a picture. But that would have meant setting up a tripod for a time-lapse shot, and it would have been more an emotion than a picture anyway.

"It will be a whole other world in there," Duncan said. "An ecosystem writing its own rules. You'll see. There are species in these mountains that no one knows exist. The *khiting vor,* practically a unicorn, like a myth, part gazelle with curlicue horns. They say it stands on its rear legs to feed, that it eats deadly snakes. There are herds of white elephants, like ghosts. Peacocks. Langur monkeys with two stomachs. Hundreds of species of moths. And the flowers."

Teak and gum trees soared. He knew them by shape, and by their Khmer names, too. They reached the outskirts of the fog, and it turned to brilliant milky smoke in their beams. Vin slowed, feeling his way forward. But they had their bearings now, that gaping hole in the forest.

Something tapped against the rooftop. A leaf. A twig.

"What about tigers?"

"These days you see more pelts than paw marks," Duncan said. "The hill tribes and ex-soldiers are trapping them out. It's obscenely easy. They take an old land mine, hide it under a dead monkey for bait, and boom, jackpot. Skin, meat, claws, and penis . . . you can make enough money for a Honda Dream. That's the bike of choice here. The tiger parts go to China for folk medicine."

Another story, another time, she idly thought.

"I wouldn't worry about the big cats. Not this deep. They've never bothered me. This far from people, they don't have a taste for us."

There was another soft pat on the roof, a light rap, an ounce of pebble, less. Then another. Molly glanced at the ceiling. Another. Tiptoes on the metal.

She frowned, wishing the noises away, guessing what they were.

"It can't be," she stated firmly. "Tell me it's not starting."

But it was. Duncan had his fingers against the roof, feeling the minute landings. "The luck," he said.

The season had beat them.

"I don't believe it," she groaned. "We're so close."

They had a deal, though. First rain, turn home. It was all the more imperative now with the river between them and the world.

More soft pats on the roof, little metallic kisses.

"I'm sorry," said Duncan.

A raindrop slapped the windshield. Molly leaned closer to see it. "That's not rain." She put her fingertip on the inside of the glass.

It was blood. Gore. With little webbed feet. Molly lifted her finger away.

"Is that a frog?" said Duncan.

He was right. It was a storm of frogs, little tree frogs. They were falling from the sky. She cranked her window shut.

You read of tadpoles being sucked into the heights and growing into young frogs among the clouds. Was this that, she wondered? Did the monsoon have that power?

Then she saw that they weren't falling. They were leaping out from the forest's high branches. Another struck the windshield. Another, and this one didn't splash to bits like the others.

Dead or stunned, the frog stuck in place. Its red and black bands glistened, backlit by the white mist.

Another hit, this one alive. It took position on the glass, head high. The tiny thing looked majestic, like a creature mounting their world, claiming it. Its miniature lungs pulsed.

"What are they doing?" she said.

"They must be drawn by the headlights," said Duncan. "Or it could be some territorial imperative."

"They're trying to drive us away?"

"I wouldn't make it too personal," Duncan said. But his voice was sober.

They began to patter, like small hail, on the hood and roof and windshield. Now that she knew what they were, Molly could see them in the lighted mist with their tiny legs and arms stretched wide.

"Or it could be the typhoon affecting them," Duncan went on. "Animals are sensitive to change. With the low-pressure cell building, their rhythms go haywire. Lemming behavior. One dives, they all dive."

"This is awful," she said.

The pat of bodies became a rattling, a squall of miniature carnage.

"But at least it's not the rain."

"It's unnatural."

"It's just a few frogs."

"A few?"

The windshield was layered with bits of tissue. They were casting themselves down by the scores, catapulting from the trees. She saw a mother, her back swarming with tiny young. The wiper blades went to work and mangled them. The hood looked like a butcher block. Molly hated it. The death and mutilation were senseless.

Plainly, Vin had never witnessed such a thing. He gripped the wheel, and the tattoos on his skinny forearms—crude lines and circles and suns, his magic symbols—rippled. He believed in other worlds. And here was this, this curse, a hailstorm of frogs.

Vin drifted to a halt. He craned his head up to see inside the strange torrent. The banging grew louder. He was staring at her. She saw his fear. It made her more afraid.

She put her hands against the roof, as if it might collapse. The metal throbbed. "We can't stay here." She had to shout over the noise.

Like vomit against the windshield, the forest puked its creatures at them. It sickened her. She glanced around.

Luke's eyes were closed. How could he sleep through this? And he was smiling.

Duncan said something in Khmer, his tone calm. He said it again. Vin nodded. They lurched into motion.

Duncan spoke into her ear. "It's okay, we're going inside now. They'll stop, Molly." His hand was on her shoulder.

She could barely see through the plastered glass. Up ahead, like the mouth of a cave, the forest parted its lips. "Faster," she whispered.

The forest yawned open.

13.

Roots and stones rose up from underneath the fog. Vin picked up speed. The Land Cruiser hopped and bounded, tools rattling in the back.

They entered.

Instantly the darkness changed. The moonlight vanished. It was like mercy. The hailstone beating quit. The frogs stopped.

The wiper blades were squealing on dry glass.

Their battle was over, but Vin didn't slow a bit.

Molly hunched over and peered through her side window like it was a porthole. Dark shapes reeled past, trees as thick as bridge pillars. The Land Cruiser lunged over roots like big swells, throwing her against the door.

Duncan barked something at Vin. The boy ignored him, still racing from the animal assault, driving blind. In a way, Molly was relieved by his dread. It validated her own. His fear gave her a fear to settle. She placed one hand on his arm and found he was quivering.

The wiper blades scratched at the crust of frogs. Forward vision returned in streaks. The mist flared in sudden white eruptions. Blackness and light.

Abruptly a huge face jumped up in front of them. Vin braked and swerved. Even so, they banged against it, not ruinously, but with a jolt.

"My God," Duncan whispered.

Molly unclenched her hands from her camera.

The stone head was as large as the car.

The wipers clawed at the rusty glass. Duncan patted Vin's shoulder. The wipers stopped. They stared at the head's tilted eyes.

Molly lifted her camera. Fog edged through the dark trees, sliding in slow, soundless white bunches between the strings of vines brewing up around the stone head.

Time had partially melted its demonic rage. The head had rolled onto one rounded jaw, part human, part animal. Its angry, bulging eyes had eroded over the ages. All around lay more pieces of toppled giant statuary.

"What on earth?" said Molly.

"A warrior icon," said Duncan. "A holy warrior."

"With fangs?"

"A wrathful deity," Duncan said. "A guardian."

"Guarding what, though?"

"That's the question. I don't know. They usually don't appear singly. There must be more like him around here, sentinels to warn the enemy away. But away from what? And look at the style, crude by Angkor standards. Primitive. Old. Molly, this goes back." His mind was churning.

She wasted a shot through the crappy windshield.

"Something's out there, Molly. This is big." His voice grew larger. "Why didn't you tell us?" he said to Luke.

But their guide was deep in REM sleep. Molly could see Luke's eyes darting beneath the closed lids, stormed by dreams.

Duncan rolled down his window for a better look, and Molly braced for the amphibious stink. But the air carried a rich, potent scent full of flowers and fertile soil and, for all she knew, tigers and old rain.

"How can this be?" he murmured to himself. His excitement infected her.

"I need pictures," she said suddenly, and fumbled in the camera bag between her feet, feeling for her wide-angle lens and the strobe flash.

She opened her door. The story quickened in her, morphing,

branching off into a completely different narrative. They had set out to find one thing, a few bones from a war, only to discover something monumental. Punt the war, this was Indiana Jones territory.

The story would begin here, she determined, fog swirling, with the blood-encrusted Land Cruiser held at bay by this ferocious head. She backed off to shoot the vehicle, its fender bent around the head. Pieces of hundreds of frogs smeared the grille and hood and rooftop.

She angled right to get Duncan's stunned expression as he approached the beast. Her flash made small explosions. He touched the carved face. He ran his palms over its blind eyes. He peeled off rug sheets of lime- and rose-colored moss.

Vin stayed inside his getaway car, engine idling, as spooked as a thoroughbred.

Light from the headlight beam played up the great flat nose, a ridiculous shot. They'd discovered a nose? She compensated with her own light, prowling for more shots.

"I know him," Duncan said. "*Ganas,* they're called. He's a kind of Buddhist/Hindi hero, like a Superman for the faithful."

"A fetish," she said, prompting him, capturing his moment of discovery.

"Much more than that," he said, "a destroyer of ignorance, a protector of the Way. A guardian, not just of a people, but of a whole cosmology."

"A hill tribe?"

"Something this large? It's the tip of an iceberg."

She liked that, a tropical iceberg. "A city?" she said. Molly wanted this for him, whatever it was. All his years of humble, anonymous, lonely searching were coming together here tonight.

The truck arrived, adding more light to the display.

Doors opened behind the rank of headlights. She heard a curse, Kleat tripping on a root. Samnang materialized from the rags of fog. She snapped him pressing his hands together in a *sampeah* to the demon head. Then he kept on walking into the darkness.

Kleat joined them, wiping the humidity from his glasses. The circles under his eyes were discolored pouches. Molly had never seen him like this, his bluff vigor drained, that muscular face betraying frailty. He fit the steel rims back onto his face.

Molly lowered her camera. Edit. Delete. Kleat wasn't going to be part of this story.

"Were you trying to have a wreck?" he said. "You took off like a bolt. Now look. You're lucky it wasn't worse."

"The frogs," she said. Now that the danger was past, she tried to make light of it. "We thought it might be a spring shower."

Kleat peered at her from beneath his thick bone of a brow, then turned to the stone head. "It would be a lot easier to go around the rocks, not through them," he said.

"Rocks?" Duncan said. "This could go back to the Funan empire, a thousand years before the Angkor regime. The time of Christ, of Rome. It's practically a myth, like Atlantis or Babylon. Funan wasn't even its real name. That's the Chinese transliteration for "phnom," or hill. It was mentioned in early Chinese travel accounts, lost fragments referenced in later accounts. And look, here we are on a hill."

"Save it for the lecture circuit," said Kleat.

Molly held her hand against the bright lights. Vin's older brothers were scolding him for damaging the bumper. Luke lay piled asleep against his door.

"We didn't come for this," said Kleat.

"But this is what we've come to," Duncan marveled.

"Irrelevant." Kleat snapped it like a whip. "They're waiting for us." His dead.

She no longer thought of them as hers. In the holes, working the screens, gathering the facts, shedding blood on the airplane metal, she had felt a contract with the bones. Not anymore. The captain had not confiscated her camera, his way of protesting what his superiors were making him do. But the exile had stolen her pride of place. The bones were meaningless to her now.

There was a movement in the darkness, and Kleat aimed his big flashlight cop-style. Samnang appeared among the trees in his neat white shirt. He blinked at the lights.

"The boulevard goes on," he announced.

Intent on the stone head, they had failed to notice the road beneath their feet. Even with roots and rocks shrugging up through its surface, it did resemble a Paris boulevard. Paved with stones, it stretched thirty feet from side to side, and extended off into the pit of the forest.

"Where does it lead?" said Duncan.

"Who knows? It goes on," said Samnang.

"Then let's keep going," Kleat said. He clapped his hands. They returned to their vehicles.

"It could be nothing," Duncan cautioned as they drove on. Molly could hear his hope. First the channel stones lining parts of the river, now the carved head and this decaying road.

She reached back and laid a fist on his knee. "But also it could just be something," she said.

He closed his hands around her fist. His palms were wet. He looked dazed and childlike.

Chastened by his accident, Vin took it slowly, steering around big stone tiles tipped up by time. Fog curdled in pools. Enormous trees bracketed the road. Their seeds had taken root with time, and younger trees grew in the middle of the avenue, rupturing more tiles.

"Look how big around these monsters are," Duncan said. "Things grow fast here. But this is old growth. Very old. I can't believe the loggers haven't plundered it."

No spindly, fibrous sugar palms in here. No fields of grass. No paddies. No sky. The trunks were like columns of skycrapers, red and gray and black and tan. Their massiveness had the look of a great cosmic weight being held aloft. As they crawled over and around the roots and rocks, it was like sliding over immense tendons and slippery bone. She could imagine the ribs of Jonah's whale.

The fog puddled in recesses as dark as side canyons. It hung like linen rags among the branches.

"Look," said Duncan, his window wide open. His wobbling light picked out another carved face watching them. There were more. Half buried among the trees, big stone *ganas*—some with the heads of monkeys and hook-beaked birds of prey—loomed among the branches. Gods appeared, their eyes half shut, their mouths half smiling. The statues kept pace with their advance. They seemed aware. The smiles seemed too serene.

Molly struggled to get a feel for their welcome. Even the times she'd visited Super Max in southern Colorado to shoot portraits of mass murderers, there had been a sense of control. This was different. They'd landed among giants. Giants wearing the masks of good and evil.

"The city wall," said Duncan.

It appeared ahead of them among the complex of vegetation. The closer they drove, the more it took shape, a long, high barrier of mineral colors in the night. It seemed to be forming from their presence, taking on detail out of their expectation of its details. The stone blocks were cabled with vines. The vines had fingers. Ferns grew from the joints.

"It must be twenty feet tall." His breathing had tripped into high gear, Molly could hear it. Then she realized it was her own breathing.

She bent to see through the windshield mottled with gruel, trying to make out the parapets or battlements, whatever you called them. Gaps plunged like missing teeth, muscled open by fat towers of trees with bark as smooth as pigskin. There was no way to tell which was winning, the forest or the dead architect.

"Here we go," Duncan said. "The gateway."

A broad, crumbling tower straddled the wall, a tunnel running through its base. Faces crowned the tower, each staring sightlessly in a different direction. The tunnel lay at the center of their collective chest. One entered through the heart of gods. Vin flipped his light beams from low to high to low. The eyes stared down at them and then away.

Vin inched in.

"It's the perfect traffic control," Duncan remarked. "You could stop any invaders with a few rocks piled inside. In fact, I wonder if this tower's rigged to drop its guts." He cast around with his flashlight.

Molly had never suffered from claustrophobia, but the moment they entered, the walls seemed to close in on her. A sort of nausea gripped her. She felt physically sick. It went beyond that. She felt trapped, as if she were calcifying inside her skin.

They emerged on the far side and the feeling lifted. She cranked at her window handle for fresh air.

"You're sweating," Duncan said.

"No, I'm cold," she said. But her face was dripping. Duncan laid his *kroma* around her bare neck, and it carried his body heat.

She had expected to drive into a city in ruins, but there was more road. Elevated upon a spine of solid, squared stone, a causeway ran in a straight line, bound on either side by vast pools of water that had degraded into swamps fouled with mangrove trees. Their serpentine roots breached and looped back into the water.

"You're looking at the wealth of kings," said Duncan. *"Barays—* reservoirs—with enough water to feed a whole people. This could be the prototype for Angkor. It could be the genesis for the very idea of Cambodia."

They came to a gauntlet of stone cobras carved along the roadside. *"Nagas,"* Duncan said, identifying them. "Water snakes that figure in all kinds of Asian creation myths. From *naga* you get *nagara,* Khmer for 'The City.' "

There were at least two dozen of the fantastic creatures arranged along the roadway. Some had snapped off at the neck and fallen into the pools. Most were intact, rising higher than the Land Cruiser, their hoods spread open to expose multiple heads with fangs bared.

As they motored slowly through the dangling moss, the water stirred. Molly could hear it down there. On an impulse, she held her camera to the open window and fired blindly, triggering the flash. Her light ricocheted off the black water. The sound stopped. She looked at the LCD to see what her camera had seen.

"Anything?" asked Duncan.

It showed a bulge in the surface, less than that, a shadow, not even a shape. "Not a thing," she said. "It reminds me of the bayous along the Gulf Coast." Just the same, she rolled her window shut.

The causeway came to an end. The broad, flat vein of solid limestone fed back into the earth. Their sculpted road top turned to dirt, and they drove on.

"There are the others," said Molly. The truck was parked at a crooked angle in a clearing between toppled pillars and scraps of fog. The men were busy unloading the vehicles.

She was glad to see them, for a minute. Then she caught sight of their guns. One of the brothers had a rifle slung over his back. Kleat had brought a pistol of his own. He wore it boldly on one hip.

Duncan whispered, looking around. "Where do we begin?"

She made herself part of it. "We'll take baby steps. A little bit at a time."

They had arrived at a terminus. There were no buildings or arches, only the end of the road. From here one climbed on foot. Behind them lay the pools. Before them, rising above their lights on three sides, squared stone terraces formed an arena of sorts. The sheer mass of stone, quarried and hauled into place, promised a kingdom. A set of stairs led into the darkness above. If there was a city, it would be up there.

They parked and dismounted, and, first thing, Vin received a rifle, too.

Kleat was stacking axes and shovels against a fallen tree. Molly stood five-eleven in her bare feet, taller than Kleat, to say nothing of the Khmers. But for a moment, faced with that gun strapped to his hip and all the other firepower floating around, she felt like a child among strangers.

"We thought you'd turned around," he said. She saw him look at the scarf Duncan had placed around her neck. He made his assumptions.

"We'll make camp here," Duncan announced. He had a tent sack in his hands.

"Sleep?" said Kleat. "The sun comes up in two hours."

"But the light will lag behind in here. That's triple canopy above us. For now, we need to rest."

"I will instruct the men," said Samnang. He had no weapons Molly noted.

He held out his hand for the tent. It was an important moment. The old man with one leg was anointing Duncan, not Kleat, as their leader. He issued an order to the brothers, who took the tents and hurried toward the ledges.

Kleat carefully laid aside a shovel. Nodding his head, he measured the alliances. His eyes flickered at the brothers moving in and out of the headlights. He studied Molly. "By all means," he said, "sleep."

Molly went to the back of the truck for her mule bag, a huge black duffle made of ripstop nylon, to root for her warmest clothes. For a month, she'd smothered in heat so thick men fell over in it. Now the slight mountain chill had her trembling, even as sweat trickled down her neck. She wished her body would make up its mind, hot or cold. A mountain girl, she knew to layer clothing and find the equilibrium.

There had been no time to sort her laundry at the hotel before their farewell dinner. Unzipping the bag was like opening a dead animal. Bad smells rushed from the interior, and when she thrust her arm inside, the contents were still warm and clammy from the dig. She grabbed the first thing that came to hand, the Vicious Cycles T-shirt, and pulled it over her sundress. It smelled like a hunter's buckskin with her body odor and weeks of soil and Off! Deep Woods cooked into the threads. Deodorant and regular mosquito spray only attracted the bugs, and she'd quickly gone native with the soldiers.

She pulled on a second shirt, then found her Gramicci climbing pants still bloodstained from her encounter with the cockpit metal. The canvas thigh was sewn back together with bright pink thread, prettier than the scar on her leg.

She wasted another minute rummaging for her toilet kit, but it was too dark to find it or, more likely, Kleat had not bothered to pack it for her. She'd have to brush her teeth with a twig. Maybe Duncan would loan her some toothpaste to use with her finger.

The Heng brothers were bustling along the terrace ledges above, farther away than she would have liked. Their lights looked small and moved rapidly up there as they assembled tents for the Americans. Molly guessed they would sleep in the back of the truck, and that would have suited her fine. But Duncan had won his showdown with

Kleat, and she wasn't about to scramble the outcome with any complaints.

She returned to the crisscross of headlights looking like a bag lady, the sundress half buried by shirts on top, toting her camera bag, pants, and a neoprene sleeping pad. Heading into the tropics, she hadn't thought to bring a sleeping bag, and her final act before leaving the dig site had been to give her sheets to a Khmer family. She could manage with her own body heat for the next couple of hours. In the morning, she'd see what covering the brothers might spare.

"I'm ready," she said.

Kleat had already started up the staircase to the tent ledges.

"In the morning," Duncan promised, "it will all look different."

14.

The birds woke her.

Her eyes came open.

She found herself curled in a fetal ball on the sleeping pad. In her sleep sometimes, her knees would pull up and she would roll onto her right side like this. It was an old arrangement of her limbs, an occasional habit. It happened in times of stress and signified surrender.

Not moving a muscle, she wondered, *Surrender to what?* What had her ears heard while she lay sleeping?

With her higher shoulder draped with Duncan's red and white *kroma* and her head pillowed on the camera bag, she listened to the birds. She listened closely, but could not connect to their alien song. The whistling and clatters and caws were more like a secret code.

She went on hugging her knees, sifting for a clue. The long ride had pummeled her, that and the hard ground and scant sleep. She ached. Even the image of those ancient stairs rising up through the night could not budge her.

Her plastic Timex said 0730, military time. Kleat was right. Maybe they should have stayed awake. Three hours of sleep felt worse than no sleep at all.

She lay there, assembling the world. At this hour yesterday, they'd been starting into exile from the crash site. Last night they'd eaten dinner in a restaurant. The colors were vivid, the red lobster, the black dirt on the white tablecloth, the sunset. The details crowded in like eager children. The moonlit highway, the green grass, the silver stream, the frogs, the fortress walls.

But none of that explained why her body was afraid. Had she heard something in her sleep? Was there danger out there?

Her fetal curl was like an early warning device. She knew it all too well. There was no controlling it; she'd tried. The trauma posture would seize her in her sleep, a dream signal that something threatened. It stemmed from tension sometimes, or simply vague bad vibes. Usually it was just echo behavior, residue from Oklahoma. Boyfriends complained that they could not hold her at night. She would clench into an animal ball at the edge of the bed, as far from them as possible. It's not you, she would explain in the morning, but then would explain no more. It freaked them out. They felt like monsters. One by one, they always left her.

Lying on her tent floor, Molly did everything in her power to stay in the moment and feel for any real menace. Recycling the past was a dead end. She'd been through it so many times with therapists. But memory has a mind of its own. This morning, spent and dull, with her bones arranged just so, she was too weak to stop it. From deep inside, it rose to the surface. Oklahoma mounted her all over again.

It was April, thirteen years past, the morning after.

I don't want you, she thought. But the memory pinned her.

The playground grass was brittle and yellow and rimed with frost. Like this, exactly like this, on her right side, eyes open, she had watched the town come awake. The cold sun climbed. A man stocked the newspaper box. After a time, a school bus had passed. No one noticed the bundle of rags in the park. It was mid-morning before the lady who owned the stationery store saw her and called the police.

They never did find the guy. They never really looked. He was just another nomad like her. Like her, he'd given up trying to thumb a ride the night before and had walked to the town park to find a little shelter. That's where they'd met.

She didn't have to be bumming rides. Her parents would have given her the money if they'd known how serious she was. But part of the exercise in running away was to hurt them the way they'd hurt her. It was stupid. They loved her more than their own lives. They said that over and over. And yet they had confined her in a fiction for all her conscious life, and how loving was that? In running off to search for her birth mother, she had invited suffering for them all.

They treated her like one more case of the suburban blues. The ER nurses were kind. They swabbed her with Q-tips and cleaned her cuts. One of the cops said that it wasn't what you would call an actual rape. She'd overheard him outside the ER room. These kids, he said, they couple up on the road and then something goes sour and all of a sudden it's a 911. She just doesn't like how it turned out.

His words had made her wonder. After the first few minutes, it was true that she'd just let the attack happen. She had quit fighting and stood off to one side and watched him go at her underneath the swing set. She'd heard of out-of-body experiences. It was true. She'd quit smelling his breath and tasting the canned spaghetti on his teeth.

When he was done, she'd gone back into herself. Her knees had drawn up into her chest like rawhide constricting. She'd hugged herself through the dawn.

She heard her name. "Molly."

She thought it was part of the memory. He'd asked her name. He'd shared his SpaghettiOs before doing it.

When the cop had come in to take a description, he'd asked her for her parents' phone number. In that instant, Molly had realized that her search could end right there. She could return to their sunny fiction, defeated by reality. Or she could accept the ugliness and get on with her journey.

He'd fucked her so hard she could barely stand. But she somehow got to her feet and took the cop's report and crumpled it into a ball to drop at his feet. With blood leaking down her thighs and one eye swollen shut, she told him, sure, she'd made it up. They released her that afternoon.

Only later, years later, did it occur to her that the animal who'd mounted her that night might have been her own father. Not her very father, of course, but a man like him. Because who could say what violence her poor mother had accepted in the name of love? Who could say where she'd come from?

"Molly."

This time the birds fell silent.

She listened. Men were calling her from far away. She clung to the sound of her name. "Moll-lee."

She stirred.

She felt earthbound. It took an act of will to get her hands to let go and her legs to straighten. Oklahoma faded. She sat up in the center of the tent.

It was her home away from home, the same dome tent she'd used to grand-slam Colorado's fourteeners and photograph the Pleiades meteor shower and sleep by high lakes and wake to vistas of light. Only this morning, she noticed, it had leeches.

Their silhouettes showed through the fabric. They were as graceful as dancers waving their bodies out there. She passed her hand underneath them and they bent to her chemical signature or whatever leeches go for. At the recovery site, she'd never seen more than a few at a time. The forest was more abundant. Here they waited for her by the dozens.

Unconcerned, Molly put herself together, what little there was to put together. She pulled off the layers of shirts and quickly shed the sundress and pulled the shirts back on and tightened the belt on her canvas pants. She folded the yellow dress and laid it in one corner. If all else failed, it could serve as her blanket tonight.

Shedding the night, warming up, she rolled her shoulders and tried a simple yoga position. But the voices called her again, dragging the syllables out, like grappling hooks. Did they think she was lost?

"Moll-lee."

They wanted to start their morning, though the day was still dim, with no hint of eastern light. "Coming," she said under her breath.

She tried rattling the tent to shake the leeches loose, but that only agitated them. She reminded herself that they were slow, blind and mindless. A little haste on the exit was all that was needed.

She scooted to the door, arranged her camera bag, and wrapped Duncan's scarf around her head. On three, she pulled down the zipper. Feet first, she slipped out through the opening and, that quickly, her *African Queen* moment was over.

Now that she was standing outside, there were even more leeches than she'd thought. The tent wall was covered with them, glistening and stretching for her, maybe not so mindless or blind after all. She zipped the door as tight as a drum to prevent any bedtime surprises, and made a note to get her hands on a flashlight.

Blue mist had replaced last night's patchy fog. Her tent stood on a wide stone ledge, and below that she could just make out another ledge. The men were invisible down by the trucks, but she could smell their cook fire and coffee and cigarettes wafting up. Oddly, their voices were coming from above. Could they have started exploring without her? Kleat wouldn't care, but surely Duncan would have come to wake her. They were in this thing together.

The stone terrace was cool and slippery under her bare feet. Her shoes were somewhere in the mule bag, a first order of business once she got down. Her flip-flops were set at the entrance to the tent, or at least one of them was. The other had been tipped upside down during the night.

Ordinarily she wouldn't have noticed, but local custom had seeped into her habits. It wasn't just a matter of taking off your shoes or sandals when entering a temple or someone's house. Footwear was always positioned neatly, side by side, and always upright. Even Samnang was superstitious about such things. And so she'd very exactly placed her sandals with the soles flat to the ground before climbing into the tent last night.

The culprit was a thin green shoot of bamboo that had grown up through a joint between the stones. It was three inches high, and she definitely hadn't seen it there last night. There was only one explanation. The bamboo had sprouted through the crack while she was sleeping, tipping her sandal out of its way. She pressed at the sharp nub, charmed in a way. Duncan was right. Things grew fast in the rain forest.

"Moll-lee." They were up there all right, and it was more than one voice calling her to join them. Possibly there hadn't been time to wake her. Duncan could be trying just to keep abreast of Kleat's predation. What were they finding?

15.

Slipping her sandals on, Molly shouldered her camera bag and hustled along the ledge toward the stairs. A red tent materialized on the lower shelf, then atomized in the mist. Giant airborne faces floated off to her right, their tonnage elevated by dharma smiles. Invisible animals shifted in the brush. Dewdrops hung like jewels.

She glanced up the steps, tempted by the pale brightening in the upper forest. Instead she started down into the thick of the mist where coffee was brewing and her socks and shoes waited in the truck. A quick cup of St. Joseph, then the proper footgear, and she'd double-time the staircase. With her long legs and jogger's lungs, she'd overtake the men before the amazement died from their eyes. The mist would bead her lenses, but this green light was gorgeous. You couldn't get more saturated color. She wanted to sprint down the steps, but they were steep and greasy with moss, forcing her to pick her way carefully.

She passed two more ledges, expecting the white Land Cruiser or the truck and the fire to appear, but the mist concealed them. Reaching the ground, she worked across her memory of the clearing. The floor had a slight tilt to it, to drain off the rain no doubt.

Trees bulged up, sudden immense pillars that evaporated overhead. Molly looked up and stopped, not trusting her eyes. Twenty feet above the ground, the remains of a name seemed to hover in the mist. She went closer and it disappeared. She backed away and it reappeared, letters carved into the skin of the tree. Years of growth had lifted them high, and their once neat incisions were stretched apart and rutted and ribbed. The scars were only slightly lighter than the smooth bark, and the wood had absorbed whole sections.

She circled around the base of the tree. "Helen," the letters said. She went a little farther, and found a final *a*. Helena.

The Blackhorse soldiers had been here.

She turned to another tree, and the name Barbara hung in the mist. There was an Ada and an Emma and a Rosita, each upon its own tree. She was in a forest of lovers. The men had taken their knives to the trees and left this much of themselves. It was magical. How much more was hidden in here?

She would have gone on wandering, but after another few minutes, she saw the fire's orange glow. Its heat had melted an opening in the mist.

Vin and his two brothers were squatting on a ledge above the bright orange flames, their eyes bloodshot from lack of sleep or from the wood smoke. They did not look like happy campers. Propped within easy reach against a fallen tree, their rifles gave them the air of bounty hunters.

"*Ah-roon soo-ah-s'dai,*" she tried. But none flashed his golden teeth for her this good morning, not even Vin. She blamed her awful accent. She was a total linguistic cripple. Some days, faced with her blank screen and a couple of thousand words to crank out, she could barely manage the King's English.

A little distance off, Kleat and Duncan were leaning over a squared foundation stone strewn with rolled maps, and that was strange. She'd heard them calling her from above. Samnang was here, too, hunkered inside the pall of smoke like a gnome, his plastic leg stowed away from the fire. She shrugged. So the forest had wiggy acoustics.

Kleat was stabbing at the forest and the sky and the map. By this point, she would have been surprised if they weren't arguing. Whatever the concern, Duncan appeared to find it pressing, too. He glanced at Molly, then returned his attention to Kleat.

That left Samnang as her official greeter. *"Bonjour, mademoiselle,"* he said, welcoming her. "I have for you a coffee."

"Is that how you keep all your wives so happy?" she said.

Samnang smiled. He had no wife or family. He had no one. The wars had eaten them all, and she knew it. But they could—and did—pretend. She played his saucy American daughter. The light would come on in his brown face.

He reached through the fire for the covered pot and poured the coffee into a white teacup on a white saucer. Probably he'd brought it from his own kitchen, probably just for her. He knew she liked it black, but went through his daily ritual of offering her sugar.

For all its noisy crackling and the billowing white smoke, the fire was a small thing. The wood was green. It was a miracle the stuff had lit at all. Then she saw the jerry can of fuel, their miracle, parked behind a stump.

"Ar kun," she said, thanking him, and sat underneath the plume of smoke by his side. The fire was warm. "I didn't mean to sleep so late."

"No matter," Samnang said. "You see this mist. Duncan said to let you sleep."

Then why, she wondered, *call her name?* "Will the mist lift soon?"

"The forest decides these things." He looked more closely at her. "Be still a moment, please." He reached over.

She knew without asking what it was. The leech clung to the skin of her throat before coming away. She touched the spot, and her finger came away bloody. She looped the *kroma* around her neck to hide the tiny wound.

Samnang held the leech for her to see. It must have fallen on her as she was exiting the tent. The wisp of a worm had bloated to a slug the length of her little finger. What surprised her more than its size and stealth was the speed of its gorging. In ten minutes, such hunger.

She watched to see what came next. Would Samnang throw it against a rock or squeeze it in his fingers? He was contemplative. "She humbles me," he said.

"That?"

"If only I could obey God with such faith." He juggled it on his palm to keep the suckers from getting hold.

"What faith is that?"

"Oh," he said, embarrassed to be preaching.

"No, go on, tell me."

"To exist in the forest with no questions, no doubt. Imagine." He smiled. "Someday, this lowly worm, a Buddha." He gently tossed it to a bed of leaves.

One of Vin's brothers went over and picked it up. He was the one named So, the middle one. He laid the leech on a twig and held it over the fire. The leech began writhing. The man grinned at Molly with yellow hepatitis eyes. She frowned, not so much distressed by the leech's fate—the thing had sucked her blood—as by the man's vandalism. It was pointed, his ruining Samnang's little act of compassion. Something was going on between them.

The oldest brother, Doc, with wisps of mustache hair and geometric suns tattooed on each shoulder, made a joke. It had to do with throwing Samnang's artificial leg into the fire. Vin glanced at Molly and did not join in the laughter. She had no idea what the problem was, but disliked seeing the old man mocked.

Samnang went back to tending the fire. He rested the pot on three neat stones above a nest of embers. The flames were trim, the heat no more or less than the morning called for.

Molly went on sitting by Samnang for another minute, mostly to show her solidarity. Then she stood casually. "Let me see what the lords of the jungle are up to," she said.

"Of course," said Samnang.

She walked to Duncan and Kleat and placed her white saucer and cup at the farthest corner of their makeshift bench, away from the maps. Like a skin drying, one map was pegged open with chunks of rock and food packets. Small pebbles on a U.S. military topo marked last night's passage. From Snuol, the logging road ran east and north, and the pebbles became bits of twigs—hypotheticals—leading off to nowhere. You could conjure up a hundred phantom rivers and streams from the wrinkles and curves, all of them descending to the Mekong.

"Got us figured out?" she said.

"Not a clue," Duncan said. He seemed frayed. He gestured at a big, boxy GPS receiver that looked almost as obsolete as his colonial-scientist compass in its brown wooden case with oiled hinges. What antiques stores had these come from? The lighted panel read "SEARCHING."

"It's like all the satellites fell from the sky," said Duncan. "We're not getting a single reading."

"Our location can wait," Kleat said. "No more fussing around."

"You don't understand. These hills may not seem like much. You can't properly call them mountains. But they can eat you alive, especially—"

"I know," said Kleat. "I know."

"We're lost," said Duncan. "It matters. We don't even know if they came in here."

"We know they crossed the river. We saw their tracks. Where else could they have gone?"

"They were here," said Molly. The two men stopped. "You didn't see the names?"

"What's this?" Kleat said.

She led them into the mist. After the fire, it seemed colder and darker out here.

Head craned back, she searched for the names. "They were carved on the trees," she said. "The names of their women. Up high."

The names had disappeared, though. There were so many trees, and she must have come in differently from the stairs. "They were here somewhere," she insisted.

"I believe you," Kleat said, though he didn't really. It was simply convenient to his argument. "Once this fucking mist thins out, we'll find them."

They went back to the fire and their maps on the stone.

"The names don't change anything," Duncan said. He didn't question that she had seen them. He took it on faith. "I still say we should backtrack, take a second look from the outside. Get a handle on the risks."

"Leave?" said Molly.

She said it with more censure than she meant. The caffeine was kicking in. But also, his apprehension confused her. He was the archaeologist. His job was to pry open the earth and raise cities from the dead. Forget the Blackhorse bones. Forget Kleat. Even forget the typhoon and the rains. In the back of her mind, they were already trapped—held under house arrest—by the river. Something stood at the top of those stairs. This was their chance to raise Atlantis.

"While we still can," Duncan said to her.

"I keep telling you," said Kleat, "he's halfway to China by now. Burma, Afghanistan, wherever the dope grows wild."

"I don't think so."

"Luke?" said Molly, jolted by the sudden awareness. "He's gone?"

"Unless he spent the night with you," Kleat said. "No one's seen him since we arrived."

Molly looked at the mist. Had he been the one calling her? "He must be here."

"That's what I keep saying," said Duncan.

"Sam took a try looking for him," Kleat said. "If anybody can track a man, it's him."

"We don't need to go through that again," Molly said.

"It's not irrelevant. Your gentle musicologist was also KR."

The brothers were all watching now. They heard the KR and began murmuring among themselves.

"We've been through this," Molly said quietly.

"And you didn't believe me."

"I agreed with Duncan. It's not our business."

Kleat gave her an owlish blink. He called across to the fire. "Tell us what you found, Sam."

"He went this way into the forest," Samnang said. "Then his footprints disappear."

"He's still here," said Duncan.

"Isn't that the direction of the gate?" Kleat asked.

"Yes. The gate is that way," Samnang said.

"He's not finished with us," Duncan insisted.

"He's harmless," said Kleat. "You're making monsters."

"He could be hiding twenty feet away and we wouldn't know it."

"Do you want this or not?"

"Maybe you want it too much," said Duncan. "Think back to last night when we saw him in the restaurant, your own words. You said he must be hunting us."

Kleat set his knuckles on the map. "Not anymore. Look around. We're the ones with all the guns."

"He brought us here for a reason," Duncan said.

"The reason of a seriously disturbed mind. He brought us here to unload a secret. A big secret. A secret that freaked him out. He found something here and needed to hand it off. Don't ask me why he chose us. What counts is that now he's freed. In his mind, he's released from his burden. We freed him." Kleat grabbed at the wood smoke and opened his hand to the air. "He's gone."

How could she have missed his absence? It seemed ungrateful and wrong to forget someone so easily.

"This was all he had," she said. "Wouldn't he hang on to it for dear life? Why leave?"

"For that, Molly," Kleat said, "you'd need to ask your mother."

Her mother, again. He was relentless, like a jackal after meat. "What on God's earth does *she* have to do with it?"

"You were all she had," Kleat said, "but she still left you. This place was Luke's baby. Now he's thrown it away. You think love heals all. But we're talking about the damned here. Love is a horror to people like them."

Molly slapped him. *The damned.* She slapped him so hard it hurt her hand. His glasses flew off. Coffee spilled across the map.

The brothers halted their low drone.

Molly pulled her hand back. She didn't know what to say. For better or worse, she wasn't wired for conflict, much less a lightning bolt like this. She shouldn't have let him get to her. She shouldn't have slapped him. Then she thought, *The hell with it, maybe she should have slapped him a long time ago.*

Kleat nodded his head, thinking, making up his mind. The bared pouches under his eyes were even darker in the daylight. After a minute, he bent to retrieve his glasses. He fit them onto his face.

"Don't apologize," Duncan said to her. "If you do, I'll have to hit him myself."

"I'm not." She'd hit Kleat too hard for that. He would take any apology as patronizing, and besides, she wasn't sorry. "You know," she said to him, "we could work together here. We came for the same reason."

Kleat looked at Duncan's scarf around her neck, red and white checkered like the KR—and millions of other Khmer people—used to wear. She couldn't tell if he distrusted the scarf or the giving of it to her, again, by Duncan. "I'm not so sure anymore," he said. "I know why I came. But there seem to be other temptations in the air."

That quickly, Molly's anger dissipated. She owed Kleat nothing, not one more emotion, not another thought, and least of all her little flight of fancy about Duncan.

One of them had emptied two MRE packets on the stone top. Molly made a show of pocketing the energy bar. She ripped open the scrambled-egg packet with her teeth and squeezed pieces of it cold into her mouth, wolfing the food down. It took sixty seconds flat. "There, done." She wiped her mouth. "Later." She started off into the mist.

"Where are you going?" Kleat said. She looked back at them. Duncan was rearranging his pebbles and twigs on the map. Kleat stood rooted in place with his hands on his hips. The Khmers seemed content hanging by the fire, waiting for the mist.

"I'm getting my socks and shoes out of the truck. Then I'm going up the stairs," she said. "The light's too fine to waste."

16.

By the time she finished tying her shoelaces, the rest were ready to go. They left Samnang and his leg by the fire to watch over the vehicles, and started off in a bunch.

The three brothers soon sprinted ahead, the slaps of their flip-flops fading into the mist above. Molly wanted to go bounding up the stairs with them, but curbed her excitement and stuck with Duncan and, by default, Kleat.

"There will be one hundred and four steps," Duncan told them. He seemed very certain of it.

"You've been here before?" Kleat said, mocking him.

"I could be wrong, of course," Duncan said. "But the place is monumental, and the statues are like half-breeds, part Buddhist, part animal. My guess is that they built it to a blueprint, one dictated by their gods. They would have dedicated a stair to each of the Buddha's hundred and four manifestations."

They were tall, steep, narrow steps, like those found on Mayan pyramids, the kind that take confidence to climb upright without hands. Greasy with fluorescent green and blue moss, they would need special care coming down. Tourists, someday, would require a handrail or a chain to hold on to. Vendors would sell them warm Cokes from the stone terraces.

"You could bleed the ecotourists white with something like this," Kleat said. "There's room down there for a parking lot and a lodge.

Put it on the water's edge. Spray the pools for mosquitoes. Clear out the trees." He pretended only to be tormenting Duncan, the purist. He accused them of giving in to the temptations of the place, and to each other, but Molly heard him warring with himself, the dutiful brother versus the building contractor, the bones versus his visions of development.

"That would destroy everything," Duncan said.

"Do you seriously think you can hold on to this for yourself? The jack is out of the box. There's no stuffing him back in again."

"We'll have to keep it secret until we can get the proper protections in place," Duncan said. "You don't rush something like this. The restoration will take years, even decades."

"First thing," Kleat said, "I'd clear the trees. The quickest way would be explosives. Give me a few pounds of C4, I could open up the sky. Better yet, bring in the loggers. Let the development pay for itself."

Duncan stopped on the stairs. "Kill the trees and you kill the city. Without the trees, it would fall to pieces."

What city? It was all conjecture. But like them, Molly was eager. She craved whatever waited above, in the mist. The stairs were building to a climax. Something was up there, she could feel it.

"After the destruction we saw coming in last night?" she said. "It looked like the forest is ripping the place to shreds."

"I know that's how it looks. But the trees are the only thing binding it together," Duncan said. "It's true, the trees have invaded the architecture, but they're also locking it in place. I've seen this at other sites. The forest is like a living glue."

He started pointing out the phantoms of trees in the mist. "Banyan trees. Giant strangler figs. And that one there, the most common invader, a form of ficus. *'Spong,'* the Cambodians call it, *Tetrameles nudiflora.* They can live for up to two hundred years, and all the while birds are scattering more seeds, spreading the forest's skeleton."

Kleat lost interest in his game. "We didn't come for this. The ruins are a distraction. Ignore the city, if that's what it is. Our mission is to find the remains of the Eleventh Cavalry men."

"You need to be prepared to find nothing," Duncan said.

"We know now they were here."

"Were. It's entirely possible they left the names of their women and headed on."

"On to where?"

"I don't know. But there's no sign they stayed. Did you see any of their tracks in the clearing?"

Kleat was quiet for a minute. His boots methodically slugged at the steps. "Our gang of mercenaries will have the place looted to the ground before we even see it," he growled. He accelerated, stumping upward, leaving them behind.

Molly held to Duncan's leisurely pace. They were going to be the last ones up. It wasn't a race, she told herself. If this proved to be half as big as it promised, Duncan was going to be the crux of her story. Let the others disperse into the ruins, out of frame. She would make him a hero. And herself a name. Kleat could find his bones. There could be something here for everyone.

As they passed the ledges leading off to the tents, she could see how the brothers had spaced them apart last night. Knowing the Americans liked privacy, they'd pitched each tent on a separate terrace. She began counting the steps from her ledge to the top so that she could find her own shelter even in the dark, but gave up. She let go. She was not alone. She was with Duncan. The two of them could manage somehow.

"How does it feel?" she asked Duncan. This could be his triumph. If only he would climb a little faster. Then she realized that he was lagging on purpose.

"I'm afraid," he said. "What if it's not what we think?"

"What do you think it is?" In her head the tape recorder was running. She had her camera out.

"I don't know. Have you ever had a dream that wouldn't let go of you? I don't know how to put it. These stairs, it's like I've climbed them before. But I've got no idea what comes next."

"You deserve this, Duncan." *And so do I, whatever comes.*

She'd paid her dues. She'd turned her sweat and blood into black ink, and made her eye the camera's eye, thinking to make the world a little better through her witnessing. But over the years, for one reason or another, she had squandered herself on trivial events and prideful men and women who tried to manipulate her pen and camera. She'd become a cynical hack. A hireling with no faith. That was about to change. The stairs were leading to something larger than life. Every writer should have that.

They worked higher into that netherworld of green mist, and when she looked down, the abyss seemed bottomless. At last she could make out the shape of cobra hoods, poised along the crest like gargoyles. The stairs reached their apex. One final step, and the ruins heaved up before them.

17.

There was no transition from below to above, no sense of arrival. They took a few steps and the architecture seemed to hurry around, enclosing them.

It was a city, a phantom city of buildings and statuary and the tangled network of the forest, a city of hints. If anything, the mist was thicker here, lush and aquamarine. Molly took a deep breath, and the air was so dense she could taste the smell of vegetation growing from its own rich compost, and flowers that were as invisible as ideas. The mist deformed the ancient metropolis. It softened the squared corners, revealing and devouring hints of towering spires, and washing against vast stone heads like a tide.

"God," said Duncan.

She got his astonishment on camera, his blank, plain daze. Every square in the red and white scarf around his neck jumped out from the mist. The background was pure Seurat, tiny dots of color flooding the air. The suggestion of a massive stone head peered over his right shoulder.

That would be the cover photo. This was a book, not an article. Done right, it might stand as a classic. She took a step and it felt like planting a footprint on the moon. They were the first, it seemed, to discover this place.

"How can this be?" she said. "A lost city in this day and age?"

"Why not?" said Duncan. "They're still finding Mayan cities and Incan tombs. There are species in these mountains that scientists thought were just myths. And look at the forest canopy. The ruins have been buried for centuries, not forgotten, just lost."

She was too stunned to arrange her thoughts. *Shoot,* she commanded herself. *Sort it out later.*

"Where did the others go?" Duncan said.

"Who cares?" For the time being, the two of them owned the ruins.

Working left to right for a digital panorama, she shot immense stacks of pyramids and squared monuments with ornately carved doorways. The mist seemed to breathe, blossoming then paling. But she realized it was her own heartbeat she was seeing through the lens, the rhythm of blood through the capillaries of her eyes.

"We need a plan," he said. "We could lose ourselves in here."

"You're driving the bus," she said.

"A basic assessment," he decided. "Yes. Describe the circle's edge, then spiral in."

They returned—with difficulty, a few steps and they were already twisted around—to the head of the staircase. The stairs plunged down into the mist. Somewhere down there Samnang was sitting by his fire.

Duncan set off along the perimeter of the chasm, following a walkway bordered by a fence with *nagas* facing outward. The walkway curved in a great semicircle along the very edge of the plateau. On their left, the architecture seemed to rush at them like a flood ready to spill over a waterfall. The *nagas'* sandstone mantles flared like pink spray.

They came to a fortress wall like the one they had passed through the night before. Standing twenty feet high, it was built of fired bricks. Some of the bricks had loosened and spilled from the top of the wall. Duncan hefted one and noticed a symbol baked into its top. "These are names," he said.

"You can read that?"

"No." He picked up a second and third brick, and they were

inscribed, too. "But certain Chinese emperors had a quality-control system like this. These are possibly the names of the brick makers. That way, any defects could be traced to its creator and corrected, or the creator punished."

As they moved on, Molly could practically feel the weight of the names holding up the wall and declaring the inside from the outside. It was like an army of magical symbols, containing the citizens and repelling outsiders.

Where the hillside rose, the wall stepped higher. A deep streambed lined with bricks and bedrock served as drainage, or possibly a moat. *A curious moat,* thought Molly. This one ran along the inside of the fortress. It was dry just now, but during the rainy season, Molly could imagine water coursing down the channel. In the slickrock country of Utah, she'd seen for herself how a small rain shower could turn the arroyos into deadly flood chutes.

The moat ascended in stages, the stone edges polished and worn by centuries of runoff. From the windows of nearby buildings, the sound of water must have been, by turns, sweet or thunderous. She wanted to veer off into the city and look out through those windows. She wanted to wander among the spires and floating heads.

But Duncan stuck to the path beneath the wall, stopping repeatedly to examine flowers and insects or animal prints and scat. They heard dogs barking in the far distance, and Molly thought there must be a village nearby, even within the ruins. Duncan explained that they were rare barking deer. He could tell the difference between one invisible bird and another by its song or even the sound of its wings. They spent ten minutes studying a spiderweb pattern, and another half hour counting the growth rings on the shells of two different species of snails.

It was maddening, almost as if he were avoiding the city. She didn't complain out loud as the wall went on and the minutes turned to hours. It took an effort not to direct his story. It would be a labyrinth in there. She had learned from the recovery team the primacy of the grid. The founding event of every dig is the driving of the first stake, traditionally at the southwest extremity. From that bench-mark emanated all the squares spreading to the north and east. That had to explain Duncan's uncertainty. He was hunting for an edge to dub southwest, a corner to the circle from which to begin.

Leaves stirred in the mist. They sounded almost like a child cry-ing very softly. As the sound drew closer, the crying became a little singsong rhyme coming from the trees, and Molly decided it could only be the birds. The sound mushroomed, rushing between the buildings with a blizzard howl. The mist churned open. A great gust of wind broke against them, nearly toppling them into the dry moat. Molly heard shouts and the clash of metal, and screams, an entire bat-tle, all within that blast of wind. Just as suddenly the air was still again.

Molly straightened. "What was that?"

Duncan chewed at his lip, staring at the mist-bound city. "The weather's changing," he said.

But there was no more wind, not even a breeze. They went on.

Molly kept looking for a breach in the wall. Surely the forest had broken it open somewhere, and they would be able to see the far side. But the wall loomed intact except along the very upper sections, where the masonry had come undone in fractions. The path and the wall went on twisting with the hill's contours.

Eventually, a gateway surfaced in the mist ahead. Like the one they had entered through the night before, it had a multiheaded turret with eyes that seemed to watch their approach. In her mind, the shapeless citadel became symmetrical. They'd entered the front door, and here was the back, and this road logically pierced the city from side to side. On the other hand, there could be a dozen more gates, with roads leading into some center like spokes.

The tunnel mouth was guarded—or had been, once upon a time—by a host of terra-cotta statues. They were life-size replicas of ancient warriors, dozens of them. "They have to be based on the sculpture army at Xi'an, in China," he said. "Or, what if the Xi'an army is based on this? Who knows how old it is?"

He kept a curious distance from the terra-cotta warriors, afraid, she thought, of disturbing the artifacts. That didn't stop her. "I'll be careful," she assured him, and moved among them with her camera. "They're so beautiful."

Extraordinary, she meant. Exquisite. But not beautiful. Each had his own distinct face, round or lean, vicious or youthful, some with little shocks of beards or delicate Fu Manchu mustaches. But their eyes destroyed the realism. They were primitive round holes, sockets, some still holding bulging, round jade pebbles.

The crudeness of the stone eyes confused her. Every other detail was so refined and lifelike, and these eyes were horrible. Was that the intent, to cow the beholder? Some still had paint remaining on them. As if the bulbous pebbles weren't frightening enough, the artists had added shocked black circles around each eye. It reminded her of war paint, or a child's drawing of a nightmare.

"Are these supposed to be like glass eyes?" she asked Duncan. "Sight for clay men?"

"Maybe. Or reminders."

"Yes?"

"That we come from the earth. I don't know. Stones for eyes in a city of stone. They could symbolize the all-seeing city. Or the forest."

Guardians at the gate, she thought. Many had shattered, and their shards still bore bits of colored paint. Others lay unbroken, on their backs or chests like store mannequins toppled by the wind.

Some still stood at attention, though these had all sunk to differing degrees into the earth. They looked like quicksand victims, dragged under to their knees or hips, some to their necks, but still vigilant. A few showed only the tops of their heads. Whatever siege—or exodus—they were designed to guard against, here they waited. They seemed ready to spring into action. Some even wore their original armor of jade plates stitched together with what looked like wire spun of gold. Gold, though? Surely thieves would have taken it long ago. Elsewhere, the wire had failed and jade plates lay scattered like pale green dragon scales. Their fists clenched empty holes where the wood shafts of spears or bows had rotted.

"There's a fortune lying here," she said.

"They came this way," Duncan said. He had stopped and was staring at the tunnel.

"Kleat and the brothers?"

"No, our soldiers, Molly. They were here."

"They went through the tunnel?"

"Not through," he said. "But they were here."

She looked into the dark maw. "How do you know?"

He opened and closed his mouth without a word. The answer man had no answer.

Molly stepped closer. The tunnel looked impassable, choked with vegetation. Ugly with it, to be honest. It disgusted her in a strange way, the messy, clenched chaos in there. She felt physically sick, and thought it might be that compressed cold egg she'd eaten for breakfast.

But as she went nearer, her uneasiness—her sense of outright disease—grew. The walls pressed down at her. The tunnel, this awful hole, made her dizzy. She remembered her repulsion as they'd entered last night, and this was worse. She was on foot. Dread and nausea shackled her. A sudden despair washed over her. What did it take to leave this place?

But she forced herself to the tunnel mouth. Vines and roots clotted its bowels. She reached to part the leaves and something bit her. She yanked her hand back, blood beading on her wrist.

"Molly," said Duncan. "Leave it alone."

Peering inside, she saw the culprit. She took a careful grip and tugged at it, dragging it into view.

"Is that barbed wire?"

"What do you think?" she snapped. Clearly this was what he'd seen.

"Molly?"

A wave of anger rocked her. "You could have warned me."

"I didn't see it."

She yanked at the rusted coil. There was a whole Slinky of

concertina wire inside, bound in place by years of undergrowth. "We'll never get out," she said. Fear seized her. Despair. They were prisoners.

"Come away from there," Duncan said.

She let loose of the wire and it drew back into the tunnel like a snake. She stared into the devouring pit.

"Molly." A command.

She turned from the tunnel.

"Come here."

She started toward him, and with each step her terrible emotions faded.

"Are you all right?" He took her arm and drew her farther away from the tunnel.

"I must be hungry," she said. "Or yesterday's still catching up with me." She sat down, emptied out.

"Drink." He gave her a water bottle.

"They closed themselves in," she said. "Why didn't they just leave?" She glanced at the tunnel, and it was just a tunnel now. But she felt scarred by it, not just scratched by the wire, but wounded by the tunnel. She wanted nothing more to do with it.

"Maybe they felt safer in the ruins," Duncan said. "One thing's certain, they didn't exit this way."

"You really didn't see the wire?"

"From here? You didn't see it until it cut you."

"Then how did you know they'd been here?"

He frowned. "It's logical. If they had time to carve names in trees down below, then they would have had time to explore up here. They would have examined the walls, don't you think, secured their perimeter, whatever soldiers do?"

Her watch read just eight-thirty. They'd left camp at eight-fifteen. The second hand was barely crawling. She pressed the stem and the little night-light glowed. The battery was working, but something was wrong with the mechanism. "The humidity," she said. So much for "water-resistant to fifty meters." "What time do you have?"

She'd forgotten that Duncan didn't wear a watch. And yet he carried an antique compass in his briefcase. She'd have to ask about the contradiction another time, one more quirk to slip into her book.

"We left camp hours ago," she said. "We should think about getting back. Don't you want to take a look at the city?" In her mind, the road leading from the tunnel would be a direct shortcut to the head of the stairs.

Duncan eyed the ruins drifting in the mist, and then the path continuing along the wall. She cut off his thinking. "The wall could go on for miles," she said. Let him connect his circle another day. The mist was thinning. She wanted to see.

"You're right." He nodded, then stepped back. She led them away from the sealed exit, in from the wall and toward the ruins they enclosed.

Only now did she discern that there was a road underfoot. Roots burst up through the ground, as high as their shoulders. The paving stones had buckled in waves, or split open in grassy zigzags. They passed between pyramids and terraced buildings. Strangler figs occupied rooftops and walls, like sea monsters with waxy brown tentacles. The careful architecture looked squashed.

Corridors branched off the main avenue, impassable, colonized from side to side with primordial trees. They crossed a bridge over a dried-out canal with little landing porches leading up to dark holes of doorways. "Like Venice," she said, "a city of water."

Every bend promised a secret. She had to discipline her photography. The Nikon would hold only so many images, and it was a battery hog. She got Duncan clambering across the wreckage of another bridge, this one pierced by a mahogany giant. She shot spires soaring like delicate, baroque rocket ships, their needles pricking the lower canopy and disappearing from view. She took six shots of a Buddha the length of two whales, lying on his side, head pillowed on one hand like a child lazing away a summer day. She could spend a whole week with him alone.

Everywhere she turned, the city offered itself to her, a prehistoric vision. Her wide-angle lens was not wide enough. The place defied her.

Baby steps, she reminded herself. She was intensely aware of the sum of the place, the notion of a grand design. Duncan was right, it would take years to decode. A lifetime.

He found a coin woven into the belly of a discarded bird's nest. Only Duncan, in the midst of a lost city, would have thought to look in a nest that had fallen from the branches.

"Do you know who this is?" He handed the coin to Molly. One side was scaled with verdigris, the other bore a crude profile. "I've seen one other like it, in a book. It's Antoninus Pius, the second-century Roman emperor." He was awestruck. "Whoever they were, these people were part of a trade network going all the way to the heart of the Roman Empire."

They entered a canyon of carved panels. Red, gray, and blue lichen plastered the bas-relief in neon blotches. It was like falling into myth. Monkey gods and human warriors waged war with exotic weapons. Concubines lounged, children played. Dancers' fingers curved like currents of water. A majestic peacock was oblivious of two crocodiles stalking it with wide-open jaws.

She and Duncan moved slowly, like lovers in an art gallery, occasionally admiring a find, then drifting apart to continue their separate investigations. The canyon seemed to contain the germs of every kind of fable and myth. The carving was peculiar in its style and demanded her concentration.

Here was a dragon rising from the sea. Here was a great fire set by invaders with spears, and a murderer stabbing his brother. She tried connecting the stories in order, and realized that every arrangement could be disconnected and rearranged to tell other tales. Was the dragon a storm? Were the invaders possibly saviors? Was the fire renewal, not destruction? Was the killer actually a hero? It went on like that.

Molly gave up with her camera. She touched the carvings. They touched her. It was hard to explain. It went beyond seduction. The walls contained her. They invited her to read herself among the carvings. It was as if she inhabited the stone.

Here was a woman exploring a garden. Here was an infant adrift on a river. Here was a woman about to stab herself. Reverse the order: Here was her mother, here the orphan, here the searcher.

She didn't know she was crying until Duncan laid one hand on her shoulder. He saw what she was looking at. It embarrassed her, and he saw that, too.

"Ancestors," he said. "The place is full with them."

"I don't know why I bother with her," said Molly. "Kleat's right. She was just a hippie chick. A suicide. One more lost child."

"It's not that easy with ghosts," he said.

"I found her, though. That should be enough."

He ran his fingers above the stone, not touching the lichen, only isolating the story. "You still have questions. What else is a ghost but a question?"

"I know everything I need to know," said Molly. "She showed up in Breckenridge with a baby in her arms. The old mining towns were going through this Neil Young *After the Gold Rush* kick, kids—hippies—settling into shacks, you know, letting their freak flags fly. She knitted hats and made candles with flowers in them. She sold them from a cardboard box. She didn't have the sense to get food stamps, so neighbors brought her meals. People stacked firewood by our trailer in the winter."

"And your father?"

"Which one? It was the Age of Aquarius. I doubt he ever knew I existed. And what would I do with him anyway?"

"You're probably right."

Molly brushed at the lichen, and if she was destroying a priceless carving, Duncan didn't reprimand her. "She would sing sad songs on the streets," she said. "An old priest told me that. She had a beautiful voice. Ballads. Hymns. Dirge music."

"Yes?"

"She died of a broken heart, he said. My poor, crazy mother."

"And so you're crazy, too?"

She looked at him, and he was not Kleat taunting her. He was Duncan. "On bad days, I wonder," she said.

"And the good days?"

"On the good days I sing."

"Sad songs?"

He had her. She could not help but smile. "Maybe."

"Then maybe, if I'm quiet, I'll hear you," he said.

"So you're counting on good days ahead, Mr. O'Brian?"

"Days?" He opened his arms to the city. "I'm counting on years. I could spend the rest of my life in here. I was born for this."

A single gunshot broke their reverie.

18.

At the crack of the bullet, as if the skin of the place had been punctured, the mist drew off in a sudden rush. It didn't burn away; the sun could not penetrate the triple canopy. It simply lifted and was gone.

They were surrounded—dwarfed—by those god heads and demon faces and the dreams of architects raised in stone and by this complicated forest. The canopy stretched overhead like an umbrella with veins. Molly felt made up, as if the giant stone heads among the trees were dreaming them all into existence.

She had forgotten about the others. Hours had passed. She could not read the green twilight. It seemed lighter without the mist, and yet dark for her sense of the time. Could it be late afternoon so soon?

Suddenly she was starving.

They followed the echo of the gunshot out of the canyon. It took some searching to locate the head of the stairs. Molly could barely distinguish between one building and another. She was in sensory overload, drained from too little sleep and too much emotion, way too much. She hadn't experienced so many raw feelings in years, all packed into the space of a single day. The city was like a fuse. One sensation seemed to trigger another in a chain reaction of old fears and repressed memories and anger and wild hope.

Luckily, Duncan had an instinct for the ruins. After a few false turns, he brought them to the rim with its pink sandstone *nagas* and the staircase. With the mist cleared, the terminus sprawled beneath them, a grand cul-de-sac in a bowl of steeply terraced walls. Trees and vines clung to the most precipitous walls.

From this height, the white Land Cruiser looked as delicate as an eggshell. The big Mercedes truck could have been a toy. The rest of them were down there, and when Kleat saw her and Duncan, he gave a big wave with his gun hand, which only made him look more miniature. The expedition suddenly seemed fragile and overreaching. Their discovery was vastly bigger than they were.

As they descended the stairs, Molly saw that Samnang had not been idle during their absence. A bright green rectangle of a hut made of leaves and poles now occupied the lowest terrace, with one side open to his little spark of a fire. The fire gave her a clue to the time. It glittered too brightly for day. Night was nearing.

They reached the ground. As she wove through the trees, Molly kept an eye out for the names of women carved in the bark, but the light had changed or she was among the wrong trees. She couldn't find the marks.

Even before entering the camp area, she saw Kleat grinning, and his reason for it. He was wearing a GI helmet with most of the canvas eaten away. Closer still, she could see fading tally marks along one side where a soldier had been counting down his days.

The brothers were in high spirits, too. A row of green bronze and jade vessels and geometrically painted jars stood along one ledge. She expected Duncan to start in about the plundering, but he only sighed.

"We're on their trail now," Kleat said. He opened his hand carefully, as if it might hold precious jewels, and three empty brass cartridges lay on his palm.

"You found those in the city?" asked Duncan.

"No, right here in the clearing. Sam found them lying over there." He knocked on the helmet. "We almost drove over it last night."

"That's all you have?"

"It's a start. Now we know where to look. Down here. Forget the city."

Molly glanced around at the forest enclosing them. You couldn't see the reservoirs from here, or their tire marks in the leaves. When it came time to leave, they would have to search just to find their way back to the causeway.

"What are those?" she asked, pointing at saplings bent into O shapes. They appeared at various distances among the trees, like animal snares.

"That's Sam's work. Landmarks. I sent him to look for the ACAVs. They have to be around here somewhere."

"Was that your gunshot?"

"No sense wasting time up there. They probably never went up into the ruins."

Molly resented that. She and Duncan had been crossing the city's threshold, drifting among its stories. And Kleat had summoned them.

"Well, they did, for your information," she blurted out.

Duncan grimaced. She bit her lip. How could she have known that was their secret?

"They were up there?" Kleat said.

It was too late to take back her words. "We found barbed wire in the gate at the back."

"You found wire?" Kleat said. "And you didn't call for me? That was the deal. I told you—"

Molly darted a glance at Duncan. It was true, they had abandoned the evidence in order to go exploring in the city. "We called for you," she lied. "We waited. You didn't hear us."

"What gate?" His eyes fell on her camera. "Show me."

She turned on the camera and showed him her pictures of the tunnel. The camera was quirking out again. The flash glare had blanched white the interior of the tunnel. The vines and roots and coiled wire were thin dark arabesques, but also there were shapes inside, trapped shapes if you wanted to embellish the image. With some imagination, one could almost make out arms and legs.

"What are those things?" Kleat said.

"Ricochet. The flash bouncing off the mist. Maybe I'm wrong about the wire. It looks like vines." Or tendons.

But his curiosity was piqued. "And what about these?" he

pounced, as she scrolled through the terra-cotta warrior series. This was what Duncan had been hoping to hide.

"Statues." She shrugged. The stone eyes stared out from the display.

"There must be fifty of them."

"I didn't count."

"Where is this gate?"

"There's no way to describe it," Duncan said. "You saw what a jumble it is."

"Then you can lead me there tomorrow," Kleat said. "But first thing, we're going to do a line sweep of the area down here. Those ACAVs are somewhere."

She started to object to his diktat. But Duncan was quicker. "Good," he agreed. "There's nothing left of today. It's getting dark. We need rest and food. We'll start fresh in the morning." Not a word more about the city, as if Kleat really might forget it.

The two men went to the hut. Before it got dark, Molly walked to the truck to grab a flashlight and another camera battery from her mule bag. Picture possibilities swarmed through her mind. There had to be a temple or a tree from which to shoot that giant reclining Buddha in its entirety, and she wanted to line up three particular spires so they took the eye to a vanishing point. And there were those sweethearts' names in the forest, so tender, so terribly mortal, the letters deformed by the years.

She was zipping shut the mule bag when Samnang returned through the dusk. He went straight to the ledge with the looted ceramics and bronze and jade bowls, and obviously this was the first he'd seen them. He approached the brothers, crouching by the fire. From the truck, she could hear him chastising them. One of the brothers rose and shouted back, shaking his rifle. Another flicked a burning twig at him. *Bad luck children,* she thought.

She joined Kleat and Duncan in the hut.

"A regular civil war out there," Kleat said. The Khmers' arguing seemed to please him. At last Samnang disengaged and hobbled off into the forest again.

Someone had put a box of MREs inside for them. Molly sorted through the packets, calling out the names of meals. She made her own selection and slit the thick plastic with her Swiss Army knife. People complained about the meals, but she'd developed a taste for them while covering a crew of hotshots one fiery season in the San Juan range.

While her chow mein heated in the bag, she gazed out at the darkening trees, unwinding for the first time in a month. After the muggy central lowlands, the forest felt cool and restoring. Even so, sweat beaded her forehead. She wiped at it.

Soon, inevitably, Kleat and Duncan began arguing. There was no excuse for it. The evening was quiet except for animal noises, and each of the men was occupied, Duncan with his sketch pad and Kleat cleaning his pistol. And it was the same argument they'd had that morning. The only difference was that now they had real artifacts to fuel their positions. They were no longer talking about the hypothetical. Duncan had found a city. Kleat had found war relics.

"We have to retreat," Duncan said. "First thing in the morning, before anything more gets destroyed or pillaged, we need to pack up and leave. We're not prepared for this. The city needs protection. We have to get this right."

Kleat rejected it with a grunt. "Not going to happen."

Molly didn't know what to say. She felt safe in here. She felt found. And yet Duncan was inviting the world in before they even had their foothold.

"But we could lose everything," she said, trying to reason with him. Once word of the find spread, the eight-hundred-pound gorillas—the *Smithsonians* and *National Geographics* and universities and celebrity professors and best-selling authors and staff photographers—would descend on the place. She would get cut out, and so would Duncan. That was how it worked.

Kleat picked up the theme. "This is what I've been saying. We're here. It's ours." He dripped solvent onto a patch and pumped the rod down the barrel.

"We'll come back again," Duncan said, "but on our terms, not theirs." He gestured at the brothers. "We can get them to drive us down to one of the towns, and bring us back with supplies to last us through the next six months. That gives us the monsoon."

"And what makes you think they'll keep the big secret down in town?" said Kleat.

"They won't. That's a given. They're human. They're poor. We're in a race against time. Which makes you, Molly, the most important one of us. Everything depends on you. You can document the city before the jackals pick it clean. It's not just these guys. Once the news breaks, the Cambodian army and government will step in. That's when the real looting begins. You're our witness to all the greatness the way it is. It means staying through the rains, though. I'd send the drivers away before the river swelled. After that, we'd be shut inside, alone."

"Yes," she answered him, though he hadn't asked the question. Yes, she wanted to be here. Shut inside. Alone.

"Get all the snapshots you want," Kleat said, "while we search for the men. They come first. There's not going to be any mission creep here. We came for the bones, not a city. We can beat the rains. Once I have the bones, this pile of rocks is all yours. You two can stay until kingdom come, I don't care." He started assembling the pistol.

"We can spend the next few days preparing," said Duncan. "And the next six months exploring."

"You and your city," Kleat said. He fit the spring onto the barrel. "What about the men?"

"If they're here, we'll find them."

"There's no if. They're here. And we're here. And we're staying."

Molly dabbed at the sweat trickling down her temples. Was she getting sick?

Now was her turn to try reasoning with Kleat. "What if we can't find them before the rain comes? Duncan has a point. It's the difference between having a few days to search or having six months."

"I need this." For a moment Kleat sounded desperate. "Before it's too late."

"I don't understand."

"The captain will come, or someone like him," Kleat said. "Once they hear it's us up here, they'll come to take it over. The river won't stop them, they'll fly right over it and banish us again. And that's not happening. They had their chance."

"Their chance?"

"These bones belong to me," Kleat declared. He fit the barrel into the frame with a metallic *click-clack*.

Molly and Duncan exchanged a look. The bones belonged to him? "John," Duncan said quietly. "That's not right. What about your talk of honor?"

"One buys the other," Kleat said. "These dead buy my dead. It's the only way I'll ever find my brother."

Molly remembered Luke laughing—barking like a monkey—at the claim that Kleat had a brother.

"That's why you're here?" said Duncan.

"The captain sent us off like traitors. Here's their wake-up call. Every year, the missing die a little more. Wives remarry. Children grow up and forget. New wars eclipse the old ones. Soon it will be too late."

"What do you think the captain and his people are doing in the dirt and mud and sun?" said Duncan. "Searching for the lost ones."

"They need to search harder, then. With the bones to shame them, I can make America sit up and listen. That's why you're important," he said to Molly. "You and your newspapers. Shame them. Destroy the old rule. We need fresh blood. New direction. My brother is out there somewhere, and one way or another I'm going to take him home."

The fire crackled outside. No one spoke for a minute.

Finally, Duncan said, "I'm sorry it's come to this, Molly. I'm trying to think of a middle way. But nothing's coming to me. It seems we have to choose between the bones and the city, and I know where I stand. And we know where John stands. But there are three of us."

He looked to Molly for the deciding vote, and she made a face. "What can I say?" She was genuinely at a loss. Kleat had all but persuaded her, and yet the city needed her. "You both have strong arguments." She was about to ask if there was really no compromise to be made, but Kleat spoke up.

"No need to fret over it," he said. He clapped the magazine into the grip and chambered a round. He looked at his pistol, then at them.

"Are you threatening us?" Molly asked.

"Please," he said. "It's just that sometimes we get carried away with this democracy thing. And we shouldn't."

19.

According to her watch next morning, she rose at 9 A.M. the previous morning. It was darker than nine, though. *Six,* she thought, and hurried from her tent.

Gray rags of fog drifted in the mist, as if the morning could not make up its mind which way to blind her. She had her bearings, though. In less than five minutes she found Samnang's bright orange fire and the men all gathered.

She feared that Kleat and Duncan were battling for the brothers' loyalties, the one to stay, the other to leave. But as she quickly learned, the brothers had their own loyalties to attend to. They wanted more money.

"Otherwise, they're leaving without us," Duncan said. He was good-natured about it. "It makes sense. Why stick around? They scored a few thousand dollars' worth of pots, and as far as they're concerned, the city belongs to them. They're bringing some friends back with them."

"What about leaving *with* us?" Molly asked.

"More money."

"Pirates," Kleat fumed.

"We knew that coming in," said Duncan.

"They'd strand us?" Molly looked around. Vin kept his eyes on the ground. The other two brothers held their chins high and their rifles prominent.

The mist was churning. The forest breathed.

Samnang brought her a coffee. "Sugar?" he asked.

"No, Samnang." It was all spoiled. They needed food to stay. Blankets. A generator to recharge her batteries. Umbrellas. More malaria pills. A toothbrush. They needed solitude.

"This is your doing," Kleat said to Duncan.

"It does me no good," Duncan said. "They've got us."

"How much?" said Molly.

"Another five hundred for the ride out. Five thousand to stay through tomorrow. They're not stupid. They keep talking about the typhoon and the river."

"I only have two hundred," Molly said.

"I'm out," said Duncan. What had they been thinking, supplies for six months?

"The statues," said Kleat.

"What?"

"Show them on your camera. The terra-cotta warriors."

"No," said Duncan. "Don't."

Samnang squatted by the fire and blew on it with pursed lips. He had breath like kerosene. The fire leaped.

"They're worth hundreds of thousands," Kleat said. "Tell them you'll show them the location. They'll deal."

"We can walk out of here on foot," Duncan said. The mist was drawing away. Trees appeared around them.

"Show them," Kleat told Molly.

She noticed Samnang watching her through the fire. Was there a right and a wrong to this? She was scared. They were in the middle of nowhere. "No," she decided.

Kleat turned to the brothers. "Statues," he said in English. He pointed up at the city. "Understand? Big money. Statues." They frowned at him.

Tails of fog flickered off through the branches. The truck stood over there, and the Land Cruiser. Molly glanced up. Her mouth fell open.

There seemed no way they could have missed such a thing yesterday.

Eyes fixed to the canopy that was their false sky, she backed away from it.

"Molly?" said Duncan. Then he saw it, too, hidden in plain sight. Kleat swore with surprise. The brothers crouched and raised their rifles.

The rusting hulk of a vehicle hung in a spur of limbs, like a Lost Dutchman, beached in the air. One long metal tread had broken and dangled from its belly. She lifted her camera and, on the flank, in plain view, a faint insignia still showed: a black horse rearing.

20.

The revelation—the relic of the Blackhorse patrol—unplugged them from their wrangling. You could not call what followed a peace. They did not reconcile so much as disengage. It was spontaneous. No one willed it. They simply forgot one another, at least for a time.

They drifted apart, staring up at the trapped war machine, struggling to make sense of it. Sixty feet up, the vehicle looked stranded by some mythical flood, but it was the forest that had lifted it.

"Impossible," Kleat said. "That's eleven tons or more."

Yet there it hung in the crook of massive branches. The helmet and cartridges had fallen from it. No one had bothered to look up. Who would have thought such a thing could happen?

Kleat paced beneath like a starving man eyeing an apple, alternately quiet and then stringing out thoughts for anyone to hear. "The first time the Vietnamese saw an APC, they called it a green dragon," he told anyone who cared to listen. "The army used them for amphibious taxis. M-113s. Armored personnel carriers. The cavalry turned them into gunships on tracks. ACAVs. 'Tracks,' the troops called them. They were fast and mean. There was usually a crew of five. They'd load them full of ammunition and go hunting in columns."

He went on about its armament, travel range, and the thickness—or thinness—of its armored skin. "They were death traps if you hit a mine or caught a rocket." Molly quit listening. She could not get over the power of the trees. Sixty feet, six stories high, in thirty years. Eleven tons.

Duncan, the dedicated scientist, went to one of the terraces and opened his steel briefcase to take notes and sketch on his pad.

The three brothers retired to the staircase in a smudge of cigarette smoke, stricken with superstition or just discussing the possible profit to be made. The market in American bones from the Vietnam era was not something the DOD talked about, Molly had learned, but they paid well for the real thing.

Samnang alone did not seem awestruck. He had unwittingly made their fire under the dead vehicle and now began shifting it to a more suitable place. A few at a time, he carried the logs with their smoldering tips to the base of a broad, flat terrace and blew the flames back to life.

Molly noticed him. His simple act declared acceptance. Everything was changed, and yet nothing. For all their differences, they were staying. He had grasped that fact. They needed a center. The fire was that, an anchor for their camp.

"This is only one of them," Kleat said. "We're looking for nine men, though. There has to be a second track somewhere."

The canopy didn't seem to be hiding any more of them. Molly looked up among the ganglia of limbs and vines, and this appeared to be the forest's sole catch.

She stood back and faced it as if facing the Sphinx. That's how it seemed, like a beast in the middle of the desert. A riddle in metal skin. They had come for bones and found a fortress. They had looked in the treetops and found a chariot. What did one have to do with the other? Some hidden hand had sewn them together, but why?

She drew out her camera and telephoto lens and sighted through the long barrel. The ACAV leaped at her. Tipped slightly downward and canting to its right, it hung up there with its machine gun aimed straight at her. She took the shot and stepped to the side, out of the line of fire.

Meandering, angling for the best shots, she ransacked the track with her high-tech spyglass. The details bounded out at her. A ramp at the rear flapped open like a drawbridge. Beside the neatly stenciled U.S. ARMY, graffiti vowed maximum savagery. There was another gun shield behind the main turret, but this one lacked a barrel in the slot.

A man was watching her from the roof of the vehicle.

It didn't register in the first instant.

She saw him, but didn't see him.

Her mind rationalized the face as a knot of wood, or a distant statue. His eyes were right on her, and she accepted them as bulbs on a limb, or openings in the leaves.

But then his nostrils moved, nothing else, just the center of his watching face, and she realized he was taking her scent.

"Christ," she said.

Her hand jerked. The camera moved, but not before she hit the shutter release. In or out of focus, she didn't know. She lifted the camera back to her eye, searching, zooming, not certain she wanted to see him again.

Duncan was at her side in moments.

Gone, he was gone. Her hands were shaking, next to worthless for holding the telephoto steady.

Kleat came over.

"A man," she said. "I saw him, his face, up there."

"Bullshit." But Kleat's gun appeared. He held it in a two-handed grip, half raised.

"See for yourself." She fiddled with the display. There was the face, or almost a face.

"You got one," Duncan congratulated her. "Too bad he moved."

"One what?"

"A gibbon, it looks like. A pileated gibbon. They're all but extinct east of the Mekong. The hill tribes loved them to death. Good meat, I hear."

Kleat holstered his gun. "A monkey," he said.

She stared at the lighted image. The focus was ragged. The turret details were perfectly sharp, but the face was a blur, barely there at all. It was charcoal gray and, granted, simian in some measure. But it wasn't quite the face she'd seen.

"Let me see," said Kleat. She passed him the camera, thinking he wanted to study the image. Instead he brought it to his eye like a marksman.

"You've done it again," he said after a minute.

"What?"

"First the pilot, now this." He handed her the camera. "That's a skull."

She steadied the camera. There the sloped breastplate, a fading white army star, up higher the snout of the machine gun, and the turret—empty now where the face had been. And behind that, all but hidden along the upper shell, she saw the head, tucked within the shadows, unmoving.

Hard and glossy, it rested on a stubby metal pole. It looked freshly plucked from the battlefield. Through her lens, the eyes gazed down. Kleat took the camera.

"The Vietnamese must have found them," Kleat said. "Or the fucking KR. Those poor guys. There could be more of them inside." The idea quickened in him. "Someone's got to go up there."

"That will be a trick," Duncan said.

"Get one of the boys to do it."

"They'll never go," Duncan said. "Especially with a dead man up there."

"Bargain with them."

"Don't force this, John. I keep telling you, part of them still lives in the tenth century, with curses and evil eyes and flying spirits. The locals give their babies charms to protect them. They stack firewood against the door to keep out the dead. You wouldn't believe some of the stories."

Kleat wheeled around and walked quickly to the brothers. For a moment, Molly didn't miss her camera. Then she realized his game.

"He's showing them the statues," she told Duncan.

They hurried after Kleat, but the damage was done. They were holding her camera and smearing the display with their fingertips. They were excited.

"What have you done?" said Duncan.

"I just gave you and me the world," Kleat said. "Now talk to them. Get whatever you want out of it, all the supplies in the world, just as long as you get us into that track."

"Forget it."

"Sam, get over here," Kleat said. "You tell them. The place is huge. They could search for days and never find these statues. And they don't have days. The typhoon's coming. We know where the statues are. I need someone to run a rope up to that vehicle. That's for starters. They're businessmen. Let's do business."

Samnang relayed the message. Doc, the eldest brother with the full *sak*—the suns and flames and lines and dots from his toes to his throat—glanced up at the ACAV and said, "*Te.*" No way.

"Come on," Kleat said in English. He pointed at the camera display. "You want these? We'll show you where they are. One of you street heroes, come on. All you have to do is climb up. Tell them, they don't even have to go inside. All we need is a rope to it. We'll take it from there."

Doc said something. Samnang said, "They want your gun."

"My gun?"

"They are saying that. The statues and your Glock."

"Why? We're already outgunned, three to one."

Outgunned? thought Molly.

"What does it matter?" said Duncan. "If the bones are there, you get what you want."

"And if they're not? Tell them no statues until we get inside the track," Kleat said. "Tell them."

"They understand," said Samnang.

Doc spoke. Vin handed the camera to them. Duncan and Samnang exchanged a wary look.

"Here's your camera. They're requesting to look at your gun. An exchange."

"The hell." Kleat's voice flattened out. A vein appeared on his scalp.

Molly took her camera.

"They want me to hand it to them?"

"Just do it," Duncan said.

"You know what they're doing," said Kleat.

"Not necessarily, John. Keep calm."

"They're pirates."

"Don't raise your voice, John."

He was going to pull his gun on them, Molly realized with sudden alarm. They were baiting him to do it. They were waiting for him. Their yellow eyes stared off into the distance. They toked their cigarettes like Marlboro men. But their fingers had shifted on their rifles. They were getting the weight of their weapons, the arc of their descent, the timing, the targets. The signs were all there.

She could almost picture herself lying among the dead.

"I'll go," she said suddenly.

Her voice startled them.

Kleat narrowed his eyes, suspicious of everyone now. "Up there?"

"You don't understand." She smiled large and stepped between the men. "I'm good at this. It's one of the hats I wear. I hang off rocks for a living. Mountain photography. Calendars and magazines. I'm not the greatest climber in the world, but I can manage a tree."

"No," said Duncan.

She smiled at him. "Baby steps," she said.

She took over, chattering brightly, getting them distracted. Samnang began relaying her decision to the brothers. Vin's eyes grew big. She reached for him and brought him down into their midst, rifle and all, disarming them one at a time.

"I'll need a rope," she said. "Do you have a rope?"

Samnang droned on softly. Vin nodded his head and started for the truck.

"And you," she said to Kleat. "Give me your gun."

Kleat backed away from her. "Now you?"

"I'm not going up there without some protection. Who knows what's living in there?"

"Forget it."

"You want me to fix a rope? That's my price. A loaner."

"I'll watch your back."

She held out her hand. "Right now." She added quietly, "You son of a bitch."

Samnang halted his translating.

She could see Kleat's gears turning. He could refuse her. But she was his only hope, and he knew it. They were locked on to his every move, and his one chance at keeping his gun was to give it away. She would take it out of the brothers' reach as well as his . . . for the time being. He handed her his Glock.

"Is the safety on?" she asked, looking at both sides of the gun.

"It's a Glock," he said.

"That's what everyone keeps saying."

"It's all internal," he said. "Don't worry about it."

She tucked the gun into the back of her waist, out of sight, out of mind.

The brothers' hands relaxed on their rifles, just as she'd hoped. "Keep this for me," she said to Duncan, and gave him her camera.

He laid one hand on top of hers, and she was shaking. His touch steadied her. He took the camera. "You want me to get a picture of you?" he asked.

That was a first. None of her subjects had ever bothered to ask if she wanted a record of herself.

21.

Vin returned with a coil of frayed, greasy brown Perlon. Molly walked to the tree and everyone followed. She turned it into a high-wire act, something to lift them from the morning of threats.

Lodged in the middle branches, the ACAV looked like a strange, small fish caught in talons of coral. She circled the tree, running her palms over the tan and white bark. "This will do."

She shook the coil loose and, without looking, tied a bowline around her waist. She shifted the knot around to the small of her back so the rope would trail behind, not between her legs. She wouldn't need it for anything until she got to the vehicle. The brothers squatted down to watch through a cloud of fresh smoke. *Razzle-dazzle 'em,* she thought.

She shucked her shoes and socks and placed them neatly by the tree. The bare feet were for extra grip, but also a bit of theater. Patting the dewlap folds of wood, she hopped up onto a massive root. "Feed me the rope," she said. "Make sure there aren't any knots." Duncan stepped forward. She started off.

The climbing went quickly. The men grew smaller, their heads tipped back, mouths open. Partway up, double-checking her grip, she faked a slip. That got an audible grunt from the audience. "No problem." She pretended to grapple her way past a perilous crux.

It was easy. The tree offered itself to her in phases, its knots and boles and branches forming a natural ladder. A whole metropolis appeared in the canopy, with limbs and looping vine bridges inter-locking the great towers of trees.

It felt good to open her wings, good to get away from the men. Things seemed much saner up here. It occurred to her that she could keep on climbing. She could vanish into the upper branches and out-wait the gunslingers.

The thought grew into a temptation. Untie from the rope and she could enter the canopy and they'd never get her back. The place abounded with food and niches for shelter. Nuts and mangos and other exotic fruits nestled like Christmas ornaments.

"Molly." Her name, so faint. Like leaves rustling.

The forest was so beautiful, and when she glanced down, her holds had withdrawn into the tree. Pathways led off along the great branches. She felt drugged.

The forest was her answer, she comprehended. But it went beyond that. The message built like a heat. All she had to do was take to the trees. Forget the men, they were deceivers. Forget the rains, they would pass. Forget the past. The forest would provide.

The ACAV broke her fantasy of dancing off into the heights.

More quickly than she'd expected, its squared metal corners and sprockets and pipes and bulldozer tread emerged around the corner. Her temptation snapped. This brute thing—not escape—was what she'd come for.

The metal ramp at the back invited her like a sturdy porch. One step and she would be inside.

"Moll-lee." The rope tugged at her waist. It was Duncan, invisible beneath the foliage. He called again, more insistent this time.

She took a breath. It was like pulling herself from a dream. "I'm good," she shouted down.

She peered at the inside of the thing. An open hatch on top helped illuminate the recesses. Stenciled warnings read DANGER—MONOX-IDE GAS. She sniffed the air, and there was only the slight odor of fuel and oil and fertilizer. Dung, she realized. Animal dung. The green dragon had become a nest for forest creatures.

"I'm going in," she called down.

"What?"

She pulled up some slack and made the small leap, landing lightly, barefoot, on the cool metal. The wedged vehicle didn't shift an inch.

The rope tugged again, Duncan fretting.

"I'm off," she shouted, and realized that the climbing lingo might confuse him. "I'm in. I'm up." She untied from the rope and knotted it to an eyebolt on the back of the ACAV. "Come on up. The rope's anchored."

Branches had infiltrated through the open cupola, and white orchids with red pistils grew here. Butterflies spiraled above the war machine, their wings bright blue and the size of her hand. Death and life. She wanted her camera.

She peeked on top, and the head was jammed onto an exhaust pipe. Its eyes and face were aimed forward, and she was grateful for that. Let the others deal with it.

As it turned out, once she'd hung the rope straight down from the ACAV, the line was too greasy and thin for them to ascend. Kleat wrapped it around his fists and hauled himself up a few feet, and the rope creaked, but that was as high as he could get. Duncan had no more luck. The brothers wanted nothing to do with it. Without a climber's Jumars to grip it, the rope was only good for a one-way ride, down.

"You've done your job," Duncan called up to her. "Come down."

"Wait," Kleat shouted. "What about the bones?"

"It's too dark to see," she called out.

"We'll send up a flashlight," he said. "And a bag for the bones."

That was the part she'd been hoping to avoid. "My camera," she shouted down on a whim. Through it she could filter any horrors before having to touch them.

"What?"

"I want my camera. And some water. And a PowerBar."

The burlap sack came to about fifteen pounds. She pulled it up hand over hand, and someone, Duncan, no doubt, had included the bag of M&M's. There were two more burlap sacks stuffed inside. Kleat was expecting a lot of bones.

She sat on the edge of the ramp with her back to the ACAV, her bare feet swinging, and ate the PowerBar and candy and drank the water. Then she stood and turned on the flashlight and went to work inside.

22.

Over the next hour, Kleat called up periodically, impatient. "What's keeping you?" she heard his tiny voice say. "Are they all there?"

Duncan only wanted to know if she was okay.

She didn't answer them. A ripple of thunder sounded in the far distance. That meant it was approaching noon. The monsoon was working up its nerve. Or else the typhoon was nearing. Would it announce itself or just open up on them?

She was thorough, exploring the deepest bay of the ACAV, poking with a stick where she was afraid of snakes. With each discovery, it became more obvious that the armored box held only questions. Their answers hid elsewhere.

She saved the head for last, climbing onto the top through the opening with the machine gun.

After an hour, there was no more to find.

She started to wrap the rope over one shoulder to descend, then had a thought. Untying the anchor knot, she threaded the end of the rope through the pistol's trigger guard, and retied the rope. Then, dangling the burlap sack from her belt, she backed off the ramp and rappelled to the ground.

As she descended from the canopy, she looked across to the top of the terraced walls and saw the city waiting for her. Her view lasted only a few feet, then she sank lower into the terminus.

Kleat and Duncan waited for her at the bottom.

"Well?" said Kleat.

She opened the sack like Santa Claus and handed him the head. "You were wrong," she said.

Kleat held it at arm's length. "What the hell is this?"

"It's a trophy. They had it mounted on their exhaust pipe."

It was one of the terra-cotta warriors' heads, its neck a long, rounded plug with a hole at the bottom. The jade pebble eyes glared up at them. The painted circles had mostly washed away, but the expression was still ghastly.

"Is this some kind of joke?" Kleat said.

The brothers, watching from the fire, saw that the head was safely inhuman. They came over from the fire. Hunkered down by his water pot, Samnang saw it, too. He approached more slowly, his expression incredulous. "Those eyes," he said.

"You've seen them before?" Molly asked. He couldn't quit staring at them.

"Once," he said. "I can never forget."

"The soldiers must have brought the head down from the gate," Duncan said. "Like Molly said, a souvenir to show they'd been here. It means they were getting ready to leave. But for some reason, they never left."

"That's all you found?" Kleat said to Molly.

"No bones," she said. "It was mostly empty. There's a big machine gun, rusted solid. And these." She gave him a handful of rotted currency.

"GI scrip," said Kleat. "They didn't use dollars in the field."

"And these." She pulled out a set of maps in plastic.

Duncan took those. "Nice," he said. "Very nice. These could tell us where they were going and why they came here. And where we are."

"Do you think that's the end of it?" Kleat said. He tossed the currency away. "Funny money and a piece of pottery and some maps?"

"No." She had wanted the city for herself and Duncan. But for a little longer they were going to have to put up with Kleat's hunger and the brothers' ransacking. Somehow she and Duncan could turn this to their advantage, but it would come at a cost. The question was, how much of a cost? "We'll keep looking for the soldiers. That comes first." His departure came second.

Kleat held out his hand. "My gun." He hadn't forgotten.

She reached behind her. She planted her feet. She'd rehearsed it in her mind. He would go ballistic when she confessed, would maybe even hit her, but not if she could help it.

Without a word, she brought her fist around in a long arc. It wasn't a graceful boxer's roundhouse, and it wasn't very fast. His surprise was almost sad. His face turned slightly away. She landed against his ear. The shock of it ran up her arm bones.

Kleat dropped to the ground with a bellow. The terra-cotta head fell from his hands and rolled across the leaves.

The brothers fell silent, astonished. First she'd slapped him, now she'd brought him to his knees. It was so strange to them, the alpha-femme twist. It was strange to her.

"I didn't bring it down." She was breathing hard, wondering how it could have come to this.

Kleat looked at her. His blank expression was changing, the rage getting traction.

"I left it," she announced loudly. "Before someone got killed."

The worm veins surfaced. "Do you know what you've done to us?" he shouted at her.

Duncan came alive, thankfully. He stepped between them, pressing his back against Molly, forcing her back. He faced Kleat. "There," he said, "it's done. Not finished, just changed. I'm with Molly."

"You two." He spat at Duncan's feet. A drop of blood trickled from his ear. She hadn't meant to draw blood. She hoped his ear was okay.

"The gun was a crutch," Duncan said. "You were a threat to us all."

Off to one side, Doc picked up the head and was gawking at the jade eyes. His brothers gathered around him.

"You're going back up that rope," Kleat said.

"No, she's not," said Duncan. "There's nothing more in the

ACAV for us. The soldiers went someplace else. We'll do what Molly said. We'll keep searching." He paused, with a glance at Doc. "And plundering."

He offered his hand to help Kleat stand, and of course Kleat pushed it away.

They ate a hurried lunch while the brothers rooted through their truck for sacks to carry relics. Molly could see the terra-cotta head resting on the front seat, a baleful passenger. Duncan studied the map she had brought down.

"You can still see traces of grease pencil," he said. "They went east at Snuol and kept on going. Who knows why? The fog of war. But the interesting thing isn't the map itself or where they thought they were or weren't. It's this little bit of marginalia."

He turned the map for Molly to see, and the old, creased plastic reflected the light. She had to separate one layer of reality from the other, the underlying contour lines and typeset names on the map from the red smudge marks on the plastic. There were four numbers beside a circle on a road.

" 'Oh-six, twenty-four,' " she read out loud. "Map coordinates?"

"It's a date, as good as an entry in a logbook. June twenty-four." She gave the map back to Duncan to give to Kleat. He was brooding over his meal, convinced they were now the Khmers' prisoners.

Duncan tried to bring Kleat into it. "You said they went missing on June twenty-third. This means that a day later they were still trying to find their way."

"But to where?" she asked.

"Not here," said Kleat. "That's certain. They were under deadline."

"How do you know that?" asked Duncan.

"Because six days later the U.S. forces pulled out of Cambodia. Nixon was under siege at home. The traitors at Kent State had started a firestorm."

She had wondered how he might get back at them.

"Those were American children who got shot there," Duncan said.

"Pawns," Kleat said.

"It's old history," she said. "You keep going backward."

"I'm dissecting an event. Establishing connections. And deceptions," said Kleat. "History is our clue. Kent State is the reason the Eleventh Cavalry men died here. While our troops were getting slaughtered in these jungles, the college spawn in their bell-bottoms and tie-dyed T-shirts were tying the hands of our president."

Duncan didn't rise to it. He let Kleat vent.

"Invading Cambodia was a masterstroke," Kleat said. "Then Kent State blew up and we had to give the hiding places and sanctuaries back to our enemy. June twenty-nine was the fallback date. That was the day the last American troops pulled out of Cambodia. All except for these men."

"I thought the motto was 'Never leave a man behind,' " Molly ventured.

"Within reason," Kleat said. "But the clock was ticking. This whole borderland was about to return to enemy control. These guys had two options. Keep driving around the countryside. Or hole up and pray. Their commanding officer chose to hole up. He made the choice. Whoever the bastard was, he as good as pulled the trigger on them."

23.

It was high noon, as best as she could tell inside the green bell jar of the canopy, when the expedition split into three teams. Kleat still seethed over the loss of his gun, but the Heng brothers treated Molly like a champion.

"Rambo," they said, still awed that a woman could hit like a man. For her reward, they paired her with Samnang and allowed her to keep her camera. Duncan was sent with the middle brother, So. Kleat went up the stairs watched over by Doc and Vin.

Doc made clear that their first priority was to locate the terra-cotta guardians at the back gate. But if they happened to find American bones along the way, that was fine, too. There was no more strike talk. For now, the issue of leaving was moot, and a few extra dollars paled beside the prospect of priceless relics.

Carrying burlap sacks and Molly's emptied-out mule bag, and even bunches of little blue plastic bags like the kind in a deli, the searchers climbed toward the city. Molly and Samnang were quickly left behind. They had the most freedom, she realized. The brothers expected little or nothing from an old man with one leg.

Every so often, she sat down "to enjoy the view" or "rest my knees."

Samnang was not fooled. "You're a dangerous woman," he teased her. "You make us believe we're stronger than we are."

"I'm serious," she said. "Climbing that tree wiped me out."

"Yes, and I have two good legs," he said, smiling.

From halfway up the stairs, their camp looked borrowed from the forest. The green hut was already surrounded by the tiptoe of grass. Their fire lay banked under gray ashes.

They heard Kleat arguing, high above them. One of the brothers, probably Doc, snapped back at him. The argument died away.

"Have I done the wrong thing?" she wondered out loud. Samnang knew what she meant. By disarming Kleat, she had made them defenseless. They were at the mercy of the brothers and the typhoon and fate now.

"You took the fangs from a serpent, and left him alive. It is up to him now, what he does with his poison. As for the others, their hearts are still uncertain."

"The brothers treat you badly."

"They blame me for their miseries," Samnang said. "That is natural. I survived, you see. Their parents did not. They have poison in them, too. We must wait for them to decide what they will do with it."

It was the closest he'd ever come to discussing the Pol Pot years with her. Molly waited for him to volunteer more, but Samnang added nothing. She could have asked him, but told herself it didn't matter who he had been, only who he had become, this gentle old pilgrim.

They reached the top of the stairs and found that the others were long gone. They started in among the ruins, strolling slowly, and it reminded her of their mornings, before the dawn, at the crash site. She thought of the pilot, and then of the Blackhorse soldiers.

"They could have gone anywhere," she said.

Samnang glanced at the ground. "Mr. O'Brian went this way with the middle boy," he said. "Mr. Kleat went through there with the other children." Children, he called them.

"The missing soldiers, I meant. Thirty years have passed."

"We have a saying, 'Don't despair on the winding river,' " Samnang said. "Patience. They will reveal themselves to us."

They went straight, following a once orderly avenue between the spires and temples and palaces. The tiles were split apart by roots and subterranean forces. The forest blocked their view. Rounding the flanks of monstrous banyan trees, they saw more trees, more buildings. Eliminate the trees, restore the order, and the city would still have been as complicated as a perfume. The canals and side streets and winding avenue formed a puzzle. If the architects had not designed it as a labyrinth, the city had accumulated a labyrinth within it. As they worked deeper into the ruins, Samnang began braiding grass into knots and bending saplings into Os to mark their path. That made her feel less stupid. She was not the only one feeling overwhelmed in here.

It was a kingdom of eyes, the enormous heads beholding their trespass. Molly tried to imagine the Blackhorse soldiers drifting through the ruins with her same hushed wonder, their rifles at the ready. There were a thousand hiding places in here, and she realized that the soldiers would not have left their bones in plain view. They were jungle fighters. They would have squirreled themselves away into the most unknowable spots, burying themselves wherever the enemy might overlook them. What chance did an untrained civilian have of finding them a generation later?

They came to a quadrangle in the center of the city. She and Samnang decided it had to be the center. Four avenues met here at a broad square, or park, mobbed with grass and trees.

In the middle of it all, dominating the city, stood a tower. It was a strange hybrid of a structure, both round and square. It had a dozen angular sides and as many levels, though they were really only one level ascending in a single, steady, candy-cane spiral. A staircase corkscrewed around the exterior, and doorways led off that. The tower rose into the trees. Parrots sailed back and forth to its upper doors.

Like in the canyon she and Duncan had found yesterday, its walls were carved with bas-relief. The tower was a giant storybook. Samnang recognized some of the images, here and there pausing to press his palms together and bend his head. He explained what he could, the scenes from the Bhagavad Gita and the stages—like the Stations of the Cross—of the Buddha's enlightenment.

"This goes back to the beginning of my people," he said. "But so much of it escapes me. The kings, the alphabet, the battles, I should know them. I'm Khmer. I do know them. Here." He touched his heart. "But not here." His head. "This comes from before the Angkor, long before."

"Duncan thinks it could be two thousand years old," she said.

"Yes, Duncan," Samnang said. "He has made this his *spécialité*."

"He said it might have been the model for Angkor Wat."

Samnang looked at her. "Angkor and this place, or the Sistine Chapel or Notre-Dame, they are expressions of an idea. Like the statues of Buddha, or Michelangelo's God with a white beard, magnificent attempts to imagine a face for what has no face."

"Have you been to the Sistine Chapel?" she asked, hoping he might offer more of his past.

"In another lifetime," he said.

She dropped it.

The green light kept dimming. Somewhere above their hemisphere of leaves and limbs, storm clouds were eclipsing a sun they could not see. Thunder rolled like a subway train.

There was a crack of rifle fire. One of the search parties had discovered the gate and the terra-cotta statues. The others would join them. "Should we go to them?" she asked.

"Are the statues something you want?"

"No. You saw the head. Those eyes. They're terrible."

"Then let us not suffer for their desire," Samnang said. "We can stay here, deaf to the world. Anyway, we will see their treasures in camp tonight."

They went on circling the base of the tower and came across a name. Carved in deep, square letters among the bas-relief it said C. K. WATTS. Underneath was a date: 8/20/70.

Molly looked up at the tower. The logic slid together. "From up there you could see the whole city," she said to Samnang. "I think that's where they went."

"Among the birds," said Samnang. "Certainly."

She ran her fingers over the incisions. According to the ACAV map, the lost souls of the Eleventh Cavalry had pulled into the fortress on or around June 24. If the graffiti's date was right, the soldiers had languished here, alive, another seven weeks or more.

The idea moved her. They hadn't just burrowed into lairs to fight it out. They'd made their home here, and found time to roam among the ruins. One of them, at least, had passed beside the stories inscribed on this wall.

She looked to see if there was a special context for the name, and it was carved beneath a monstrous warrior, one of Duncan's wrathful deities, with a tiger circling his legs. He wore a necklace of severed heads.

She snapped a picture of the name and the demon slayer. She doubted C. K. Watts ever knew this was a ritual slayer of ignorance. But what irony, an American kid with a gun and a knife, off course and vulnerable, unconsciously appealing for wisdom. More likely he'd been taken with the image's ferocity.

"That makes four of them," she said. "Him, plus the three dog tags."

The tower reached into the middle canopy. The stairs stretched up and around, offering access to scores of gaping doorways. There would be a hundred and four of them, she remembered. Maybe she was getting the hang of the place after all.

"I think this will be of interest to Mr. O'Brian and Mr. Kleat," Samnang said. "They will want to be here."

She promised to wait at the base of the tower while Samnang went to find the others. He disappeared into a thicket of spires and trees in the direction of the rifle shot.

Her watch read 10 A.M. yesterday. The second hand crept. She tried to restrain herself. With her macro lens, she stalked a small white gecko with red spots.

But as the everlasting seconds dragged by, she chafed. The stairs lay right here before her. And the brothers might have shanghaied Samnang to carry down their plunder. Even if they released Kleat and Duncan to explore the tower, another hour or two could pass before they arrived. The afternoon was marching on. The tower might go unexplored until tomorrow. And tomorrow was a toss of the dice. It was senseless to wait.

24.

She took the winding staircase slowly.

The tower held answers, she was certain of it. Once it would have commanded a view of the entire city, maybe even of the far plains to the west, a man-made mountain on top of a mountain. Even with the encroaching forest, the tower was still the ultimate high ground. It would have given the soldiers a vertical fortress, with a honeycomb of doorways to watch for their enemies.

The deep, wide steps spiraled in a clockwise direction. When she was a kid, her stepparents had taken her to Washington, D.C., and she still remembered the marble steps eroded by millions of feet passing up and down. Add to that twenty centuries of rainfall and you had these stairs. The inner half of the steps had melted into a single sluice for running water. It forced her to walk along the outer edge where the steps wobbled under her weight, and a slip could be deadly. But she felt only a growing sense of authority.

On her left, always her left, the city unwound its maze, a great crossroads with the tower at its center. She spied more canals and lanes and corridors veining off without landmarks that she could see. Even from this height, satellite pyramids looked identical. The place seemed built to be lost in.

On her right, the doorways yawned like ornate caves. She glimpsed statues and carvings inside, and it was entirely possible the rooms held more Eleventh Cavalry relics and graffiti. Their discovery would have to wait for another day. She wanted to see what lay at the top.

Thunder rolled through the heavens. Vines hung like slow-motion rain. She came to a summit deck, and it held a crowning structure. Molly hesitated outside the entrance, a final door.

The statue of a female lay in rubble to one side. Her twin, a half-naked Amazon with breasts as round as bowling balls, guarded the other side of the entrance with a stone sword, its point resting between her feet. Standing head and shoulders above Molly, the sentinel was voluptuous and beautiful, a change from the bestial glare of the warrior statues. She passed on the photo for now. It needed Duncan or Samnang for human scale. Not Kleat. When it came time to write the account, she didn't want to have to explain him.

From this height, the faces carved on distant spires seemed to be lowering their eyes before the tower. She peered down from the edge for the others. She could hear their voices in the forest; they were speaking her name. But the plaza was empty. Her gain, she reckoned. For a few minutes more, the tower room belonged to her.

She stepped across the stone doorsill, and the room was richly lighted inside. The roof had a rectangular opening so large she thought it must have been built as an observatory. There were no sun or stars to see now, only the green jacket of the canopy. Leaves formed a thick, moldering carpet from one wall to the other. It smelled, not unpleasantly, like a compost pile.

Buddhas lined the far wall, or what was left of them. Side by side, each sat tucked within his own niche. She counted them: thirteen. The skylight had been built to illuminate them. At one time, the display must have been awesome.

The centuries had not been kind, however. The far end of the statue wall had collapsed into rubble. The faces were chewed down to raw stone. At least their lower bodies had been spared the ravages of time. Their long, elegant fingers twisted in ritual shapes, like gang members' hand signals. She imagined princes and monks meditating here, issuing prayers up through the aperture, to the heavens. Long ago, this must have been a transit station to the sacred.

After a minute, she pulled her eyes from the Buddhas, and remnants of the Eleventh Cavalry lay all around her in the shadows to the sides and rear. She turned in place, discovering a tangle of green web gear with worn grommets, and a rotting boot, and a snaking length of unspent machine-gun bullets. Mounds and heaps of things lined the wall. The soldiers—some of them, anyway—had retreated to this room.

She treated it like a crime scene, touching nothing, documenting everything with her camera, memorizing the line of her motions. She planted her feet as meticulously as a tai chi artist.

Using her telephoto, she reached across the leaves to a heap of emptied metal ammunition boxes with hinged lids. Two lay on their sides, one stood upright, half filled with old water. A black-and-white dragonfly hovered there, and that was a photo.

She found—but did not touch—a toothbrush with the bristles mashed wide from overuse. Some boy's mother had taught him well. Dental hygiene right up to cause of death.

Stacked boxes had rotted and collapsed, avalanching their contents out from the walls. There was a flashlight with a red lens, like something out of *Dick Tracy*. A flak jacket was propped up and empty. A broken M-16 rifle lay to one side. A tendril had grown up the barrel and out through the jammed chamber. A small white flower hung like a shell in mid-ejection.

It was as if the soldiers had shed themselves here.

As her eyes adjusted to the light, the room became more defined. The Buddhas had been defaced, not by the elements, but by gunfire. The collapsed section had been dynamited or hit by a rocket.

Bullets—hundreds of them—scarred the statue wall in long, slashing bursts. She tried to piece together their desperate firefight. Had the enemy dropped down through the roof? Or had they come running through the door and sprayed the Americans crouching beneath the Buddhas?

The place should have been heaped with bones. But there were none that she could see. Had they been scattered by animals, or had the victors carted them out and pitched them off the tower? Had she passed bits and pieces of them on her ascent without knowing it? Part of her didn't want to find them. She fastened on the idea of them rising up through the hole in the roof, body and spirit, rescued on their Judgment Day.

She passed over the hands twice before recognizing them.

There were two of them beneath a scorch mark in one corner, the bones gloved in dried black skin.

She pulled the image closer with her telephoto, not willing to cross over to them. To the side, were those more bones? Sticks, she saw, charred firewood. A cremation? But the pyre was too small. This was no bigger than Samnang's cool fire.

The hands had mummified over the years. Or been smoked by the fire. Someone had lopped them off at the wrists.

It came to her.

Cannibalism.

Trapped, battered by fear, out of food, they must have taken to eating their comrades.

A laugh—a yap—cracked through the room. It fell upon her, Luke's animal laugh. But it wasn't Luke up there. Molly looked, and there were three of them this time, like the one she'd seen in the ACAV turret. While she prowled through the room, the gibbons had stolen up and perched along the skylight rim. They had black masks and gray arms. Her pulse slowed. She took a picture of them, just to regain control.

"Hey," she said. "Just looking."

One leaned forward. He opened his mouth. He bared his teeth. Were they going to attack? But his eyes stayed fixed on hers, and he seemed to be trying out her language. That made her more afraid than the bared teeth.

They were studying her, and she was alone.

Careful not to turn her back to them, Molly began retreating from the center of the room. Something gave a muffled crunch beneath the carpet of leaves. Nut shells within the mast? She moved her foot and whatever it was shifted under there. Bones, she thought. What did anthropologists call it? The midden. She was walking across the cannibals' scattered garbage.

The monkeys suddenly bolted away.

"What are you doing here, Molly?" It was Kleat's voice at the doorway. "Sam said you'd wait."

She exhaled softly. "I knew you were coming. I heard your voices."

"Our voices? I don't think so. The old cripple had us running to save you. We were too busy catching our breath to talk."

Then she'd heard birdsong, or trees creaking. Or monkeys discussing. No matter.

"We located another gateway," Kleat said. "With clay warriors, and rooms with pottery and jars. And a tunnel blocked with barbed wire. That makes three entrances, including the one Samnang said you found."

He stood in the doorway. Something about the room troubled him. It disrupted his bravado. He wouldn't come in.

"Where's Duncan?" she asked.

"Halfway up the stairs. Crawling. I've never seen such a fear of heights." Kleat would not cross the threshold. "You shouldn't have come here alone. You could have destroyed evidence."

Duncan appeared, and there was indeed dirt on his knees. The two men stood there, blocking the light. Did they need an invitation?

"They were here," she said.

Samnang arrived last. Edging between the two Americans, he caught sight of the ruined Buddhas, and his palms clapped together like magnets. He bowed his head solemnly.

Samnang's entrance seemed to break the spell. The other two stepped inside. Molly imagined Kleat would set upon the room like a wolf, but he moved tentatively, scarcely nibbling at the relics.

She watched what drew them. Kleat went for the rifle with the broken stock. Samnang gravitated to the wall holding the statues. Duncan vacillated. He moved along the edges. He lifted the web gear and dropped it, and ran his fingers along the foot of one damaged

Buddha, and shook his head sadly. Then he found the husk of a radio set propped against one wall, and that occupied him.

Molly remained near the center, surrounded by their motion, shooting them making their discoveries, waiting.

The radio was partially disassembled. Duncan flipped switches on and off and the thing was dead, of course.

"There are two hands," she said, pointing at the fire ring.

"Hands?" said Kleat. He took the pieces of rifle with him to the corner. He nudged aside the sticks of firewood and laid one of the dried hands along his outstretched palm. It was small. Too small, she realized.

"Monkeys," Kleat said.

"Monkeys?"

"The men ran out of food."

Kleat glanced from the hand to her. "Did you think they were human? Don't tell me. Ghouls in camouflage."

"No."

Duncan returned to his tinkering. "Huh," he said and pulled out a transistor tube. He held it up to the light. "Look at that."

Duncan brought it over to Molly, and Kleat joined them. He heard the crunching sound underfoot. "What's that?" He pressed at the leaves with his boot.

Duncan held out his find. "It's a condom," he said. "And there's something inside."

It was in fact a condom stretched long over a short tube and knotted at the end. He tore off the knot and peeled down the sheath, baring a roll of papers torn from a pocket-size notebook. The pages were brittle, and he didn't try to force them open.

"It must have been a journal. Or a will." He studied the outside of the roll. "But the rain got in. The ink's run. It's spoiled."

"There are still some words," said Molly. "Maybe with better light—"

"What *is* this?" Kleat said again, rocking his weight over the leaves.

Bones breaking, she thought. Monkey or squirrel or parrot bones, whatever hungry men might take from the forest. Kleat worked his fingers under the carpet of leaves.

He lifted a long fragment to expose the red stone of the floor. They weren't bones, but cartridge shells. Duncan pocketed the papers, and Molly helped clear more of the floor. Brass shells littered the floor.

"Now we know where the side guns on the ACAV went," Kleat said. "These are shells from an M-60. They must have pulled the big guns out of the tracks and brought them up here. Look at it all, like Armageddon in here."

Molly picked one of the cartridges from the floor, and a beetle crawled out. She dropped it.

"There's something more here," Duncan said. He ran his fingers along a wide black stripe.

The three of them rolled back more of the thick mat. A big serpentine line emerged, painted onto the floor with engine grease. To its side, another line appeared.

"It's an SOS," Duncan said. They didn't need to unpeel the whole thing. Stretching thirty-feet from end to end, it lay directly beneath the skylight. They looked up at the forest ceiling.

"They must have chopped a hole in the canopy, or burned it open with fuel," Kleat said. "They were trying to signal for help."

"But who would see it?" said Molly.

"A passing helicopter. Spotter planes. Our pilot."

Like a child's prayer, Molly thought. The soldiers had died making wishes to the sky.

"It's coming together," said Kleat. "They made their last stand in the tower. You couldn't ask for a better field of fire. The enemy would have had to come up the stairs one at a time. But how long could nine men hold out? It must have been hand-to-hand combat in the end."

"I thought of that, too," said Duncan. "But then there should be bones all over the place."

"This is quite odd," Samnang said behind them. He had moved

from the Buddhas to the doorway and was running his hands along the back wall. He walked over to them.

He stirred the shells with a stick, and a whole colony of beetles began scuttling around their feet.

"All of these come from American guns," Samnang said. "M-60, here, M-16, this one, and this."

Molly felt Kleat's eyes on her, and knew what he was thinking: KR. The old guerrilla was exposing himself.

"This is detonation cord for plastic explosive." Samnang held up a coil. "That explains the damage at the far end. C4 *plastique*. And these I dug from the wall."

Samnang opened his hand to show a half dozen lead slugs. "All from American guns. Also, you would think their fire would be directed at the door, yes? But the walls are smooth and untouched, you see. Only the wall of statues is scarred. They alone were targeted."

"What are you getting at?" Kleat said.

"I have looked," said Samnang, "and there is no sign of an enemy."

Kleat's voice dropped to a growl. "They were fighting for their lives."

"Perhaps," said Samnang. "But against whom?"

"Okay." Kleat mocked him. "Whom?"

Samnang let the mashed slugs fall from his palm. *"Âme damnée,"* he said. His French sounded like a song.

Kleat jerked. "What?" His voice thinned to a whisper. His hard-boiled expression crumpled. He stepped back as if the slugs were poisoned. Molly saw he was retreating from Samnang. Eyes round behind his thick lenses, he looked stricken.

Not certain what to make of Kleat's sudden affliction, Molly said, "Damned men?"

"Fallen from grace," Samnang said. He acted oblivious to Kleat's recoil. "It is only my conjecture. But what if the men turned against one another?"

"Bullshit," Kleat said. Molly wasn't sure what he was denouncing though, the guesswork or its author. Or something else. He was staring at Samnang.

"How then to interpret the knife?" Samnang asked.

Kleat blinked. "What knife?"

They followed Samnang to the wall of Buddhas. Molly had not spied it through her telephoto. You had to see it from the side, jammed to the hilt in a seam between the stone blocks, the handle protruding.

Samnang let them consider the knife. Up close, the Buddhas looked eaten by disease. The knife's presence was deliberate, like a judgment rendered, or a desecration.

"A K-Bar knife," Kleat said, his certainty returning. "That's how I interpret it."

"But why would anyone stab it into a stone wall?" said Molly. "Here of all places, this wall."

"How would I know?"

"It looks so angry. Like adding insult to injury."

"We're talking about a piece of stone," said Kleat. "A dead city."

"Molly's right," Duncan said. "It does look . . . excessive."

"Excessive," Kleat scoffed. "They were fighting for their lives."

"Samnang's got a point, though. The only damaged wall is this one. And see how the faces of the Buddhas were targeted? This knife didn't end up here by accident. Someone found a joint in the stone and hammered it in with all his strength. This looks less like a battle than a signature."

"What does it matter?" Kleat said. "A bunch of old statues."

He grabbed at the handle. He was arming himself, Molly realized. Let him have it. The knife would be a rusty old thing.

He pulled, but the wall held on. He braced his other hand against the stone to pull again. Just then a clap of thunder exploded directly above the canopy.

It was so close, Molly's knees buckled. She smelled ozone, a whiff of the upper stratosphere. The men's eyes went wide and white. They looked at each other.

The seconds passed, her ears ringing. More thunder rippled in the far distance. The sense of nature returned.

The knife and the sky had nothing to do with each other. It had been thundering since morning. Just the same, Kleat released the stubborn handle with disgust.

In the silence that followed, another sound descended to them, the hushing sound leaves make when they tremble. But it wasn't the leaves.

After a minute, water began dripping through the canopy.

The rain had finally come.

25.

They fled the tower slowly. Rain fell in rivulets from the canopy. Water raced down the furrow in the winding staircase, forcing them to the edge. Molly had the advantage with her climber's balance and her youth. Twice she caught Kleat when he slipped. For a few minutes, the dangers unified them.

The forest grew darker by ounces. The rain diminished. Samnang guided them through the city to the stairs that led to camp.

The brothers had already returned from the gate. The thatch hut and campfire waited below like a lighthouse in a deep harbor. By the time they reached ground level, Molly's cold sweat had returned.

It couldn't be malaria, she thought. She was on proquanil. Then again, she was on proquanil because the Cambodian strain of malaria had grown resistant to chloroquine. Maybe the bug had morphed again.

The brothers, by the fire, were in high spirits, their gold teeth flickering like sparks in the darkness, their tattoos glistening from the canopy's slow drip. Molly arrived at the hut to find two dry green ponchos spread as a floor. Vin bustled over with a cup of steaming black tea loaded with so much sugar it made her teeth ache. She thanked him.

Kleat arrived, his bronze skull as slick as a muscle car. He was wearing the flak jacket from the tower room. Now he could pretend to be bulletproof like the brothers. The superstitions were layering over them. He didn't bother to remove his boots. Molly scooted deeper into the hut to make room for him.

He thumped her knee. "We're saved," he said.

Molly tried to evade his good cheer. But it was hard not to feel some camaraderie. Two nights ago they'd been licking their wounds in a restaurant, banished and irrelevant. All that was changed. Fame and wealth and great dreams were almost within their grasp. It did feel like salvation. She had her camera in her lap. The display screen flickered with images of the strange, beautiful city.

Duncan came in from the darkness. "Have you looked in the truck? There must be ten heads in there. You've got to get a photo of it," he said to Molly. "It's like they've decapitated the city. The heads are always the first things to be plundered. They're portable. Collectors go wild for them. They move like lightning on the art market."

Samnang entered from the night, wordless, and crossed his legs. Raindrops clung to his white burr cut. Cutting a glance at him, Kleat looked confused and at the same time annoyed, like a man who has misplaced his keys.

"They must not do this," Samnang said. "Taking the heads like barbarians."

"It's a small price to pay," said Kleat. "Play it through with them. You'll get what you want. We all will."

"You don't understand?" Samnang asked Kleat.

Kleat tsk-tsked. Dumb question. End of discussion. The fire snapped in their silence.

The Americans and Samnang dried off under the thatch roof, all except Molly, who could not quit sweating. Suddenly ravenous, she pulled the box of MREs toward her. "Spaghetti and meatballs," she said.

She offered the MREs to Vin and his brothers, out by the fire, but they waved off her hospitality, too intent on toting up their riches with a hand calculator. She would have to think up some other way to mother them. It was imperative that they not forsake the Americans.

The canopy leaked in episodes, dripping like a metronome, then spilling in vertical columns that released here, then there. It was all cause and effect, no mystery. A leaf brimming with rainwater would flip over, creating a chain reaction among lower leaves. Every few minutes another gush of water splashed in the darkness. It would go on until the canopy had lightened its load.

One of the miniature waterfalls scored a direct hit on their fire. White steam billowed up and the hut went dark. The brothers jumped to their feet. "Ho," they shouted, laughing. Then the flames jumped high again.

The brothers settled back along the edge of the fire. The dirt and embers at one end of the pit seemed to twitch on their own, like someone struggling to break free from below. Molly passed it off as shadows.

Vin was dispatched to offer the Americans a bottle of clear liquid, which he poured into their empty tea cups. Kleat took a sip. "God, you could clean paint off with that," he said.

"Not good," Samnang murmured after Vin left.

"As long as they're happy."

"The happy part won't last," Duncan said. The brothers looked over, and he smiled and raised a toast to them. "I've seen men go at each other with hatchets on this stuff."

"And us without a gun," Kleat said. He toasted Molly and took another sip of the hooch and adjusted his flak jacket.

Molly wished she'd thought of the flak jacket, not for the armoring, but the warmth. Was she the only one who felt the cold? If only they would build the fire a little higher.

Back in Kampong Cham, they had pledged to turn around at the first sign of rain. There was no question about staying through the night, though. It would be absurd to try to retrace the oxcart trail at night, and the river would not recede until morning. Neither Samnang nor Duncan could predict tomorrow's weather. Without a radio or even a view of the sky, they were reduced to speculation. The mountain would act as a natural magnet for the first precipitation, and maybe this little shower was all the sky contained for now.

They came up with every excuse to stay. They pretended the decision was theirs to make, that they were in full command of themselves. They pretended emotion had nothing to do with wanting to stay, that the very fact they were discussing caution meant caution still ruled. But the ruins were inciting them. Everyone had something to gain here. The nearness of the bones had Kleat in high gear, and the marvels of the city excited Duncan, and the plunder wound up the brothers. Even old Samnang had desires. Molly saw him lay out a row of incense sticks and knew he meant to return to the tower. They were all obsessed, herself included.

It was agreed that the rain signified the beginning of the wet monsoon and had nothing to do with the typhoon. The typhoon might have died in the South China Sea, or it might still strike them.

The bigger uncertainty was the brothers. Duncan guessed the truck held a half million dollars' worth of relics now. They could simply drive away in the morning and leave the Americans. It was all a matter of their whim. Samnang said they meant to stay. They wanted more.

The fire stirred again. Something was under there. Molly saw it again, like an invisible hand moving its fingers within the red coals. A root, she decided. The heat was drying its sap, making the root contract and twist.

Kleat spread the pieces of the broken M-16 on the poncho. The rifle clip was empty. "Once his ammunition ran out, he clubbed the rifle. How many of the little bastards did he take with him?"

"I saw that movie," said Molly. "John Wayne. *The Alamo.*"

"Explain this then." Kleat held up the shattered rifle.

"We've been there," she said. "If there was a battle, there should be other signs. Not just in the tower, but down in the city. Bullets in trees or in the sandstone."

"Laterite," Duncan corrected her. "Technically speaking. It's a soft stone when it's first quarried. Perfect for carving before it hardens."

"Other signs," she continued. "Rocket scars on the walls. Things blown up."

"You'll see. The bones will tell."

"They could have left or been taken prisoner."

"Explain the dog tags then."

"Explain Luke," said Duncan.

Circles within circles. The sweat stung her eyes.

Night was a frame of mind. The ACAV flickered in the heights like a box-shaped moon. There were even stars, the fireflies and sparks. And constellations of animal eyes glittering red and yellow in the trees.

Like a museum curator, Duncan began delicately appraising the pages from inside the radio set. They might have been the Dead Sea Scrolls, the four curled pages of lined notepaper. Minuscule termites had wormed their way across the pages, etching in their own account of time. Ink foxed the paper in blotches. Duncan teased the pages apart and held them to the firelight, trying to candle out any legible words. When that didn't work, he gently pressed them flat, and the pages crumbled like dead leaves.

Kleat seemed gratified. "They wouldn't have told us anything anyway."

Duncan pieced the fragments together as best he could, side by side, and pored over them with Kleat's big krypton flashlight. There was precious little to decipher: " ' . . . can't not stay anymore, where else . . . darkest before dawn, oh, God, your false promise . . . in the life of the stone . . . ' "

"No atheists in the foxholes," Kleat said. "The boy was stoked on the Bible."

"Here's part of an inventory: 'morphine, 7 amps, .50 cal, 3. . . .' " Duncan leaned down and ran out of words.

"That's all?" said Kleat.

It took another five minutes to turn the fragments onto their flip side. Duncan found a little more. " ' . . . he was right, but we were wrong to listen . . . let him go like Cain, but west, from Eden on foot. Maybe we should have' . . . And this, 'another visit last night. They come every night now. I know I shouldn't speak to them, but we spoke . . . ' "

"What's that all about?" Molly said.

"Regrets," Kleat said. "The 'he' must have been their commanding officer. And it sounds like one of them got out of Dodge before it was too late. Obviously, they wished they'd never listened to their commander. And they wished they'd followed the man who left."

"But who are his visitors at night, the ones he shouldn't speak to? Maybe tribal people coming in?"

"Here we go, a bit more in pencil, along the margin." Duncan read several lines of a poem, something about wild cats growling, wind howling, and two riders approaching. He looked up. "They must have heard a tiger. The monsoon was coming. And they were the two riders, you know, their two ACAVs approaching the city walls."

"Useless," Kleat said. He seemed, Molly thought, glad to be done with it.

But Samnang bent closer. "Bob Dylan," he said.

They looked at him.

"Yes, those are the final words of a famous song." Samnang was excited by his discovery. 'All Along the Watchtower.' One of my students wrote an essay on its true meaning."

"What true meaning?" said Kleat. "It's plain. They were trapped. They were dying. They wanted out of here."

"And yet the soldier chose this song," said Samnang. "A song about revolution. Why?"

"Forget the watchtower crap," Kleat said. "Forget last wills and testaments. What we need is positive identification."

"Let me take a turn," Molly interrupted.

"You have better eyes?"

She held up her camera. "Let's see what it sees."

She knelt above the fragments and took a picture of the front side of each page. Duncan began patiently turning them over.

Out by the fire, Doc snapped a command. Hands planted on his folded legs, elbows out, he looked almost like one of the kings she'd seen carved in the stone. His voice was too loud. He was drunk.

Vin hopped to do his bidding, shoveling at the coals with his machete. After a minute, he levered up the edge of a helmet. At least that's what Molly thought it was, the helmet that Kleat had found. They were using it to cook their dinner. She was wrong, though. It was a turtle.

They must have trapped it from the *baray* swamps and buried it under the coals to roast. Molly lifted her camera and zoomed in. She'd never seen a turtle eaten. Steam vented from the leg holes. The camera autofocused in the witchy light, blurring, centering, blurring. She thumbed the focus to manual and stabilized the image.

It was still alive.

Molly kept the camera between her and it. Through its glass and mirrors, she could stand almost anything.

The turtle filled her frame. There was no mistake. Its legs paddled at the air. Its neck stretched and moved. That explained the embers stirring.

The middle brother snatched the machete from Vin. He gave a light, expert chop across the belly plate. The turtle opened like magic.

The firelight pulsed. The stewpot of organs pulsed separately from the light. Alive, still alive. They used sticks and knives to spear pieces. Doc saw her shooting and, with exaggerated hospitality, held up a slippery organ to her. She shook her head no, and they laughed. Kleat laughed, too.

"There," announced Duncan, unaware of the little incident. His puzzle of fragments was ready for her. She leaned over and snapped pictures of the reverse sides. A drop of her sweat fell on one page, staining it as black as blood.

Samnang was frowning at her. He'd noticed her sweat. She rested against the box.

"Whoever the man was," Duncan said, "he rolled the pages up, closed them in a layer of condoms, and hid them inside a radio that was dead. A message in a bottle."

"No name, no date." Kleat shrugged.

"Did Samnang show you the name at the base of the tower?" Molly asked. She referenced it on her camera display. " 'C. K. Watts. August 20.' It gives us some context. And the monkey remains," she added, keeping her eyes away from the turtle, "more context. We're not without clues."

"It's a dead end, I'm telling you," Kleat said. He fished a cigar butt from his shirt pocket and whistled at Vin, who brought a lighted twig.

Molly frowned. Kleat was acting so oddly, so detached, even hostile to the possibilities. But, to borrow Samnang's French, this was her *spécialité.* She was a journalist, a detective. "We know the approximate date of their arrival. We know they left at least one of their vehicles here. They took gear and weapons and barbed wire, and some or all of them climbed into the city and apparently made a decision to hide here."

"A bad decision." With the stogie and the flak jacket, Kleat made a poor General Patton.

"Once the decision was made," she went on, "they were stuck with it. They tried to radio for help, but the radio was dead. They tried to signal passing aircraft, but no one saw them."

"A lot of nothing." It was as if he were trying to sabotage her.

"Seven weeks later," she said, "at least one of them was still left to carve his name on the tower. We know they were hungry, and despairing. There's that fragment about darkest before dawn and God's false promise. The boy sounds so desolate, like there's no hope on earth."

"The only relevant question is where they died," said Kleat. "I need teeth, whole jaws, the entire skull if possible. Pieces of bone for DNA analysis. Wedding bands, class rings, wristwatches with initials. Words don't matter."

"Of course they matter," Molly said. "They're our best clues at this point." She continued scrolling through the images on her display, landing on the photos of the journal pages. The LCD was chewing through the batteries, stealing from the future to pay for the past, so to speak, using up power she could be saving to take more pictures. But she justified it as part of the interview process. The evidence was speaking to them.

She studied the images, goosing the light, enlarging sections, penetrating the inky ruins of the manuscript. "There's more," she said. "I can't tell what order the pages go in. And anyway, he seems to have written things wherever there was space"—she turned her camera— "even upside down. Here's more of the inventory list. And some words to fill in around the segments, and a number on this page, '7/17/70.' "

"Three weeks after they arrived," said Duncan. "A month before C. K. Watts carved his name."

She tilted the display, straining to see. " 'We can't not stay any-more,' " she read. " 'Where else could we have gone? It was finished the minute the TC took the wrong turn. Now we have to live with what we've done. The TC gets the tower for his tomb, the first of us to go. And now we know it's not true that he loved the city more than us. He was only trying to preserve us all.' "

"The TC?" she said.

"The team commander," Kleat said. "There would have been two of them, one for each ACAV. But one would have had seniority. He was the fool who brought them here."

She returned to the display. " 'There is death in the life of the stone. We see that more every day. We try not to notice, but the walls talk to us. The statues speak. The city sings. The eyes see. The rain is killing us. Every day gets worse. We hide from each other, not sure who is who now. I've never been so lonely.' "

"Out of his mind," said Kleat.

Molly scrolled to another section. " ' . . . he was right, but we were more wrong to become his rebels. It was mutiny . . . ' And this. 'We let him go like Cain, but west from Eden on foot. Maybe we should have killed him for it. But we let him lead us into sin. So we were part of it, and now it's done. And now we are scattered.' "

They were quiet for a minute.

"And?" said Kleat.

"They were at war all right," she said. "You want glory. You want heroes. They were scared. They were boys trying to deal with an ugly, dirty little dead end. And they had themselves a mutiny. A revolution. And then they died off like animals."

"Journalists," Kleat snorted.

"Something happened here," she said.

"How about this?" Kleat said. "Their commander fucked up.

They believed in him, and he betrayed them with his stupidity. They could have killed him, but they spared him and drove him out like Cain. The man who led them wrong. He's lucky they didn't put a bullet through his head."

"There are other ways to read this," said Molly. "This says the commander got the tower for his tomb."

"Whatever that means."

"Part of this was written three weeks into their confinement. The rest of it sounds like it was written later, maybe over the coming weeks or months. But one thing is clear, they were at odds with one another. He talks about rebels, *his* rebels. There was a troublemaker. Tensions must have been running high. Nine men found themselves caught in a cage. Think about it. They were bound to start laying blame for their troubles. And somehow their commander died. Whoever wrote this sounds guilty. He talks about sin."

"He also talks about talking statues and a singing city," said Kleat.

Molly stopped. "Which is it, Kleat? Either the writer was insane and none of it mattered, or his words are fact, but muddled by time. You can't have it both ways."

Kleat released a cloud of smoke. His steel rims glittered. "None of it matters."

The brothers had finished the turtle. They were passing the shell back and forth, sipping the gray broth.

Molly flipped the off switch. The camera display went black. "I'm going to bed," she said.

She fit her camera into the bag, got her shoes and flashlight, and climbed down from the hut. Duncan started to follow. "Please don't," she said. She didn't want to talk anymore.

He lagged back. "Don't give up on us, Molly," he said. "You're right. I don't know what, but something happened here."

26.

She woke suddenly, in the middle of the night. Samnang's fire cast a glimmer on her tent wall. Hours had passed. Her clothes had dried. Some second sense told her not to move.

It was raining again. Water grazed the outer skin of the forest with a muffled hiss. A rain to sleep by, she thought, drifting off.

Then she saw the shapes. The fire animated them. Their silhouettes trickled across the panels of her dome tent, bent low and ranging their rifles back and forth. *The brothers.* They'd come for her.

Crouched like cats, they stole along the terrace edge. She held her breath, looking for Vin's thin figure. Maybe he could stop his brothers. Then she saw that there were more than three out there. That made no sense.

Just then, gunfire crackled up from the depths of the camp. Molly huddled behind her screen of nylon and fiberglass poles, thinking these stalking men must be the target. She braced for the explosions they would unleash in turn.

But none of the silhouette men returned fire. Instead they grew more misshapen, even their rifles, twisted and melting. Their arms trailed tendrils and became vines. The metamorphosis left her wondering what she'd seen in the first place. Pieces of the forest, nothing more.

The gunfire rattled again in the distance. That much was real. Her knees drew up against her chest. Her eyes squeezed shut.

The tent wall rustled. One of them was trying the door.

She willed herself invisible.

"Molly," the man whispered.

He was the dark apparition of Oklahoma. She couldn't help herself. *Be a good girl.* Fear squeezed the air from her lungs.

"Molly."

Quiet, she instructed herself. Stand aside. Don't be part of it. Return when all is safe again.

More gunfire.

"Molly." Louder this time.

The door unzipped. She saw herself backed as far as possible into the corner. She saw herself with her eyes squeezed shut.

"It's me," he whispered.

She saw herself open her eyes. In the scant, cold light, Duncan hunkered at the doorway. His hair hung in long, wet strands.

The rifles crackled, on full automatic. She glanced at the tent wall. The images had fled. He was alone.

"Don't be afraid," he whispered.

She began to return to herself.

"I thought you might be afraid."

She was shaking with fever fits. Her jaw unlocked. "Duncan."

"Keep your voice down. They're drunk. It will pass."

She was convulsing. He couldn't see it from out there.

"I just wanted to make sure you're okay."

She wasn't. She had demons.

"Lie low," he said. "Keep your light off. The bullets fall back to earth, but the canopy will protect us. You're safe."

He started to raise her door to seal her inside with herself again. "Don't," she said.

He paused.

"Don't leave."

"If you need me, I'm here." He started to zip the door shut again, still outside.

"What are you doing?" she said.

"I'm here, I promise." His chivalry bewildered her. He meant to sit in the rain like some warrior monk? She needed more.

"Come in." It was so cold.

Backing inside, he zipped the door closed and sat beside her with his legs crossed.

Her teeth chattered. It finally occurred to him. His palm covered her forehead. "You're sick."

"I'm cold."

"I can't take you to the fire," he said. "Not with them like this."

"Hold me."

It surprised him. She read his surprise. The halting way he opened his arm for her to lay her head on was like a remembered act. He had forgotten human touch.

She pressed her back to him. He was warm. They didn't talk. Eventually the gunfire tapered off. She quit shaking and fell asleep in his arms.

27.

The birds woke her.

The rain had stopped. The city waited. She opened her eyes.

Duncan startled her. She startled herself.

During the night, she had twisted. In her sleep, she had thrown one arm across Duncan. She had one ear against his chest. She could hear his heartbeat. His ribs rose and fell in slow waves.

She never woke this way with a man, holding him and being held. It did not happen, even with lovers she trusted. And while he wasn't a stranger, he wasn't a lover either. She barely knew him. And yet her sleeping self had folded against him.

Molly lay very still, trying to sort out this new development. He was warm, and she'd been afraid. She remembered the gunfire, and those silhouettes. But they weren't enough to explain her trust.

He looked almost boyish sleeping in the blue-green light. There was a powerful scent of flowers. Her eyes traveled to his shirt pocket. He'd collected an orchid yesterday.

Part of her wanted to shake him and climb back into the city. They knew their way into the ruins. She had dreamed about them last night, dreamed madly. The city was starting to inhabit her.

But she lingered, reluctant to shatter this remarkable contact. Twice men had proposed marriage to her—seriously proposed— thinking they could overcome her nightmares. As gently as possible, she'd spared them their gallantry. They couldn't save her. The rape had burned her. Molly had resigned herself to her clenching scars.

What could explain this? She was a serial disbeliever. She required truth, good, bad, or ugly. Offer her a wound for proof and she would plunge her fingers right in. Which had made the search for the bones so fitting. The missing soldiers were an unhealed wound, like a hand-hold, both a story and, deeper, an appeal to her missionary instinct. So how did Duncan fit into that?

It wasn't that he could protect her from the perils. The plotting brothers and the typhoon and Kleat's paranoia endangered him as much as her. Was it that she seemed to occupy him the way the ruins occupied her? He had been her welcome to Cambodia. When she was at her weakest, he had shielded her from the sun with his scarf. When the guns started going off last night, his first thought had been for her safekeeping. He'd crawled out into the rain to guard her.

He looked twenty-something this morning. The soft light smoothed his crow's-feet and softened the hawk profile, but it was something more. Years had melted from his face. His beard line looked . . . diminished. There was just stubble on his chin and upper lip. His throat was smooth. The jugular throbbed. It was like watching her own heart beat.

A long, welted scar ran in a line above his left ear. She'd never seen it before. Normally his long hair hid it. He'd survived some terrible violence, but had never mentioned it. She'd have to ask him about that someday.

She wondered. *What would he be like in Boulder?* With his long hair and seven-league boots, they'd take him for one more globe-trotter with an athlete's veins. Every other man and woman you met there seemed to be in training for some imaginary Olympics or Everest. She'd written an article on the legend of Boulder, average age 29.5 years, average body fat 11 percent. She'd dubbed it an orthopedist's paradise, with all the skiers' knees and climbers' shoulders you could wish for. Duncan would move among them like an aging lion. They could go to the movies on snowy afternoons, drink tea at Turley's, chart new travels. With Duncan, she might finally feel at home.

But there were the ruins to decipher. His destiny was here, and hers, too. She felt it powerfully. She had not ended up here by accident.

Her thoughts wheeled pleasantly.

Slowly she noticed the bamboo. It stood on the far side of his face, a slender, glossy green shoot poised almost like a snake. The trespass surprised her. The forest had invaded her tent.

She lifted her head from Duncan's chest. The bamboo had pierced the tent floor and pushed right through the thin sleeping pad. Its point was hard and sharp, the shaft slick and phallic. They could have been impaled in their sleep. That was too dramatic, of course. They would have woken at its first touch.

Only then did she notice her tent wall. It was deformed. Half caved in. A tree limb must have fallen across them.

A wall tent or pup tent would have collapsed altogether. Her dome tent had spread the weight through a system of poles. The rain must have torn the limb loose from the canopy and it had dropped during the night.

Duncan woke. He started to smile, then jerked his head away from the bamboo. He saw the deformed tent wall. "How could we have slept through that?" he said.

He pushed at the branch with his foot, but that only tightened its pressure. The tent creaked.

"These poles might not hold it," she said.

Despite the quiet destruction of her tent, Molly was grateful for the quick exit. It was too soon for pillow talk and holding hands. In escaping the tent, they would be escaping any awkwardness.

They couldn't sit upright. Then they saw more bamboo shoots sticking through the floor. Duncan got over her on his hands and knees, and put his back against the tree limb. She slid between his legs.

Unzipping the door dumped the dome's remaining strength. One of the long poles snapped, then another. She slid out and helped Duncan crawl from the shambles. They faced the wreckage.

It wasn't a fallen branch, but a vine. The thing had come untethered from the ledge above and was strapped across the tent. Its tip had burrowed into a joint in the stone. In the space of a few hours, it had muscled down and broken her tent. Molly looked around at the mist and its shapes. A giant god floated with his serene smile, and sank away.

"It's like a tidal wave, a green tidal wave," she said. "Do things really grow so fast here?"

"The forest must have been thirsty. The first taste of rain and it takes off like a rocket." Duncan aimed for levity, but it troubled him.

"I'll come back for it later." Who was she kidding? The tent was a write-off. She felt violated and put on notice. This place was not her friend. She jerked her camera bag from the collapsed doorway.

Duncan had to use his Swiss Army knife to free their shoes. A filament of roots had invaded a rip in the floor and corded them to the ground. He pretended it was normal. "Man versus monsoon," he intoned. "Who will win the primordial struggle?" But it bothered him, she could tell.

They walked along the ledge around little pickets of bamboo growing through the joints, and stepped across cablelike vines. His tent was collapsed as well. Lowering himself to what remained of it, Duncan cut an opening through the side and extracted his steel briefcase.

They finished descending to the terminus floor and wended their way through the mist.

Molly kept looking for the names carved into the trees. "There they are." She tugged Duncan after her, but then she got a closer look.

The letters were bleeding.

"It's tree sap," Duncan said.

"But they weren't like this before."

"The forest is having a growth spurt. The bark pulled apart. It's only sap."

Thick and crimson, it seeped down from the beloved names. She regretted waiting to take the picture. Yesterday morning, they had been radiant on the gleaming bark. Now they wept, though maybe that was the more appropriate mood for the photo.

Farther on, they heard a low roar building.

"Is that the truck running?" she asked.

They hurried, thinking the brothers were leaving.

But the roar was the sound of the fire. Kleat was there, piling logs onto a small inferno. The flames leaped taller than the hut, eating a jagged hole in the fog, throwing sparks with pistol shots of sap.

The furnace heat had him pouring sweat. He'd shed his shirt, but was wearing the flak jacket. His face and scalp were as bright as mercury. He looked insane.

"What are you doing?" asked Duncan.

Kleat loaded on another fat log and straightened on the far side of the flames. His glasses reflected the light. He had showers of red and orange sparks for eyes. Inside his fury, he looked afraid. "Up late?" he yelled at them.

Molly had been almost ready to pity him. "We heard the shooting last night," she said.

His chest hair was singed to black steel wool. She smelled the burned hair and Caucasian sweat, but also caught other smells in the smoke, potent smells, the scent of different kinds of wood, of ferns, flowers, nuts, coconut, even cinnamon. Once part of a royal garden, spices grew wild here. The fire was opening up the forest's abundance.

"You missed the hunt," Kleat said.

"Is that what they were doing, hunting?"

Kleat looked at them. "He should have known better."

The fire forced her back with its hot breath. Her chills were gone. She felt fine this morning. Molly glanced around. At the edges of dissolved mist, half-formed shapes moved between the vaporous white Land Cruiser and the larger bulk of the truck. She counted three shapes with rifles. There was only one man unaccounted for.

"Where's Samnang?" Duncan asked.

"He brought it on himself."

"Be clear," said Molly.

"He fucked up."

"What happened, Kleat?"

"He waited until they were drunk, then he got his revenge. But there was no way he was going to get away with it. Of course they found out." He toppled a decaying stump into the flames. White termites came flooding from its cavities.

"What revenge, what are you talking about?"

"He destroyed their artifacts, smashed them to pieces, the pots. Hid the rest. All the heads, they're missing. That's what they were trying to beat out of him. Don't ask me. I don't speak the language. One thing led to another."

"You saw it? They beat him?" While she slept soundly.

"I only came for the bones." Kleat glared at her. "You know that."

"But you were down here."

"I heard them arguing. I came down and they had him. They were pushing him around, hitting him with their rifles. He's KR, I keep telling you. They hated him enough as it was. Then he pulls a stunt like this."

They'd gone hunting.

"What did they do to him, Kleat?"

"I didn't see anything." He bent for more wood.

It was obvious. "They killed him."

She cast around for bloodstains, but the rain must have flushed them into the earth. It occurred to her that they were scorching the evidence out of existence. That would explain this manic bonfire at the crack of dawn.

"They were working themselves up to it," Kleat said. "But then I came down. They weren't going to do it in front of me. So they gave him a head start. That's the last I saw of him."

"Where is he?"

"He went off into the night. He's a slippery old bastard, and they were drunk. They chased him and came back and went out again. They were afraid to leave the fire for very long. It went on for hours. You heard the gunfire, they were all over the place."

"And you just sat here?"

"I kept the fire going. That was my job. They made it clear. A big fire. That's the important thing. I kept them on our side. Someone had to make sure they wouldn't leave us. They could have driven off. They still could." He threw on more wood. "But not for a while."

"This is murder," she said. "And you did nothing."

Kleat's glasses flashed. "I stopped an execution. I came down and they set him loose. I saved his life." He had it all worked out in his head.

Samnang was dead somewhere, she could picture it, floating in the *baray* pools or slung over a root. "How did you save him? They hunted him. You said so."

"Three street kids against an old killer. Some hunt. They lost him." Kleat stood on the far side of the flames. "Or he left, like Luke, out the front gate. Or he's dead, okay? He's gone."

He shoved in another log. It struck her suddenly. "What's in the fire?" She dragged the log out. She reached for another.

Duncan took her arm. "That won't help, Molly."

"He's under there," she said. "They're burning his body. They're burning the evidence."

"Molly . . ." Duncan murmured.

"Get a grip, woman," Kleat said. "First cannibals, what next?"

"He was an old man." She turned away, tears blurring her vision.

"He was KR. They think he killed their mother and father, I got that much. You must have heard them," he said to Duncan.

"How would they know?" said Molly. "Vin would have been an infant. Doc would have been four."

"They've got it in their minds," Duncan said. "They say it's the reason they agreed to come along, to confront him and get the truth. I'm kind of surprised Samnang invited them. It's almost like he wanted to get it over with."

"They're thieves. They were beating him to find their plunder, not to ask about their parents," Molly said.

"Why can't it be both?" said Kleat. "They're thieves. And the old man was a butcher."

They were quiet for a minute. Finally Molly said, "He watched over me."

"So he went down in glory," Kleat said, "doing his holy deeds."

Duncan peered through the mist. "What are they up to over there?"

"Working up their nerve," Kleat said. "Go see for yourself."

28.

They left Kleat building his fire higher.

"Stay with me," Duncan said to her. "Keep your temper, do you hear me? Don't make it worse." He squeezed her arm.

"I heard you."

Broken shards lay scattered across the clearing. The forest floor was chopped and muddy. Pieces of pottery had been trod into the ground.

"This is strange," Duncan said. "Look at how deep some of these footprints are. It's like a herd of horses came through. But the prints are human."

"The rain must have softened the earth," Molly said.

"Not enough for this." Duncan stomped at the ground but didn't make a dent. "It's hard to believe Samnang could have done so much damage. And why only the pots and not the heads? There must have been fifteen heads. How could one man carry them off so quickly?"

"No idea, Duncan." She didn't care about pots and heads and footprints. Samnang was dead.

The brothers materialized in the mist. They were circulating back and forth, from the Land Cruiser to the enshrouded truck. Their rifles twitched at Molly and Duncan's approach.

At first she paid no attention to the vehicles. She'd never had a gun pointed at her. The bluing on the gun metal had worn through in places, like the finish on secondhand guitars. The guns had traveled many miles through many wars before ending up in these tattooed hands.

Duncan announced himself, arms wide, and they lowered the barrels. Toting his silver briefcase like an insurance adjuster, he spoke in quiet tones. Doc, with his full armor of body ink, shouted back at him and shook his rifle. Duncan went on talking, moving closer.

Molly stayed back, hating them for what they had done. It took her a minute to even look at their faces. She expected hangover scowls or bully glares, but their eyes were filled with voodoo fear. Their panic caught her off guard.

Then she noticed the Land Cruiser, and the truck, and was frightened, too. Tilted at ridiculous angles, gripped by vines, the vehicles were trapped. The forest was car-jacking them.

A fast-growing tree root had hoisted the rear of the Land Cruiser a foot off the ground. The back tires dangled. She went with Duncan to it.

Creepers had infiltrated a crack in the windshield. She peered inside. Vines wrapped the plastic steering wheel and were rooting into the underside of the dash panel.

The old Mercedes truck was being overrun, too. Vines roped its hood and doors, but it was being sucked backward into the earth. The rear wheels had sunk to the hub, tilting up the front end like a bull struggling from quicksand.

In a different setting, in a museum of modern art, it would have been sardonic, nature's revenge. Here, this morning, it scared her. Her mind careered through explanations. The rain had created a mire under the truck. In the darkness, the first night, they'd inadvertently parked on top of a tree trunk. The vines were genetically programmed to raid. Mother Nature was tripping on speed. Nothing human was to blame. There was some consolation in that. They were all victims. They were in this together now.

The brothers were in a state. Vin had the machete they'd used on the turtle last night. His brother So carried an ax. She glanced at the tools, looking for blood. There was none, and her hopes rose, foolishly, she knew.

Duncan opened his briefcase and gave Doc a pack of Camels still wrapped in cellophane. What else did he harbor in there? A sketch pad, she knew, though he was too shy to show her his sketches. Maps, surely, his obsession. A day journal, perhaps, and photos of some long-lost loved one. Had he kept the stub of his air ticket from the States as a memento?

The pack of cigarettes went around the circle, and Duncan accepted one. The Heng boys skirted their smashed plunder, gawking at their precious vehicles, afraid to touch anything.

"How could they sleep through this?" she said. It was a silly question. The same way she had slept through the destruction of her tent.

"I'm not sure any of them did sleep," said Duncan. "They were drunk. And busy." Hunting in the forest.

"What do we do now?"

"We need to work with them, Molly."

"Work with them, after what they did?"

"They have the wheels."

"We should just go," she whispered to him. "This very minute, Duncan." They could fade into the mist and find the causeway, and cross between the *barays,* and slide through the gateway. There was still more forest to negotiate beyond the fortress walls, but once they reached the sun, or at least the sky, they could navigate their way back down the mountain. Villagers would feed them. Loggers would pick them up.

"Without Kleat?"

"He'd leave us and you know it."

Duncan shook his head. "We're in this together."

"That's very high-minded. But look around. You can't make this better."

"No." He had his mind made up. "The best thing is to try and help them. We'll be okay."

He joined the brothers again, moving with them, taking stock of the damage. He laid his hands on the metal and glass, and that simple act did more than anything else to break their terror. At least Doc quit shouting.

The brothers' tight faces loosened. Duncan made a suggestion, and Vin handed him the machete without hesitation.

With the care of a surgeon, meticulous so as not to scratch the white paint, he slipped the blade under a creeper binding one door and sliced it free. He cut away more vines and, opening the door, made a show of returning their machete.

Little by little, he showed them how to regain control. He got So to begin unraveling the vines from the wiring. He called Molly over, and four of them manhandled a rock into place under one of the Land Cruiser's wheels. "We'll get this straightened out," he said. He put Molly to work with a shovel.

After fifteen minutes or so, he came from the Land Cruiser carrying a burlap sack stuffed with other sacks. Vin trailed behind him with his machete and rifle. "All right, let's get Kleat," he said. He propped her shovel against the truck.

"What are we doing?" She didn't mean for her voice to be shrill.

"Everything's going to be okay."

Kleat was dragging another log from the brush. Sweat ringed his flak jacket at the neck and armpits. "We've got a deal," Duncan said. "We're all leaving today, before the rains return. But first we have a job to do."

Kleat guessed from the sacks. "They want us to mule down more loot for them."

"A little salvage work." Duncan spoke to Kleat in the same soothing tone he'd used with Doc. "They need to be made whole, that's how they see it. They'll keep digging while we go up into the ruins. Vin's going with us."

The kid had found a pebble and was playing soccer with it, batting it between his toes, waiting, with the AK-47 on his back.

Kleat had a dark thought. "You know he's taking us off to shoot us."

"No he's not. They want their share of the city, that's all."

"Then they'll do it down here," Kleat said. "Later, when they're done with us."

"Show some faith, John. We scratch their backs, they scratch ours. Everything will be fine."

"They're not on our side," Kleat said. "They could do anything to us in here. Look what happened to Samnang."

"I talked to them about that. They said he ran away. They were only searching for him. They wanted to bring him back to the camp."

"They were trying to save him?" Kleat snorted. "They had a gun at his head."

"They know that was wrong. But they say what he did was wrong, too. They only wanted to know where he hid the rest of their possessions."

"They were hunting him like an animal."

"They say it was the other way around."

"The old man was hunting them?"

"No." Duncan grew quiet. "The *prêt.* They say."

Vin heard the word and stopped his little soccer game.

"The what?" said Molly.

"They're a forest legend, like what the Romans called their night-walkers, *lemures,* or *larva,* the Latin for spirits still forming. If you die violently—"

Kleat's face screwed up. "Not this again." He upended the log and let it fall into the fire. Sparks belched. The wet skin of the limb sizzled.

"They claim the forest is full of them," Duncan said.

"And you believe that?"

Duncan hesitated. "Of course not. But they do. Strip away the layers of Buddhism and Hinduism and you have an animistic religion dedicated to neutralizing the dead and pushing their spirits as far away and as quickly as possible. They were drunk. It was dark. We're looking for American remains. I'd be surprised if they hadn't seen things out there."

"Then add one more *prêt* to the collection," Kleat said. "The old man won't make it far on a plastic leg."

Molly still wanted to run for the causeway and find their own way back to civilization. "What if it's a trick?" she said. "He could be leading us up so they can desert us."

"They would never leave their own brother. Don't you see? He's our greatest assurance."

"That's the part I can't believe," Kleat said. "They're giving us a hostage."

"That's not the right attitude, John."

The fire glinted on Kleat's glasses. "I'll bear that in mind," he said.

29.

It should have been straightforward. They had all visited one or the other of the gates and its statues at least once, but the city was more alien than ever. The mist was like quicksand. Within minutes they were lost.

Molly had begun to memorize her way into and out of the heart of the ruins, but overnight the rapid forest had undone what little was familiar. Samnang had tied knots in the grass, but new grass had sprung up, higher and more lush, taking over the ruins. The saplings he'd bent into careful circles had sprung loose in the rain and grown beyond recognition. It was like entering a different city.

Vin kept sweeping his rifle back and forth at shapes materializing among the trees and temples. With the machete scabbard strapped to his back and its handle standing above his head like an exclamation point, the boy looked overloaded and self-conscious. The American soldiers with RE-1 had taught him how to moonwalk and chew Red Man. Molly and Duncan had treated him like a man, asking about his warrior *sak*. She could tell it was awkward for him to be using them as pack animals. Vin spoke softly to Duncan. The only word Molly understood was "please."

"Basically, he's asking for our cooperation," Duncan said. "The sooner we find the gate and the statues, the sooner we can leave."

"He wants to be friends?" Kleat said. He had his eye on the boy's rifle.

"Does anybody recognize anything?"

"If we could just find the tower," Molly said.

She longed to return to the room of the Buddhas. The yearning filled her. It overrode her fear of what was happening to them, their disintegration and the creeping violence. As a landmark, the tower might help orient them, but that was only an excuse. It was the room on that man-made summit that drew her. It held . . . something.

But this morning, with visibility cut to twenty feet, the tower seemed to have dismantled itself. As they penetrated the waist-high grass, nothing was the same. The avenue and side lanes and bridges and canals were all reconfigured. The massive faces projecting from lesser towers and the crests of flattened pyramids were no help. Their serene smiles only added to the sense of entanglement and maddening circles. Molly found herself resenting the tranquil stone expressions.

They chose a canal and followed its trickle of water uphill, reasoning that vertical gain was a direction of sorts. At least, Duncan said, they would not be going in circles. The same trickle of water could not round back on itself.

As they marched higher through the ruins, Vin kept Kleat in the front of the line, where he could watch him. The boy might be naive, but his brothers had instructed him well. As Samnang had put it, with or without his fangs, Kleat was still toxic.

As if hearing her thoughts, Kleat flashed Molly a look, then another one. She was following behind Vin, which put her within easy reach of the machete riding between his shoulder blades, practically a gift to them. She understood Kleat perfectly. He wanted her to kill the boy.

She tried to convince herself that Vin was her mortal enemy, and even that didn't work. She wondered, if things came to it, if she could even kill an animal to eat. Kleat glared at her. Her thoughts returned to the tower.

After a half hour, they found themselves back at the bridge on the canal where they'd begun. Impossibly, the downhill trickle of water had circled back on itself. "That can't be," Kleat objected.

Vin didn't question it. To him, the perpetual circling of water was just another arcane loop in a city of riddles. He and Duncan had a discussion using the lines on Duncan's palm as a map.

After a minute, Duncan said, "Okay, a slight revision. We're going to split into pairs and spread out the search. It should be simple. All we have to do is find one section of the wall, then we can follow it to one of the gates and get what we need."

Vin chose the teams, himself with Duncan, and Molly with Kleat. Kleat frightened him, and Molly frightened him, too, though differently. His puppy love was obvious, and out of decorum and modesty he did not choose her. It was almost cute.

"What are we supposed to do if we find something, whistle?" Kleat said.

"Stay within earshot," Duncan said. "Let's not lose each other."

They separated into pairs. As Molly wove through the piles of temples and narrow corridors, Kleat railed at her. "The machete was right in front of you. They want heads? We'll give them a head."

"He's a kid. He's not going to hurt us," she said.

"He's one of them. And we're going to need his rifle and machete. Think."

"Leave him alone, Kleat."

Kleat put his face close to hers. "Do you want to live or not?"

She had witnessed paranoia in her career. She'd photographed it in prisons and asylums and at a treatment center for foreign torture victims. She'd even argued with it, her own fears, in therapy and alone. But Kleat's was a species all its own.

She stood her ground, or tried to. "What kind of question is that?" she snapped.

"Don't think I'm going to die caged in like this," Kleat said. "Now's no time for bleeding hearts. When the time comes, just stand out of my way."

He bulled on, and Molly slowed. The sound of his crashing through the brush dimmed. Thunder grumbled far away. It seemed early. Without thinking, Molly glanced at her useless watch. The mist was thinning. The morning was getting on.

She strayed alongside a panel of more bas-reliefs, and, like yesterday, they were dense with stories both alien and familiar. The carvings seemed to whisper to her. She imagined herself written in the stone, the lone bird-woman living in a tree, the queen—or goddess—watching over the city, or that infant being held up to the sky by her mother.

Then her eye chanced up, and she was being watched again. This time there was a small troop of the ghostly gray monkeys, perched in the branches and sitting on ancient masonry and terraces. They unsettled her, like in the tower room that afternoon.

It wasn't that she thought they might attack. They were cute and fuzzy, with a few infants at the long nipples and some wide-eyed youngsters. But they were wild, and there were no bars separating her from them. And they were watching her, not eating or playing, just watching, like the huge, inescapable god heads. Even the infants were staring at her.

They'd been fighting. Slowly she detected the blood. It was mostly on the larger males, whose red penises jutted out from the furred hoods between their legs. The rain must have washed much of it away, but there had been a lot of blood and it stained them in patches.

They had something up there on the ledge with them, and it occurred to her that they had taken a piece of an animal. These adorable vegetarians were feeding on some kind of meat. She started to back away. Let them feed.

One stood on the shelf and she couldn't help but look when it lifted the thing. It was a pink human leg, smeared with blood. Her mind shunted the possibility away. Then she recognized the blue high-top sneaker wired at the ankle. It was Samnang's prosthesis.

She froze. *What have you done to him?*

The monkey pounded the leg on the ledge, foot down. The sneaker didn't make a sound. But the message was clear. She was trespassing.

Stand or run, she couldn't decide. In the Rockies, you made yourself larger. You put your hands over your head to appear taller and lowered your eyes. If a bear attacked, you played dead. If it was a mountain lion, you fought. This wasn't the Rockies.

Before she had time to decide, the canopy stirred. It was the softest of breezes, just a whisper. The monkeys shifted. They looked around them, at the trees, down the corridor of ruins. The whisper was approaching. Molly remembered the gust of wind that had crashed on her and Duncan their first day up here, and this had the same rising force to it. Molly glanced up to see where it was coming from and how it would strike her.

The monkeys fled.

It was that simple. They bolted into the branches and were gone. The gust of wind rushed overhead. It missed her, and plunged on with a howl.

She was left alone. White and orange flower petals drifted down onto her head and shoulders. It was so quiet she could almost hear them land.

"Kleat," she shouted. "Kleat. Duncan." She waited. No one answered.

After a minute, bracing herself for the carnage, she climbed up onto the ledge. It was both worse and better than she was ready for. Samnang's leg lay where the monkey had dropped it, and clearly it had been clawed and wrenched from his body in a great struggle. But the object of their feast was not his body. One of the monkeys had been killed, perhaps in the fight with Samnang. They had been eating one of their own.

30.

"Samnang?" she called out.

From the ledge, she could see a thicket of towering bamboo. It swayed gently. The canopy stirred again. The breeze was starting up. Somewhere the forest was letting it in. This time she could smell the coming rain on it.

The bamboo shivered. The feathery tops soared to various heights. The stalks clattered, lines and shadows luring her. Samnang might have escaped into there, she decided.

It was like entering a giant wind chime as she sidled among the green and yellow rods. They were a grass, not a tree, she knew that much, but some of the stems were as thick around as small kegs.

"Samnang," she called again.

The stand was many generations old. On the outskirts, youngsters stood no taller than her thigh, their stems as thin as pencils. Deeper in, the stand was older and taller and denser. Dried, gray, dead monsters—thirty, fifty, a hundred years old—had pierced the canopy.

The breeze stirred their long wings of leaves, sending tremors down the stems. The shafts quivered under her open palms. They pressed against her, then pulled away. They jostled her with long, arcing nudges. Samnang slipped from her mind. She was barely aware that her attention was shifting from him to the forest.

How did you capture this in a photo? It rose in her like a desire, the urge to hold the green light and the moment. There was no controlling the sensation with her lens. *Surrender,* she thought. It came to her in a whisper.

Yesterday they had been in a race against the rain. Today she felt in synch with it. In a strange way, the rain gave them an advantage over their captors, if that's what Vin and his brothers truly were. Unless the Khmers made a quick exit, the river would trap them and the forest would devour their vehicles. By contrast, the only thing the Americans stood to lose was a season stranded, and probably some weight.

Surrender. The idea grew. She and Duncan could melt off into the forest and outwait the others and inherit the ruins. If it was in the stars—in this starless place—they might become lovers. They would survive. The city—the forest—would provide.

The quaking leaves reminded her of aspen. Their shape was different, like minnows, not coins, but they shuddered and flipped with the same playful motion, and their colors ranged from blood red to green to yellow veined with gold.

The stand tightened around her. Her senses took on new intensity. Every stem had its own pulse. She could practically taste the light.

Molly went slowly, trying to balance her progress with the bamboo's rhythm. At first she looked for a simple left-to-right or back-and-forth pattern, but it was more complicated than that. You had to feel for it, yielding and then invading, stealing through its openings. Resist, push back, and it only wore you out.

It became—absurdly—erotic. The forest was dancing with her, bending her, carrying her. Like yesterday while climbing the tree, she felt pieced away from the greed and confusion and dangers of the expedition. But it was more powerful than that. She felt embraced. She felt desired.

The stand grew thicker. She found herself snaking between the stems in brief surges. The way a boatman rests among the waves, gauging the sea and hoarding his strength, Molly paused. She stopped. It took a minute to register that she was, in a way, trapped.

One green rod pressed between her thighs, another lined up against her spine, more a saddle than a scissors. There was nothing awkward or alarming about it. She would simply have to wait for the bamboo to shift and release her.

The bamboo chattered all around her. The fat stem running between her legs vibrated. *Absurd,* she thought again. *But nice.*

The stalks had tangled their leaves high above. *Patience, a moment more,* she thought to herself. *A wicked moment more.*

It happened again. The stem pulsed from the top down, a velvet jolt traveling from the sky into the forest floor. She struggled, though not for long. *Surrender.* Another tremor, and she felt lifted off the earth.

It was unspeakable, literally . . . getting humped by a tree. Not another person in the world could ever know. She couldn't even speak it to herself. But really, what was her alternative? To fight? To cry out for help? In a moment, the leaves would untangle. The bamboo would part. She would get back control of herself.

The wood throbbed again. It was like the devil down there between her legs. It took her breath.

She pushed with her back. The bamboo bowed with her. She bent sideways, but her camera strap tangled. *Surrender.* How was this different from a sunset or a flower's perfume or the meat of a fruit? It pleased her. And where was the decency in nature anyway? The soft earth gave her feet stirrups. Bamboo appeared between her fists. She hung on.

The high leaves shivered. She let her hips tilt and would have gone through with it, would have let the bamboo finish her. But as her head settled back along the one stem, she saw the soldier.

The skeleton wore a uniform of rags. The pieces of him lay in a patch so dense it formed a forest within the forest. The bamboo shafts opened and closed like seaweed in a crosscurrent.

Molly straightened. She pushed against the bamboo, really pushed, and this time the forest released her. She freed her legs and stumbled upright.

The thicket had her penned in now, unable to move forward, unable to retreat. The breeze was blowing stronger. The bamboo quickened its jangle, changing from wind music to the clatter of teeth. There was a skull in there, its eyes covered by the helmet.

"Kleat," she shouted. "Duncan."

The rattle rose to a clashing of wood against hollow wood. She shouted again.

Thunder fell against the top of the canopy.

She yelled herself hoarse.

It was an American uniform. He had a rifle.

The breeze became a wind. The wind became a gale.

At last she saw a distant figure approaching from the outside, chopping with machinelike double strokes, a forehand from the right, a backhand from the left. A second man appeared behind him.

"Here," she shouted.

Duncan was in front with the machete. "Are you hurt?" he called. "Can you get to us?"

"Just come," she shouted. She didn't tell them more. They had to see for themselves.

The closer Duncan got, the farther away he sounded. The *toc-toc* of the machete blade paled in the mounting racket.

Vin was not with them. She feared Kleat had done something to him. But she didn't see the boy's rifle, and Kleat would have taken that.

The rain began. It wasn't like yesterday's slow leak. Driven by the wind, the drops had real velocity. They stung her face. While the men worked closer, she tried once more to move nearer the skeleton. But the bamboo held her out like iron bars.

Finally, Duncan cut through to her. He laid one hand on her shoulder, as if to take her back from the forest.

"Where's Vin?" She had to shout over the crash of bamboo and thunder.

"We sent him down for help. We thought you must have broken a leg. Or that a tiger was at you. He gave us his machete just in case."

"Not his rifle, though," Kleat shouted. He looked almost disappointed that she was in one piece. "What are you doing in here?"

"Samnang's leg," she said. "You didn't see it?"

"See what?"

"His leg. The monkeys must have stolen it again."

"Samnang's in here?"

"I came to find him. And look."

She pointed. The bones were all but invisible through the thrashing bamboo. It took them a minute to see.

"How did you know he was in here?" Kleat shouted.

"I didn't." And yet she'd come almost directly to the skeleton. Molly tried to remember the phases of her entry, her reasoning for this detour. The monkeys had gotten her attention, and there had been the music of the bamboo, and the light, and the dance. Now, with the bamboo smashing together and the rain whipping them, it seemed off the wall.

"We can't stay in here," Duncan said. "The wind is getting worse."

"Give me that." Kleat grabbed the machete from his hand.

Molly and Duncan stood back while Kleat attacked the bamboo. He threw his raw emotions at the barrier, grunting and cursing. The blade caught each time the stalks bent in the wind, pulling the handle from his grip.

In the movies, a single swipe would have opened a small highway. Here the bamboo fought them, knocking them sideways and backward. Caught at their tops, each severed stalk bucked and stabbed in wild directions, their bottoms like tubular knives. Each stem had to be yanked loose from the canopy and laid flat before the machete could be used again.

"This is no good," Duncan shouted.

Kleat gave up. He'd gotten them closer. But the bamboo still kept them out. They could clearly see the soldier, wearing a tanker's helmet with padded ears. His rifle was trussed to his ribs by vines, barrel up, the way it had fallen from his hands. The skeleton was amazingly whole. Green shoots had grown up between the long bones. Creepers held the ribs and spine in place. Like the city, the bones were both raided and preserved by the forest.

"He shot himself," Duncan said. "Look at the back of his helmet, the hole. And see the way his rifle's lying?"

"What?" The rain glanced off Kleat's head.

"He ate his gun," Duncan yelled. "Look. The recoil tore out his teeth."

"What was he doing out here?" Molly said.

"It's an old jungle fighter's trick," Kleat said. "E and E. Escape and evasion. Bamboo makes the perfect hiding place. It guards you in your sleep. The minute anything approaches, the bamboo wakes you up."

Duncan scanned their sky of furious leaves and cane. It sounded like the clash of spears and the scream of men. His hair whipped like a mare's tail. "The storm's growing," he said. "Listen."

Molly listened. Deep beneath the clatter of bamboo, some monstrous entity was grinding its stone teeth together. The earth vibrated with it.

"It's the wind," he shouted. "There's a sail effect on the canopy. The canopy rocks the trees. The trees rock the ruins. The wind is moving the whole city. We have to return to camp."

"But this is my proof," Kleat said. "I only need one of them. I need him." His knuckles were white on the handle.

"It could take another hour to get in there." Duncan pointed at the sky. "This is the big one."

Mekkhala, Molly thought. The angel of thunder was here. But it would pass. The city could be theirs. This was their chance to be rid of Kleat.

"Let me try," she said.

Duncan ignored her. "The bones aren't going anywhere," he said. "We can come back for them."

"A typhoon could bring the whole forest down," Kleat said.

She gave her camera bag to Duncan.

Kleat had brought them to within ten feet of the remains. She pressed her palms against the wall of bamboo, feeling for its tempo. Two towering stalks parted and clashed together. When they opened again, she was ready, slipping through with a skip. The stalks clapped shut. She waited again.

Her body swayed with the stand. She waited and stepped again, and waited. Like that, she insinuated herself all the way to the bones.

31.

She stood astride the skeleton, not sure what to do next. Here was this mortal thing in her keeping. The bamboo raged around her. The rain was coming down harder now.

The uniform was just threads held together with tendrils. Moss grew in the spaces of his remaining teeth. The barrel's recoil had ripped most of his front teeth outward. Three stuck up at odd angles.

Bullied by the stand, she bent and unfastened the dog tag. They would need more, she knew. Teeth. The mandible. The whole skull.

Fastened together, the straps of the helmet would make a handle for the bucket. But when she tried to lift it, the helmet rolled away, exposing the upper face.

His jade eyes stared at her.

Molly barked and straightened bolt upright. The bamboo promptly clubbed her to her knees.

Someone had pressed the jade balls into his eye sockets years ago. Pale green, they bulged from the bones of his face. A skein of rootlets had grown across the skull and stone eyes, a mask of vegetation.

"Moll-lee." They were calling her, though it came to her as a whisper.

The J school Ws crashed through her mind: who, what, when, where, why. The bamboo shoved at her. She couldn't think. The typhoon was coming.

The helmet had preserved his blond hair. The skull, she told herself. It was wet. His hair was coarse.

She worked her fingers under the bone to get a purchase, and the back of his head was a ragged cave. Her hand slipped, and the whole carpet of his scalp came away.

She was almost sick. "God," she yelped. The skull was fused to the earth.

"Moll-lee."

A branch of leaves whipped her face. Leave the skull. The forensics people would have to make do with pieces. She plucked the three loosened teeth from their sockets and folded them, with the dog tag, in the pouch of the scalp, and shoved the bundle into one pocket of her pants. She stood, half bent, and began her exit.

The bamboo punched her ribs. It creaked and banged. The rhythm eluded her. She went too fast, then too slow. The stand struck at her. It caught her hand. She fell, then got to her feet.

Then Duncan was pulling her through. Without a word, he gripped her arms and propelled her along their narrow path through the bamboo. Kleat was already out of sight.

She cast a last glance back at the skeleton, knowing the skull would be wearing its death grin. What she didn't expect was its knowing authority. It seemed to be nodding to her. The remains floated on sea swells of vegetation, the arms and legs spreading and rising and beckoning her back, or waving good-bye, the eyes staring.

They emerged from the bamboo, and Duncan did not stop. The clash of bamboo faded, and now she heard that deep-ocean scraping of stone on stone. Dazed by her beating in the stand, Molly looked to see if walls were shifting or spires bending. Surely the city was tearing to pieces. But it stood intact. It was nestling. The ruins were rearranging themselves deep in their foundation, settling a fraction more into the forest.

In the rain and green gloom, they could have been on a giant ark of stone. The floods were coming. Molly smelled wet fur, and it was monkeys—dozens of them now—huddled on the temples' edges and on top of giant faces, watching them, passing them from one pair of eyes to the next.

Kleat was waiting for them in the mouth of a building, out of the rain. The bamboo had knocked one lens from his steel-rimmed glasses. The remaining lens was misted over. He seemed fractured and only half present.

His one visible eye looked a hundred years old, bloodshot and milky. For all his ugliness over the past weeks, Molly felt pity for him, even a kind of respect. At an age when many men were retiring to the links or cursing the financial pages, Kleat was getting broiled by the sun and horsewhipped by bamboo, faithful to his brother.

He had the machete. Slow water bled from the metal. With the scar along his throat, he might have just returned from battle. "What did you get?" he said.

"Sit," Duncan said to her. She was shivering.

Molly brought out the bundled pelt. The soldier's hair was three or four inches long. It had grown during his exile among the ruins. She unfolded the scalp, and there were dark veins along the inside of the leather. The teeth lay on top, yellow with coffee and the decades. The dog tag was so tarnished it appeared to be blank.

"Good," said Kleat. "Very good."

She felt ghoulish crouching over the bits and pieces of a man. She set the artifacts on a stone and wiped her hands on the wall, trying to clean away the feel of his hair. Kleat could carry the thing from here on. She'd done her duty.

"There's something else," she said. "He had jade eyes."

"What are you talking about?" Kleat said.

"They were hidden by the helmet. I moved the helmet and someone had put stones in his eye sockets. It was almost like he could see."

"Who would do that?" said Kleat.

"Maybe it's a funeral rite," Duncan said. "But I've never heard of any of the mountain tribes doing a thing like that. And the only people inside the city were the soldiers."

"Get out of here," Kleat said.

"Who knows?" said Duncan. "After a few months in here, the survivors might have been losing their grip on things. Going native. Going wild. Making things up. Maybe they buried him that way, modern warriors copying ancient warriors."

"But he wasn't buried," said Molly. "He was lying in the open. He shot himself where no one could find him."

Duncan fell silent.

"This fucking city," Kleat said. He took off his glasses and cleaned his fogged lens and fit what was left of it onto his face. "At least we'll know who he was."

He held the tag up in the light. Molly watched his expression. He blinked. The muscles twitched in his cheeks. "Ridiculous," he said. His lens clouded over again. He said it a second time, in a whisper.

Duncan took the tag from him and tilted it to read the embossing. His face drew into itself. "I don't understand," he said.

Molly pulled the tag from his fingers.

" 'Yale,' " she read aloud. " 'Lucas M.' "

32.

"He's playing with us," Kleat shouted over his shoulder. He was angry.

"It's tattooed on his arm," said Duncan. "We all saw it. Lucas Yale."

They were on the move again, heading for the stairs. *Nagas* reared up along the rim. Water shot from their cobra mouths into the depths of the terminus. Channels hidden within the terraces sped it toward the waiting reservoirs. Duncan had said the history of Cambodia lay in its hydraulics. She was beginning to see this empire built on shaping the shapeless, capturing the rain with its ancient geometry.

The wind was picking up. It struck the canopy in bursts, creating huge green pinwheels that moved overhead. Maelstroms in the sky. Molly thought of Van Gogh's *The Starry Night,* and that panicked her because night was not far enough away. They needed all the day that was left for their escape.

She tried to see their camp in the abyss, but the rain drove at her eyes. Roots and fallen leaves skated underfoot. The rain was as warm as blood. She put it out of her mind. She was putting a lot of things out of her mind.

"He had free run of the place. He found the bones," said Kleat. "He saw the dog tag. He got the tattoo. Or he had this made and planted it there. Who do you think put the stones in his eyes?"

"But why do that?" Molly wondered out loud.

Kleat whirled on her. "Defiling the dead, that's what he's done," he shouted. "He's a lunatic."

His outrage was out of proportion to the event. Kleat was possibly right. Luke had somehow written himself into the last days of the Blackhorse missing. There would be some reasonable explanation. But the remains of the soldier had not been desecrated so much as adorned. Luke hadn't moved a bone. At most, he'd decorated them.

What disturbed her was Kleat. With his cockeyed steel rims and the missing lens, and that machete, he looked unraveled. His furious rationalizing was irrational. The soldier's real identity wasn't lost, only temporarily lifted. They had flesh, hair, and bone to present to the forensics lab. The soldier would get his name back. Luke's act baffled her. Identity theft was one thing, but in the middle of a jungle? What did he gain? Nothing added up.

"You're saying a madman went to the trouble of forging something so common, a dog tag?" Molly said. "And then hid it where we would probably never find it? All so we *could* find it?"

"He brought us here, didn't he? He lured us with the tags."

"I'm not so sure anymore. We brought ourselves. With our needs."

"The gypsy kid walked right up to our table in the restaurant. He'd watched us for a month and selected us out of all the others. It's so plain in hindsight."

"It's not plain at all. What does he get out of it? Why us?"

"Maybe he needed to get resupplied. Look at all the food and gear we brought with us. Plus two vehicles, with pirates to drive his riches out of here." He added, "And a woman."

"You said he'd gone. Halfway to China, you said."

"Maybe I was wrong."

Kleat was talking nonsense. He wanted things to make sense. He wanted them to connect even if they made no sense.

He strode ahead, arms swinging, that machete like a pendulum. The blade sparked against a wall. She wanted to get it away from him. Regardless of whether they escaped today or in a week or in six months, they were going to need the machete to build camps and cut wood and butcher game and keep them sustained. In Kleat's hand, it was only a weapon.

"What if he's one of them?" Duncan asked from the back. He had been quiet ever since leaving their shelter.

"One of who?" Kleat's voice was cautionary. He'd had a bellyful of ghost talk.

"One of the Blackhorse men."

"Christ." Kleat quickened the pace, leaving the thought behind.

Molly pondered it. "One of the original soldiers?"

"We know they were here. What if not all of them died?"

"A living MIA?"

She felt boosted. Amped up. Here was the ultimate survivor tale. A Robinson Crusoe in fatigues, subsisting in a lost city for thirty years, dodging enemies, and eluding the $2.6 million reward for his capture. In Luke, not the city, lay her story. If it was true.

But it couldn't be. That quickly, she dismissed it. "He's just a boy. Twenty years old." Except for his eyes, the thousand-year-old eyes.

"I thought of that, too," said Duncan, undeterred. "But what if he's a different kind of MIA? What if he's Luke's son? Or the son of one of them?"

She stopped. Kleat came back to them.

"You're saying Luke came looking for his father?" she asked. Then she remembered his young face. The war was thirty years ago, and the boy was twenty, not thirty. Once you've crossed the thirty mark, you know the difference. "He's still too young."

"Not if his father did survive."

"I don't get it."

"They were trapped. Some of them died. Maybe only one was left. He didn't dare descend. One war after another raged out there. Maybe he went mad. Maybe he was injured and suffering from amnesia. What if he went off into the mountains and some tribe took him in? And twenty years ago, he had a son. A son who could watch over the remains."

A son dressed in peasant pants and Vietcong sandals. *All borrowed together.*

"A half-breed guardian angel?" said Kleat.

"I'm only saying what if," said Duncan.

"Okay, what if he is the sentinel and this is like his own tomb of the unknowns. That doesn't explain why he went down and chose us and gave away his secret."

"Maybe that was his job. To find someone to take them home."

"That's crazy," said Kleat. "The kid's a Westerner. Blue eyes, blond hair, white skin. And where did he learn his English?"

"That's a problem," Duncan admitted.

"Not just his English, his American," said Molly. "You can't fake an accent like that. I heard it. He's from West Texas, not the Cambodian highlands."

"You're right," said Duncan. "I was just trying to come up with something other than ghosts."

33.

A surprise awaited them partway down the staircase. From there they could see into the clearing, and the brothers had not left. The Land Cruiser stood ready to go, its engine running. Molly could smell its exhaust through the rain.

"By God," Kleat said.

Her relief took over. She wanted to collapse. She didn't have to hold it all together anymore. Everything was going to be fine. They were going to drive out of here.

"Hello," Kleat shouted down. He waved the machete in the air. A tiny figure appeared on the far side of the truck and waved up at them.

"There's luck for you," Duncan said.

They passed the ledges, and Molly saw the splintered poles and shredded fabric of their tents among the relentless vegetation. Across the way, Kleat's immense bonfire was nothing but mud and charred logs. The thatch hut looked as desolate as the ACAV stranded in the tree above.

The next time she came, the forest would have consumed it all, the hut, the fire pit, and the leftovers of their tents. It would be as if they'd never been here. She felt a twinge of regret. Above and behind her, the waterways were coursing and gurgling. She wanted to see the city the way the people had seen it twenty centuries ago, with the water animating its canals and gargoyles. The city would never belong to her again the way it did at this moment. *Surrender.* Now was her opportunity.

At the base of the staircase, Kleat paused. "All right, listen up. We're going to have to work as a team on this."

"We are a team," Molly assured him. She heard the havoc in his voice. And now he had the machete.

Raindrops spattered off his scalp. The veins were rising. He took out a bundle of dollars. "We're coming down empty-handed. But we still have cash. Don't offer anything at first," he said to Duncan. "Let's see where we stand with them."

"Good idea, John," Duncan said.

"You stay to the right. I'll go in from the left." He fastened the flak jacket shut.

"That won't be necessary, John."

"Stay separated."

"It's going to work out," Molly said.

"We've got what we came for," Kleat said. He patted the pocket along his thigh. It bulged with the scalp and teeth and dog tag.

"Don't do anything," she said.

Kleat looked at her with his one fogged lens and that aged eye. He started across the clearing.

"He's going to kill them," she whispered to Duncan. "Or get us killed. Warn them."

"They'd shoot us for sure."

"But we're not with him."

"We're Americans, Molly. Do you think they see a difference?"

"We should go back up the stairs."

"How far do you think we'd make it?"

"Stop him then."

They hurried to catch up with Kleat. In their absence, Doc and So had shimmed wood and stones under the wheels of the Land Cruiser and rolled it down to safety. The engine was idling.

The truck was another matter. Its front end pitched up like the stem of a sinking ship, deeper than ever. It was a goner, but the brothers weren't giving up. With axes and shovels, they had spent the morning chewing down to the wheels and axle. Their hole looked more like a grave than true hope. A rusty cable fed from the front hitch, ready to attach to the Land Cruiser for a heroic tow.

As the three Americans approached, Doc climbed from the muddy pit, ax in hand. Molly's stomach knotted. Their rifles were probably on the front seat of the truck, out of the rain. She looked for Vin, a friendly face.

So poked his head up from the pit. Plastered with black mud, the two Khmers looked the way God's Adam must have looked like in his first moments, mud with two eyes. Molly did not reach for her camera.

Duncan greeted them. Doc spoke. "He wants to know, where's their cargo."

"Start bargaining," Kleat said, moving to flank the pit.

It was beginning. Molly wanted to freeze them all, make them as still as carvings.

Doc wasn't fooled.

"He wants to know how you got Vin's machete," Duncan said. "He wants to know where their brother is."

So pulled himself from the pit. The mud made sucking noises. He was armed with a shovel.

"Tell them." Kleat was smiling, all innocence. "We sent him to get help."

So barked at them.

"They say he never came down."

"Then he must have gotten lost. He's on his way." Kleat held up his money. Water sluiced off the bright steel blade.

Duncan frowned. He spoke with the brothers.

"I told them we should start searching for him. The ruins are moving around. A stone might have fallen on him. There are animals, too. And the typhoon will get much worse, I think. We don't want to be inside here tonight."

"Good," Kleat said, smiling. "We're on their side. Keep talking."

Duncan knelt to draw in the mud with a twig. Maps, always maps with him. Doc sat on his heels to add his own lines to the diagram. So looked over their shoulders. Molly stepped closer.

No one noticed Kleat until the door slammed shut up ahead. He gunned the engine, and with a wild glance back through his broken glasses, he took off. The Land Cruiser shot a rooster tail of leaves into the air and bucked forward over roots and tipped paving stones.

He was leaving them.

Molly was surprised by her surprise. Of course he was leaving them. He was Kleat.

The brothers gave a shout. Duncan, too. A waste of breath.

Molly watched it unfold. Duncan waved his arms in the air. The two Khmers raced around to the truck and grabbed their rifles. Duncan yelled at them not to fire. They cut loose anyway and gave chase.

34.

From behind, Molly couldn't tell one mud figure from the other. One let off a long burst that emptied his banana clip, and he changed to a fresh one without missing a step. She ran after them.

Picking up speed, Kleat reached the green mineral causeway that ran between the ancient reservoirs. He veered to miss the remains of a *naga*, putting more distance between them. There was going to be no stopping him.

The brothers ran on. The faster one sprinted ahead, not bothering to shoot, maybe gambling that Kleat would clip a statue or that one of his brother's bullets might puncture a tire. Molly continued after them. She didn't want to see Kleat punished, but she didn't want him to escape either. She just wanted to see.

She had reached halfway across the long causeway. The mouth of the gateway appeared in front of them, like the eye of a needle. Through there it would be blue sky, or almost.

One brother fired. The other chased.

The Land Cruiser suddenly lifted up on an orange blossom.

That was the first antitank mine detonating the fuel tank.

A heavy boom echoed across the water. From Molly's distance, the Land Cruiser seemed to be launching into space. It spiraled forward through the plume of fuel and smoke.

The truck started to land on one side, then jumped again, thrown by the second mine. It flipped onto its roof, still moving, and the screech of metal rippled back to her in stereo along the tops of both ponds.

Flames shot up. Smoke spilled like ink.

The reserve fuel tank went off. The fireball created a temporary sun in the rainfall. It even cast an artificial rainbow.

An arm appeared from one window. Somehow Kleat had survived the explosions. He was trying to drag himself from the burning car.

The sight of him struggling to escape renewed the brothers' fury. Molly thought of the turtle in their fire last night. They would have no mercy.

She was sure the wreck had quit sliding. But then it moved again. From her distance, it looked like translucent animals rushing up from the water and bunching around the fiery vehicle. It was the rain in her eyes, she thought.

The Land Cruiser shifted. It hit a third mine. What was left of it flipped off the road.

The water was deeper than she'd guessed. The flaming ball of metal didn't float and go under in a lather of bubbles. It vanished. The man-made lake swallowed the man-made sun in a single bite.

Molly came to a standstill.

Kleat was gone.

Plastered in mud, the two brothers howled and fired their rifles into the water, cheated of their enemy.

She wasn't sure what obligation she had to Kleat. He had left them to die. Let the prehistoric fishes have him. But someone needed to witness what was left. Someone had to say a few words over the water.

Grimly, she started forward.

In the space of an instant, she felt a hand wrap around her left ankle, rooting her foot in place. She felt its fingers squeeze.

Even as she glanced down, the image of a fist disappeared. There was the echo of a sensation, a physical resonance. Then it was as if it had never been.

She lifted her foot. A piece of green waterweed led over the road's rim, limp and flat. Her imagination was in overdrive. She had invented the hand to halt herself.

She peered over the edge to see if a wave had flung up the weed. The wreck might have caused a ripple or runoff from the city. But the water was flat and dimpled by rain. And occupied.

Something was in there. Molly moved her head to one side.

It was the other ACAV. It had sunk to the bottom and was lodged in mud. Weeds floated up from the machine-gun barrels. A goldfish the size of a carp swam from one hatch. Another peered up at her from the depths of the second hatch. She leaned out over the water, angling for a better view. Their eyes weren't spaced like the eyes of a fish. They were almost human.

"Molly!"

She pulled back from the water. Duncan was standing at the forest's edge. The machete hung from one hand. The pacifist had armed himself.

"Come back," he said.

"Kleat's gone," she announced. She heard her unnatural calm. "And I found something in the water."

"Molly, before they start back. Their blood will be up. We have to hide."

She glanced down the road at the brothers. They were prowling from side to side, searching for any trace of their vehicle or Kleat. "But we didn't do anything. Kleat betrayed us all, you and me, too."

"They'll figure that out eventually. But it will be better if we're not around when they return. Come back. We'll take some food and spend the night in the ruins. We'll go find Vin. That will satisfy them. It will all work out."

That sounded sensible. Good old Duncan. She turned.

There was a fourth detonation out on the road.

Molly looked in time to see a man flying from the road, like a puppet getting jerked from the stage. There was no ceremony to it, barely a bang.

Abruptly he stopped, in midair.

She thought that it was an illusion, that time had stopped. The arc of his flight would continue in the next moment, it had to.

Then she saw the tree branch quivering. He'd been impaled on its tip. There he hung, like an ornament. Less than that, like a bit of trash caught in the trees.

Fifty yards ahead of Molly, the remaining man froze in place. The brothers were children of the mine fields. They knew them with the same dread and familiarity the Dark Ages had known hell. One step more, forward, backward, or to the side, and the man knew he might be maimed or killed. He stood there as if his very soul was at risk. And for him, it was. Samnang had told her that to die away from home, away from burial rites and family, meant wandering for eternity.

For a full minute, the young man didn't move. Covered in mud, anonymous to her, he was like a tar baby with a rifle stuck in his hand. Next to him, rising higher than his head, a *naga* bared its stone fangs.

The man groaned. It wasn't a word, just a noise escaping his lungs, the start of grief.

"Stay where you are, Molly."

Duncan started out to her slowly with a stick in his hand, touching gravel and leaves as if reading braille, scanning all around his feet for trip wires or metal buds or any evidence of mines.

He took hours, it seemed. Molly didn't move. The lone brother didn't move. She kept her eyes away from the man hanging in the tree.

Molly felt heavy, and yet light, magnificently light. Released. Anointed, in a way. She had been spared, but more important, she had seen. That was the crux of it.

As a photographer and a journalist, she had made a living from catching the meta-moments. In an article on a day in the life of an emergency room, she'd captured birth, suffering, and the still toes of a traffic fatality, and thought she'd seen it all, and in a sense she had, through her glass lens. No glass this time. No mirrors.

She stood obediently. Duncan was coming for her. He was almost here.

Once again, as in the bamboo thicket and when she had descended from the tree, Duncan laid claim to her. He was taking her back from the jaws of this place.

Beyond his shoulder, one of those giant god heads was smiling across the water, eyes closed but aware, deep in his dream of them. That was probably all she needed to know. They were figments of a stone imagination. And yet she wondered at it all. There was Samnang's cosmic stream, but then there were the day-to-day riddles, like land mines where there had been none before.

"How could this happen?" she asked.

"The soldiers," said Duncan. "Thirty years ago. They must have laid them."

"But we drove in this way. And now look."

"Chance," he said. "The robots of destiny. Like they say, mines are infinite war."

"No. Someone placed them here for us." She was utterly certain about that.

Duncan corrected her. "For someone like us. The soldiers were guarding themselves."

"It's like we're not being allowed to leave," she said.

"Don't say that," said Duncan.

"They were laid to keep us here."

"Not so loud," he said.

That frightened her. He wasn't disagreeing. It came to her. "Luke?" she said.

"Not now, Molly. One thing at a time."

"What about him?" The tar baby.

"I'll go for him next."

35.

It all might have worked as Duncan said. He would have led Molly to the forest and returned for the final brother. But an animal began to cry. It started as a tiny, thin keening, and Molly was sure it was some macabre birdsong.

Then she realized it was coming from the corpse skewered on the tree. The mine had lopped away his lower legs. His arms were broken at the elbows. But even with the spike of the branch punched through his chest, what remained of him was not yet dead. There he hung, above the water.

The cry rose an octave. It was awful. He didn't seem to take a breath. Like some inelegant jungle bird up there, he rustled his wings weakly, whistling a one-note song. The rain spoiled her make-believe. The mud was being washed away. She could see the red meat underneath.

The man on the road appealed to his brother. He reached up. They were only twenty feet apart, separated by the span of air and water. The dying brother gave no sign of recognition. His cry went on.

Thunder shook the pond. It came up through the mineral vein carved into the shape of the road.

The wind howled and skipped across the canopy's surface, and the branch moved. The impaled man rocked in space. His brother laid down his rifle and knelt before the carcass in the tree, hands pressed together.

Molly could barely breathe. The man shuffled forward on his knees, unnerved by the death song, drawn to it.

"He'll never last," Duncan said. Did he mean that living corpse or his brother?

"Don't move," he said to her. "Do you hear me?"

Stay with me, she thought. But he was Duncan, the savior. "Yes," she said.

Off he went, twig in hand, calling to the young man. The brother had entered a trance. He took no notice of Duncan scolding and commanding him. Duncan advanced by inches, touching the road, testing the fabric.

The part of a man continued singing from the tree, a grotesque siren drawing his brother to wreck himself, too.

Duncan refused to hurry. He tested each fallen leaf on the road, turning them with the tip of his stick. He skirted a patch of dirt and stepped over random pebbles.

There didn't seem to be any possible place to hide a mine out there. The road was all of a single piece, carved flat from a volcanic extrusion. Olivine, she guessed, keying on the color of the word. *What a photo.* Like the devil whispering in her ear.

Duncan reached the rifle and stooped to take it. *They would need that,* she thought. The summer stretched before them, her forest idyll after all. They would subsist on fruit and nuts, and meat brought down from the trees.

The brother was almost to the water's edge. There his knee touched the mine.

There was nothing flashy or pyrotechnic about the explosion, a sharp blast smaller than the heavy booming that had thrown the truck. Mostly it was a matter of dust. As the air cleared, Molly saw that the brother was gone. He had been pitched into the devouring water, though she hadn't actually seen that.

Duncan was standing in place, looking off across the pond. He turned to her, and his chest seemed to be smoking, though that could have been the rain driving against him. The rifle was missing from his hands, and his twig was only a few inches long now. He started back to her, more quickly on the return, his path memorized.

Molly saw the wound gradually.

Her T-shirt with the mountain-bike wheels was bleeding.

Oh, Molly, she thought. Amazed, she plucked at the wet cloth and found a small hole through the spokes of one wheel. She lifted her shirt, and the hole went through her bra. She pried it open and looked inside at the top of her white, freckled flesh, and blood welled up where the shrapnel had entered her. The wicked thing was in there somewhere. But suddenly she didn't want to know more. She let the shirt drop down again. Later.

"Molly?" She heard the anguish in his voice.

She managed to ask him first. "Are you all right?"

Miraculously, the shrapnel had missed him. The gods were protecting one of them anyway. "You need to lie down," he said.

"No," she said. "While I'm still on my feet, take me home." To camp, she meant to say. Suddenly her legs quit on her. She sank to sitting. The red blood blanched to Barbie pink as it fanned lower across her wet shirt. There was no pain, really. She just had a need to sit.

She looked out over the green water. Lily pads the size of doormats floated on the surface. Raindrops pattered the glass. That horrible birdsong had stopped. Thank God.

Duncan materialized behind her. She felt his big hands on her shoulders.

"It's only a splinter," she said.

"I need to take a look."

It wasn't how she wanted him to see them the first time, clinically, with her on her back in the rain, filling with fear. They were nice breasts, really, one of her best features. She would have liked to make him aware that a woman can blind a man with her body.

He didn't waste time with the bra hooks. She saw the clasp knife. The elastic released. She watched his eyes. He blinked. At her beauty? At her ruin?

He lifted her breast with the fingertips of both hands, careful beyond need, though she appreciated the tenderness. Now she could feel the splinter of steel. It was lodged deep in the tissue, a metal tumor. "Can you feel it?" she pleaded. She suddenly, intensely, wanted it out of her.

He glanced up with frightened eyes. "I'm trying." He spider-walked his fingertips across the rest of her body, probing here and there. "Tell me if this hurts," he kept saying.

"No," she said. "No."

He ran his hands down each leg. Nothing broken. Only the splinter.

"Can you sit?" He lowered her shirt and fashioned a sling with his red and white *kroma*. The scarves were a whole magazine article unto themselves. Someday.

Then she saw over his shoulder. "Oh God," she whispered.

Monkeys were flocking to the body in the tree. They were playing with it, pulling at the clothes, flopping the head. Looting him the way he had looted their city.

Duncan moved to block her view. "Stick with me, kid," he said.

They were massing at the body, fighting over it. She'd never seen such a thing. He raised her to her feet. "I can carry you," he said. "But it will be better if you can follow me. Can you do that?"

"We'll be fine," she said.

36.

The wind mounted, but could not penetrate the canopy. It shrieked and beat at the forest, and great whirlpools appeared among the leaves. But the membrane held, and for now they were spared the full brunt of the typhoon.

Her bleeding slowed.

Here in camp, with the terminus walls at their back, Molly felt almost sheltered. The rain didn't drive so hard. It spilled from the canopy in long, thick, silver shafts, and funneled through the barrel of the ACAV's machine gun like a cherub peeing. Night seemed near, but she was learning that this was a constant in the permanent twilight of day.

She lay propped on her side in the thatch hut in front of the fire that Duncan had revived with gasoline and a car flare. He was reviving it all, the whole camp, and their appearance of settling in. In fact, the fire and camp were his illusion. He intended for them to escape once darkness fell.

There were two possibilities. Either Luke had rigged the mines on his way out, trapping them inside his shell, or he was still nearby, armed with a Vietnam-vintage arsenal, playing cat and mouse with them.

"He thinks he's God," Duncan said to her. "Whether he's watching or not, he thinks the walls contain us now. We're like animals in his zoo. But even zookeepers sleep."

But God does not, she thought to herself. From the hut, she could see the half-closed Buddha eyes looming in the forest, and they seemed menacing with their wakeful dreams.

Duncan stayed as busy as a beaver. She watched through the flames and the plumes of rain steam as he came and went, stripping the truck like a castaway. The brothers' pit, dug to free the truck, brimmed with water now. The prow tipped higher as the truck slid backward into the earth in slow motion. With the machete, Duncan knifed open the canvas covering the truck bed, looting it from the side, lifting out whatever remained.

He brought whatever he could carry, waxy boxes full of MREs, jerry cans of fuel, shovels, axes, burlap sacks, pieces of plastic and canvas, a screen for sifting relics from dirt, even a pair of sunglasses and a set of keys from the ignition. He stockpiled it at one end of the hut or cut big leathery wild banana leaves to cover it, more stuff than two people could use in a month, much less what was left of the afternoon. She drifted in and out of sleep.

The wires of the truck spilled from one open door like colorful entrails, tangled by creeper vines tugging at them. The forest had disemboweled the beast.

"You should fix the wires," she told him. "You can make it run."

He bent to look at her eyes. She was cold again. Shock this time, or her fever? He wrapped a strip of canvas around her shoulders. It was hard and rough and reeked of fuel.

"The truck's gone," he said. "We don't want it anyway. The road's a mantrap. Our only way out is through the ruins and over the wall."

Up the hundred and four stairs, through the labyrinth at night? "Are you sure?" she said.

"Up and over the mountain. While the storm's still raging. He'll never expect that."

She wished he would just take her in his arms. She remembered that morning. It seemed so long ago.

He made a steeple of wood above the fire so the wet branches would dry and burn. Kleat would have been proud. Another few hours and they would have themselves an Aggie-size bonfire. He brought her a tin cup filled with hot water sprinkled with ashes. He stirred in instant coffee from an MRE.

"Rest," he said. "Eat. Drink. Gather your strength. If I could just find the med kit. And a rifle. Just in case."

"I know where there's a gun." She gave him a secret smile.

He glanced at her doubtfully. "Is that so?"

"Go to the tree," she said. "Pull the rope to the side, toward the tree. Pull it hard."

He wagged a finger at her, delighted by the trick. "Kleat's gun? You said you left it in the ACAV."

"I did. But it should slide down to you. Unless the monkeys took it." The wicked monkeys.

"After dark," he decided, "in case he's watching. For now, keep up the charade. I'll keep salvaging and gathering firewood. And you . . . you keep bleeding. I want him to think we're on our last legs."

He went back into the rain. The truck had sunk to the windshield. Duncan balanced on the hood and hit the glass with a pry bar. The windshield crazed and pouched in, and he hooked it out like a carcass. Then he lowered himself inside.

She didn't like his disappearing into the earth this way. Minutes passed. At last some packages heaved into sight. She recognized his steel briefcase, and then came more boxes of gear and food.

He emerged through the windshield muddy and with his face beaming. He held aloft the med kit like it was the greatest treasure.

Her wound became the first order of business. He untied the sling and opened the med kit, and it even had a pair of latex gloves for him.

It was different this time. Out on the bridge, they had both been frightened. Here the moment was more considered. She watched him trying to confront her breast, and it amused her. He blinked diligently. He cleared his throat.

Part of his dismay was the forbidden fruit itself. Her areola was wide and brown, and though she was thirty-something there was still no southern drift, no stretch marks, no erosion of her supremacy.

But also he was perplexed, and she was, too. A broken bone you straightened. A cut you stitched, a burn you bandaged. But a soft breast with a tiny wound? He clenched his gloved hands.

The shrapnel seemed to have migrated deeper. Again she felt panic and loathing, and again she made herself remote from it. "It's in there," she said. "It's hard to describe. I can feel the sense of it."

He tore open a Betadine swab and painted the area orange. She feared he would make himself brusque and surgical and go digging into her flesh. Instead, he confessed.

"I don't know what to do," he said. "It will get infected if we leave it in there, but I'd probably infect you trying to get it out."

In the end, he simply placed a Band-Aid over the hole and lowered her shirt and retied the sling. He rummaged through the med kit, picking up vials and packets and reading their contents. "I haven't heard of half this stuff."

"Let me look," she said. She found a bottle of Cipro. It wasn't penicillin, but she figured something was better than nothing. She downed a capsule with some coffee and pocketed the bottle.

"We'll get you to a doctor," he declared. He covered her with the canvas again and built the fire higher. The flames licked close enough to curl the edges of the green thatch. But she couldn't seem to get warm.

"Eat," he urged. "We have a long night ahead of us."

"Tomorrow morning," she bargained. "I'll be better then."

"You'll only stiffen up," he said. "Besides, we need the storm. It will give us wings."

He went back into the clearing to haul gear and further their illusion of staying. He positioned jerry cans of gas and diesel along the walls inside the hut, which worried her. With the fire so close, they seemed like bombs waiting to go off. But she trusted his judgment.

When everything that could be pulled from the vehicles had been collected, he started making rounds of the clearing, pulling up rotten stumps and hauling more firewood. His ruse even fooled her. Coming in from one of his forays, he dumped an armful of wood on the pile, and slipped the gun to her.

"You are so clever," he said. That cheered her.

The hurricane roar rotated in Dolby surround sound from one side to the other. Logs fell into the fire, setting off explosions of sparks. The rain hissed and vaporized in bursts of haze.

"How can I help?" she asked.

"We're going to need your camera bag, but without the camera. It's got to stay. I'm sorry. My stuff stays, too. We can't afford the weight, and we have no backpacks. I'll need your bag to carry food and meds. We have a long trek ahead of us."

She wanted to argue. But they were running for their lives.

"Don't make a big show of it," he said. "Just take the camera and lenses out. Line them up. Polish the glass. Remember, he could be watching."

37.

Duncan left again, carrying on with his charade of inhabiting this island. It was getting dark beyond the flames. Molly wondered when he meant for them to make their move.

She emptied the camera bag, polishing the lenses, drying the camera, and setting the lenses in a neat row. Ten grand in glass and mirrors. Let the forest and the monkeys have them. The real treasures were her images. Those she could still keep.

It took a few minutes to transfer the last of her images to her digital wallet. Little bigger than a hand calculator, it held close to a thousand of her best shots. Wrapped in a plastic bag, it would fit into her pants pocket. Duncan would never know. If she couldn't manage to carry the extra few ounces, she wasn't going to make it anyway.

While she was at it, she decided to surprise Duncan with some of his own treasures. Just because he was sacrificing his briefcase didn't mean losing everything in it. Once they reached Phnom Penh and their escape was just a memory, she would present him with a few of his most precious mementos.

She reached for the briefcase. From the first day she'd met him, Molly had wondered what it held. The stainless steel was dented and raked with scratch marks. The hinges on the bottom and the lock combination were rusted. She'd never once seen him clean the mud or dust from it. In a way, his neglect made the contents that much more mysterious, because the case was nothing to him, only a shell.

She raised the lid and the smell of mildew poured out. Inside lay a clutter of papers, photos, news clippings, postcards, and letters mixed with rotted rubber bands and rusty paper clips. At first she only registered the strata of his accumulating. There were decades of stuff in here. The bottom layers were mottled with fungus and yellowed with time. On top, his most recent acquisitions were still unspoiled by the tropics.

Only then did she see what his newest artifacts actually were, the memorabilia he'd stolen from RE-1.

Duncan was their camp thief.

Here was the stolen *Hustler* the two marines had fought over. Here were the snapshots and mail that men had reported missing.

She was dumbfounded.

Here was a page of the *Wall Street Journal* dated six years earlier, and on it the bygone dot.coms and their stock earnings that he'd talked about with such freshness and authority.

Here was a monograph on Cambodian flora and fauna written in French in 1903.

Here was his sketchbook, and it was filled from end to end with mindless squiggles and scrawl.

Here was a chapter torn from a British text on pre-Angkor archaeology, word for word the lectures he'd given them.

Here was an article from the *New York Times,* "Giant Trees Hold Ancient Temples in a Deadly Embrace,' complete with *spong* and its scientific name, *Tetrameles nudiflora.*

Here was the kitchen he had built by hand, the zebrawood cabinets, the butcher-block table, and the panel of green and brown and blue bottle bottoms leaded together like a stained-glass window. Only it wasn't his kitchen, it was a magazine ad.

Here was the red setter with the bandit's neckerchief that he'd grown up with, except the setter and the neckerchief belonged to three children in a snapshot with a digitized date, two months ago.

Here was Kent State in all its bloody details—in a paperback history of the war.

Here was Duncan, the scraps of him gathered like stolen homework.

He had dissected each thing. He had underlined sections, circled faces in snapshots, written marginalia, and then dropped it in here to be layered over with more of the same. He had memorized a life.

Who was he?

She looked out into the night. Logs detonated, splitting open with loud snaps and bangs, offering their white meat to be burned, renewing the fuel. The rain evaporated in a cloud above the fire. Eventually one would win out, the rain or the inferno. For now they were in perfect balance.

Duncan came in from the darkness. "Feeling better?" He began weaving shut the hut like a giant cocoon, braiding strips of bark into a front wall. "Once we close the front door," he said, "we'll escape through the back door."

"There is no back door, Duncan." Samnang had woven solid walls to the rear and sides.

"That's what Luke will be thinking, too." He went on knitting the raw strips into a screen.

She mopped the sweat from her face. Chills shook her. The hut seemed to be spinning. If only her body would make up its mind, hot or cold.

He was either her murderer or her savior. Maybe he was both, like a Jekyll and Hyde. Was he the one who had mined the road that he was so desperately trying to lead them away from? Could this explain his reluctance to follow Luke here, the knowledge that his other self, his forest self, was waiting to stalk him? But then, who was Luke? The son of a soldier who had lost his mind in the Cambodian wilderness? Had Duncan told her everything already?

Molly struggled to piece it together. Sweat poisoned her vision. The smoke was hard to breathe. While she was still able to aim the gun, she had to judge this man. Should she confront his fiction or let herself raft along on it and hope for the best? Would he confess his mimicry or stick to his innocence? Or was he so insane that he was incapable of guilt anymore? And what about her? If it came down to it, could she pull the trigger?

He didn't look like a monster sitting there, weaving strips of green bark. But he was Oklahoma all over again, sharing some food and talk while they waited for the night to pass and the highway to carry them on. This very morning she had lain in his arms and spun a romance in her head. She had trusted him.

She gripped the gun. This had to be done. "Who are you?" she asked.

He looked up with his farm-boy smile. "Me?"

She kept the gun along her leg, out of sight.

"I looked in your briefcase," she said.

He looked at the briefcase and back at her. He was confused. "Yes?"

"I know who you're not," she said. "I want to know who you are."

"Molly?"

She had made a mistake. She didn't have the strength for this. He was too practiced at his masquerade, or too far over the edge. But she had started it now. "I'm trying to understand," she said.

"What is it?" He was earnest. He pulled the briefcase onto his lap and opened it. He lifted up papers, his sketchbook of nonsense, someone's plastic booklet of snapshots from MotoPhoto, a decomposing British passport, a plastic badge that said UNTAC. He saw what she had seen, and none of the musty pile seemed out of order to him. Was he more harmless out of his mind than in it?

"Where did you get those things, Duncan?"

He frowned, trying to grasp her point. "My documents?" He spoke without a hint of self-defense.

"Are these your children?"

"My children?"

"In that photo of the setter."

He studied it. A frown appeared. He had not seen the children before. Then his eyes clarified. "You mean my brother and sisters," he said. "With Bandit. He was a dog's dog. There's his scarf I told you about." He showed her.

"But you're not in the photo," she said.

He looked at it again. He thought. "Dad was teaching me how to use the camera."

"How old were you?"

"Gee, probably eight. I liked Cheerios." There was a box of Cheerios in another photo.

"Duncan." She didn't know what else to call him. "Look at the date."

He couldn't see it. He opened one hand helplessly.

"The digital numbers along the side," she said. "It was taken two months ago."

His lips moved. He held the photo closer and rubbed at the date with his thumb. Then he flinched.

His face aged. It was the firelight shifting, she thought. The laugh lines turned into deep creases. His forehead blossomed with worry.

"What's this?" he muttered.

"I thought you could tell me."

He was trying to think. The date confounded him. Plainly, he'd never seen the children before. He'd plagiarized the photo for a dog, nothing more. Where was the harm in that?

He pawed through more of his documents. The *Hustler* spilled open, all tits and labia. Postcards, photos, yellow news clippings.

"How long have you been doing this?" she asked.

"How long, what?" He was disoriented.

She chose her words carefully. No harsh accusations. He looked so frail suddenly. "Borrowing," she said. "Stitching together a masquerade."

"Molly?" He spoke her name as if it were a lifeline.

She wanted to believe in him. Amnesia would pardon him. It would make him a virgin almost, an understudy to everyone he'd ever stolen from. That would make sense of the skin mag and its nudes and all the rest. He was simply trying to catch up with the world.

She kept hold of the gun. Someone had planted those mines on the bridge. Someone had trapped them in here.

The light twisted again, and his face drew into itself. It didn't collapse exactly, but some aspect of him seemed hollowed out. The shadows were invading. The furnace blast of light dimmed.

The rain, she despaired, not taking her eyes from him. *It was winning.* She'd made a mistake. Wounded and ill, she'd chosen the middle of a storm at the beginning of night to unlock this man's asylum.

"The fire," she said to him. If she could keep the light strong, if she could keep Duncan occupied, if she could wear him down, if she could make it to dawn, some opening would present itself.

He peered at her. His eyes had a glaze to them, a cataract glaze. *Old,* she thought again. "Sorry?" he said.

"The fire needs more wood."

"Yes, I'll do that." He spoke softly. He sounded broken inside.

It took willpower not to reach across and pat his arm. He had saved her time and again. She didn't want to have to pronounce sentence on him. What difference was there between an angel and the devil except for a fall from grace? Was it his fault that he had stumbled among the ruins?

He closed his briefcase and laid aside the plaited strips of bark. He brushed his legs clean. His big hands looked thinned. The fingers trembled.

He had never seemed frail to her. Her heart was racing. Had she broken his mind? Or was he only pretending . . . again?

He started to scoot out through the doorway, then stopped. Something stopped him.

Molly tightened her grip, praying he wouldn't turn to her. But he kept staring ahead. She darted a glance through the doorway.

Luke was out there, waiting for them on the far side of the fire.

38.

Duncan's steeple of logs collapsed. Sparks and steam erupted. Molly turned her face away from the fiery heat, and when she looked again, the flames were strong and Luke was still there.

He stood so close to the fire his rags of clothing were smoking. His shirt had torn open, exposing one very white shoulder, his mortality on display. The rain poured off the planes of his face as if over ceramic. His hair was gone. He'd shaved himself bald.

He was the trickster, all along. Who else? Their captor. The devil.

Duncan was frozen. He couldn't move. It occurred to her that he was Duncan's monster. Or his master. Which was it?

As a photographer, she'd learned to shoot first, ask later. But that was with photos. And what if she was wrong? She kept Kleat's Glock hidden behind her thigh.

"Where have you been, Luke?" she said. "We missed you."

Luke didn't answer. He was staring at Duncan. Into Duncan.

"You had us worried," she said. "We called for you. We thought you'd left."

"Our wandering brother." Luke spoke to Duncan. Brother, not father. And Duncan had left, she understood. But now was back.

She tried bravado. "What the hell do you want?"

She brought the gun up from its hiding place. It held Kleat's bidding in it, like a spirit resident. How else could she explain pointing it at another human being? This was her hand, but it couldn't possibly be her willpower. The gun found its perch in the space between them.

"Did you lay those mines?" she said.

Luke turned to look at her. She remembered his eyes in the restaurant, cornflower blue. Now they were rolled up into his head, only the whites of them showing. She'd known a prisoner who did that. Every time she started to snap his picture, he would roll his eyes into his skull, a one-man Black Sabbath.

"You have a job to do," he said to her. Just as she'd feared, they weren't being allowed to leave.

"Duncan," she pleaded. She didn't know what to demand with this weapon. A declaration of guilt? A promise of aid? Surrender? An end to the war? *Say something,* she thought to Duncan. But he was connected to Luke, or Luke to him.

"We saw what you did to the bones," she said.

"There's more," he promised. More carnage? Or bones?

A movement caught her eye. The darkness shifted over Luke's shoulder. She squinted through the flames. Animal eyes flickered in and out of view. A shape climbed down from the trees, then another. The monkeys were descending, she thought. Becoming jackals.

"What do you want?" Duncan's voice broke. He was afraid.

"It's time," Luke said.

Duncan didn't move. "You don't make sense." His neck was stooped.

"We said we'd follow you to hell and back," Luke said. "We did. Only it took this long." *Out of his mind,* she thought, *him and us. Possessed by the remains of war.*

Why hadn't she listened to Kleat? He'd warned them in the restaurant. He'd said the man was a predator. And yet Kleat hadn't believed his own warning. It was he who had pushed the hardest to follow Luke into this limbo of trees with bleeding names and the labyrinth and the hiding bones.

"Leave her out of it," Duncan said. He sounded tentative. His brow tensed. He was trying to navigate. Searching for safe harbor.

"Out of what, Duncan?" she whispered.

"I don't know," he pleaded.

"It's almost over," Luke said.

"It was you," said Molly. "You mined the road."

The fire sank under the downpour. For a second, Luke's empty sockets stared at her. It was the darkness. Then the flames leaped up. His eyes returned.

"I told you to tell him," Luke said. "He lost his place with us. Now Johnny's not ever going to leave."

"Johnny," Duncan repeated, trying to remember.

"Leave him alone," Molly said. She reminded herself that she was the one with the gun.

"Molly," Luke whispered. But his jaw didn't move. It wasn't his voice. *Us.* They whispered from behind him.

The monkeys gained in size. They straightened. She was wrong. These weren't monkeys, what she could see of them. Some were naked among them. Others wore rags. Some had skin. Not all of them.

She tore her eyes from the shadow shapes. They weren't real. It was her fever.

The gun took on weight. It wavered. She slipped her arm from the sling to steady her aim.

"What do you want with him?" she said.

"Him?" Luke said.

They wanted her.

"What do you want?" She could barely hear herself.

"We've been waiting long enough, don't you think?" said Luke.

The words came back to her, Duncan's refrain at the dig.

Luke smiled at her, and she recognized them, the ruins of his teeth green with moss. Only now three more were gone, the three she'd plucked from his skull that morning. He hadn't shaved his hair off. It was gone. She'd carried his scalp off in her pocket. Lucas Yale was no forgery. He was dead.

Molly pulled the trigger.

He had not made a move. He'd done nothing but smile. No witness on earth would have called it self-defense. And yet she fired. She killed his impossibility.

There was a cry, and the sound of a body pitching into the fire. Torches of wood catapulted from the flames.

The rain hissed. Steam and smoke pumped upward, sucked by the wind. The light nearly died.

"Duncan," she shouted.

He looked at her, at the gun, at the body smoldering on the logs. He finished getting out of the hut. The shadow men—the monkeys—had fled.

Molly crawled from the hut with the gun in one hand. The rain whipped at her like cold stones. Her wound seemed distant, no longer clutched in the crook of her arm and held close to her face. It was, for now, beneath her attention.

Together, she and Duncan rounded the fire to the body. His clothes were too wet to combust quite yet. But there was that smell again, the stink of burning hair. *What hair?* And when had this rifle appeared across his back?

Duncan dragged the body, hair flaming, from the fire. They turned him faceup, and it wasn't Luke staring at them with jade eyes, not with the crude tattoos along his arms and the gold teeth sparkling between his burned lips. She had just killed Vin.

Molly let the gun drop from her hand. In her fever state, she had mistaken the missing boy for a phantom. Or the rain had infected her. It was dark. The night was diseased with shadows.

Duncan picked up the gun.

She was too horrified to care.

He aimed the gun. She saw it through a foggy lens. Her mind was shutting down. The bang of shots rang in her ears. He was firing point-blank into the hut.

She had forgotten the jerry cans stacked inside. The smell of fuel reminded her. It was leaking downhill, toward the fire.

Before her eyes, he'd built a bomb.

"Run," Duncan said.

She tried, and fell.

He caught her, and she thought he would carry her up the stairs. They would fly into the night, the typhoon for their wings.

But he was too weak. After a few steps, Duncan groaned, "I can't."

Her superhero lowered her back to the ground. He seemed frail, or injured. As they set off with her arm draped over his thin shoulder, Molly couldn't be sure who was carrying whom.

39.

The clearing lit like a chalice of light. Like Lot's wife, Molly could not resist glancing back at the destruction. Jerry cans pinwheeled out of the hut walls, whipping tails of flame. The hut was just fire squared on the edges, an idea of civilization. The ACAV glinted among the branches.

She looked for her phantom ape-men, but the light had banished them. All that remained was the body. She had imagined Luke, a dead man, even spoken to him, and then pulled the trigger. But in killing off a hallucination, she had murdered a poor lost boy. Blinded with stones. Or had she imagined his eyes, too?

She wanted to blame her fever, but feared the worst. Madness was built into her genes. Her birth mother had finally come home to roost.

"Climb," Duncan said.

Another jerry can ignited. The faces of stone giants throbbed among the trees. Shadows fled and reassembled.

"We need to go back," she said. "I need to bury him."

Who were they running from except themselves? Luke was imaginary and she had killed a child and panicked this fragile hermit into detonating the fuel. It occurred to her that she might have imagined that, too, that she was the one who had emptied the gun into the jerry cans and destroyed their final hopes for survival. It was in keeping with the family tradition, slow suicide, only by jungle, not by snow.

"Climb," Duncan whispered. "They'll be coming for us."

She forced him to stop, a matter of leaning on his shoulder. Where had all his strength gone?

"You saw them?" She spelled out her delusion. "Those others in the shadows?"

"I don't know." But his urgency was certain. "We need to keep moving."

They were being hunted. Duncan didn't speak it out loud. Maybe he thought she would stop functioning.

By midway up the stairs, the rain had drowned the scattered fires and the hut and their bonfire. The darkness gave her hope. Maybe Luke and his death squad would be reduced to hers and Duncan's same blind groping.

They climbed the stairs, resting more often than they wanted. Duncan's exhaustion mirrored hers. He seemed every bit as weak and confused as she was. She faltered, he faltered. She had wounded him with her doubt. It had to be more than that, of course. She remembered the smoke coming from his chest that afternoon, and feared he'd caught some of the shrapnel after all. Had she been so preoccupied with her own wound that she had missed his?

Near the top they huddled like invalids. Resting her head on his back, she could feel his ribs against her cheekbone. In her mind, his grip was big and meaty, but now his hand felt narrow. She blamed herself. He had shielded her so often that she'd built him into more than he was, a man, a tired man at the end of a long, terrible day.

They finished the stairs at last.

The city was alive tonight. She remembered Duncan's embrace that morning, and his marvelous heartbeat and the swelling of his lungs, and the city was like that. It pulsed with water. Its clockwork was in motion. The rain had resurrected it.

The rain had stopped, even the wind. But the city was activated. Runoff coursed through its veins.

Molly thought the storm was over. The raindrops quit biting at her eyes. The great sea roar above the canopy was silent. But Duncan wanted the calm to be just the eye of the typhoon. He wanted more tempest and fury to cover their escape. "It's our only hope," he said.

Moonlight trickled through the leaves, not in straight pencils of light, but reflecting, from one leaf to the next. It alloted a silver murk to the ruins, enough to give her sight.

To their right and left, all along the rim, water poured from the cobra mouths of *naga* gargoyles. Monuments and spires formed silhouettes with flame and flower profiles along their edges. Massive heads drifted like asteroids bearing human features.

They crept deeper into the ruins.

The city was a hydraulic monument, a celebration of the water that had once powered an empire. Even terrified and hurting, Molly was astonished by the intellect within the ruins. Two thousand years ago, architects had designed the buildings to make music with the water.

Stealing among the moon shadows, she could hear the notes. Water overflowed from one huge bowl to another, cascading harmoniously. It streamed through stone flutes, forcing air through whistling pipes. It beat rhythms against panels lining the canals.

Each structure seemed to have a song built into its vent holes and gutters. The trenches and pipes were more than simple veins to drain away the water. They were throats designed to sing.

The Blackhorse men had heard it, the journal fragments said so. Had they felt her marvel? Had they listened to the music? It called to her from side paths and stairways, even from underfoot, beneath the paving stones. She wanted to linger and search the city, listening to its parts.

"Listen," she said. It mesmerized her. The music overruled their pursuers. It seemed more powerful than any danger. It drew her. She couldn't explain it.

Duncan kept himself immune to the temptation. "Keep going," he whispered.

They came to the tower, and she would have been happy to rest in its summit. From up there they could scout for Luke and his shadows, and Duncan could warm her in his arms. They could forget with the city's song rising up to them.

Duncan forged on. Each time she lagged, he said, "The gates."

"But the gates are closed," she said. "They're choked with wire and vines."

"One or the other will go," he told her. "I know." He stated it as an article of faith.

"I'm tired, Duncan."

"A little more."

"We can rest in the tower."

"They'd find us."

He pulled her by the hand, hustling her across a bridge. The architecture began to diminish in size. The high, dark snake back of the fortress wall appeared. The interior moat was bellowing with runoff. How many enemies had been sucked to their deaths trying to leap across that monster?

Duncan grew more wary, moving them from one pool of shadows to the next. The light began failing. The storm was returning. Clouds rushed the unseen moon. The intervals of silver gloom shortened, swallowed by darkness. The wind was finding its lungs again. The patter of leaves gave way to branches thudding like giant footsteps. Duncan was going to get the other half of his typhoon.

"There it is," whispered Duncan.

The multiheaded gate tower straddled the wall. Another bank of clouds shuttered out the moon. But they had their bearings.

"I'll go in front," Duncan said.

He was afraid of mines, she thought. Luke had sealed one entrance, why not the others? That was the mischief they had to test. And if anyone could unravel the knot of wire and vegetation, it was Duncan. They had desperation on their side, and their hunters had a whole city to search.

They edged through the darkness, connected by her fingertips on his shoulder. The noise rose as the wind hit and the sail effect began to grind the city's foundation.

Even blind, Molly could sense the gate's nearness. That vague, familiar claustrophobia began to press at her. With each step, it grew, an undertow of disease and despair. What were they thinking? The barrier was impenetrable. A curse upon trespassers. The thought drove at her.

In the next instant, she heard a sudden dull crack. Duncan gave a startled cry and collapsed backward, against her. They both fell, and she thought, *Now we are dead.*

40.

He struggled for air. His feet scraped against the slippery stone. She was certain he'd been shot.

"What is it?" she whispered. He was pushing, she realized, to get back from the gate.

She stood and dragged him by his shirt, away from the gate. It surprised her. He weighed little more than a child.

Duncan coughed in animal bursts and sucked for air. Above the canopy, the clouds parted for a brief minute. The swamp glow lit them.

Black oil—blood—spread from his broken nose and mouth and a gash across one eye.

"What?" she moaned. She had to be strong. It was her turn to play savior.

He couldn't form words, only noises, strangled and nasal, through the blood and the damage. His jaw was crooked. Had they shot him in the face? She rested beside him, searching for their attackers.

A small forest of ceramic warriors stood before the tunnel. Their heads had been returned. Their jade eyes surged with menace.

Molly tried to take it in. They had risen up. Shoulder to shoulder, they no longer lay toppled or sunk into the earth. Someone—Luke, or Samnang, or others—had dug them from the ground and propped them upright to block the exit. They were ranked in columns, more than she could quickly count.

The tumble of light made them seem alive. They were nothing but hollow shells. But with their incandescent eyes, it was almost as if they were the ones who had maimed Duncan. She searched for Luke hiding among the statues. But all was still among the legs and jade armor.

The moon died again. Darkness swamped them. She held Duncan on her lap.

He kept reaching for his face. She could feel him touching it, probing his own wounds, and that made her more afraid. They were like deep-sea creatures reduced to learning the world with feelers.

Terrified of hurting him more, Molly made herself touch his face. She deciphered blood and the bony protrusion at his jaw, and that scar above his ear. She ran one hand through his wet hair, and it pulled away in long strands. It was weeds or moss, she told herself. But it felt like hair as she untangled it from her fingers.

The stones grated under her knees. He groaned.

"I'm sorry," she whispered.

He patted her hand reassuringly.

She felt him grip his jawbone, and knew what he meant to do. He got his thumbs underneath and clutched the sides, and tugged at the bone. The bones gave a gristly pop and he groaned. But the jaw would not go back into joint. She was almost sick.

The moon returned. Duncan leaned forward to let the blood run from his nose and mouth. She got to her knees and unknotted her sling, his checkered *kroma,* and wrapped it around the gash on his forehead. What now?

The statues scared her. Luke had posed them as a warning, obviously. What other tricks had he arranged in the tunnel?

She got Duncan to his feet. He was so thin. "Put your arm over my shoulder."

Holding him gave her strength. *The endorphins were kicking in,* she thought. He seemed almost light enough to carry in her arms.

Clouds gobbled up the moon again. The gate was out of the question, and it would be foolhardy to try for the tower at the center of the city. By now their pursuers would be hounding the ruins.

She led Duncan along the moat path, following it by ear. She planted each foot with care. One slip and they would both be swept away. They shuffled higher, alongside the wall.

The wind began to scream, clamoring to tear the canopy open.

Thunder fell upon the mountain. She heard the bamboo chattering at her, and vines lashing like bullwhips. The ruins grated like the bowels of a glacier.

She felt helpless. They were the walking wounded. Even if there were a breach in the wall, how far could they hope to get? What lay out there in the night?

While she still had strength, Molly turned Duncan toward the city.

There were no more holes in the darkness, no more moon. The storm sprang at them. Molly found her way by the songs of the ancient buildings.

She listened for hollowness and found a doorway. That got them out of the rain, but the floor was half flooded. She felt her way up a short staircase to a ledge.

By touch, quivering with fever, she tucked Duncan along the back wall and foraged moss and leaves to pile over him. When he was well covered, she burrowed under to hold him. The rain would wash away their tracks and scent and any last evidence of them. In the morning, they could start over.

41.

She woke holding an armful of leaves on a ledge, an ancient veranda that faced out upon the ruins. Maybe lovers had once cooled themselves here and shared this secret view of the street below. The light was blue turning green, and the mist was sinking in the street below. It was dawn in the city.

She lay unmoving above the ghost river. A dragonfly appeared, a jewel with wings. Gods—their wandering faces—invited her back into the great dream.

The typhoon had passed. The stones no longer grated. The water songs had dried to a faint trickle.

Duncan was gone.

She looked at her empty hand sticking through the leaves. He had gone to draw them away from her. That was Duncan.

Whispers threaded up from the mist. "Molly," she heard. They knew she was here somewhere. They were backtracking for her, which could only mean they'd run Duncan to earth. His footprints or scent, whatever they were following, led this way.

Her hand drew into the leaves. Eyes wide, she watched them from above.

They surfaced in the street mist, phantom hints of them, a bare shoulder, a hunched back, a wisp of black hair, khaki-green rags. It was a parade of apparitions, of fragments of apparitions, even of relics.

Held by no one she could see, a rifle barrel, beaded with dew, swiveled from side to side.

They were mere pieces in the mist, silent except for their hiss of words. They might have been a giant serpent gliding through the labyrinth, its skin whispering against the walls.

Molly waited, hating the adrenaline that woke her body. The shrapnel wound burned with infection. She could feel the tickle of insects on her legs, the gentle suckling of leeches.

At last her hunters faded away.

She forced herself to wait, counting time in her head, devising plans. The gods smiled at her foolishness. The fortress walls stood whole. There was no exit.

She crawled out from the decay. Her vision swam in broken auto-focus, soft to sharp, near to far. Glossy black leeches clung to her arms. The forest was stealing her. It took all her strength to stand, and when she glanced down, her bed looked like an animal lair.

Her thighs trembled as she descended to the street. She went the opposite way from her pursuers, both to avoid them and to find the origin of their tracking. That was where they would have left Duncan.

As the mist cleared, the spires grew taller. All around, buildings leaked their lungs of fog. It ushered out of blank doors and cascaded down stairs. It exhaled from the mouths of giant heads. Between the flags of it, she saw parrots and smaller birds wheeling in the morning air. Monkeys sprinted overhead like spies. Invisible deer barked at her progress.

They were giving her away. But her presence was already known. She accepted that.

Here and there weapons and rusted C-ration cans fanned across the road, tossed from doorways like garbage. Had the soldiers become so careless, even discarding their rifles? It was the animals, she knew. Over the years, they had rooted through the fragments and pulled them outside. Her mother had been scattered over a mile of moun-tainside.

It was all she could do to stay on her feet.

She peered inside a room, and it was like a lunatic's cage. Hand-sketched maps were plastered to the walls like wet leaves. Their ink had bled, but it was still possible to see the attempts to map the ruins. Each map bore a date in one corner, July, then August, and one made in late September . . . three months after their arrival. Each was scratched out, drawn over, crumpled, and smoothed. The mapmakers never had gotten the hang of this place. The ruins had defied them to the end.

When she stepped from the room, Molly saw the black bead of a gun barrel aimed straight at her. The sniper's nest was practically invisible among the leaves, but her eye went straight to it. She could not explain her gift for finding them.

The sniper sat in a fork, tied to the tree. His rifle was rooted in place, stitched to his shoulder by vines. His skull leaned against the stock, taking infinite aim with round stone eyes. Like Luke, he had been fitted with the vision of jade. It was as if the city watched itself through their eyes.

Nothing remained of his uniform, though he still wore web gear and a towel around his neck vertebrae, and the skull sported a do-rag. His leg bones and boots had long ago fallen to the ground, but his upper half still maintained a bull's-eye on the street.

Duty was one thing, this was something else. Besides tying himself to the tree, the man had cooped himself up inside a cocoon of barbed wire. His last act—hauling up the wire and constructing a shapeless ball of it—bewildered her. What had he hoped the wire would protect him against? Starvation, despair, madness? Had he caged himself to prevent his own wandering?

She recalled the monkeys plundering the body yesterday. Had he chosen the tree for his tomb and wired shut his mortal remains against the animals? Who else could he have feared among his dead and dying comrades?

Molly stumbled on, passing beneath his aim. One of the soldiers—or perhaps some of Duncan's seventeenth-century Dutchmen trekking through Indochina—had carved a cross into the wall. A red and white painted Confederate flag graced one sheltered wall, and beside it a black-and-white peace symbol. They had scratched the names of wives and girlfriends among dancing, round-breasted *aspara* nymphs.

She passed through the canyon of story panels that she and Duncan had shared, and the carvings had altered. Now the train of prisoners lay beheaded. The dragon had retreated back into the sea. The monkey-gods had defeated the humans. The crocodiles had caught the peacock and were dragging it feet first into the carved waters. She got it, she got it all, the death of the captives, the passing of the typhoon, the triumph of the monkeys, and their bodies and spirits being pulled into the underworld.

She came to a little cemetery. They had buried their dead, or at least, while they still had their strength and sanity, their early dead. But thirty years of animals had undone their labor. White bones lay strewn across the hillside by the hundreds.

The bones and relics were so obvious to her this morning. It was as if the Blackhorse soldiers were coming out of hiding. She thought the storm must have thinned the canopy to allow more light, or that the fever made her senses more acute. The bones practically greeted her.

She had no idea how many men the cemetery had held. Duncan or Kleat could have judged by the bones; they had trained themselves to puzzle together the remains. But they were gone. She was the last one left. That was her first conscious admission of the fact.

She was dying.

If Luke didn't find her, the fever would take her, or the infection. It was only a matter of time. But then who would take the soldiers home?

A rifle stood, jammed barrel down in the black earth with a helmet on top, a classic shot. She framed the picture in her mind, the rifle, the white bones, the black earth. Molly blinked. She recognized this dirt. It was the same rich black soil they had shed on their white tablecloth in the restaurant. This was where Luke had grabbed his fistfuls of mud and dog tags. Here was where her journey had started. The circle was tightening. She was getting to its center.

42.

She found the tower by looking not up, but down. Overnight, the rain had filled a long, rectangular reflecting pool that extended beneath the trees. This was a new approach, different from her other forays into the city's center. The image of the tower hovered at its far end, upside down in the mirror. There between the branches, a hundred yards ahead, stood the root of the tower. *Lost no more,* she thought. There was her destination.

As she skirted the pool, a ripple spanked the stone. She paused and the water went still. The lily pads lay motionless. She waited and, like yesterday at the reservoir, something shifted in the depths. The surface seemed to open.

Tangled with weeds, a big machine gun rested on the bottom. Coils of belted ammunition were turning green, like old pennies. The gun was not mounted on a tripod or neatly positioned. It had the look of a thing thrown away without care.

Then the surface sealed over. It became a mirror again, and she found herself facing the gunner, or his reflected image. She lifted her eyes. What remained of his skeleton—the limp spine and his skull and a few ribs—dangled from a noose. The rope twisted. The skull turned, and he had jade eyes, also.

First Luke, then the sniper in his coil of wire, now this man. Despair had swept them like a virus. She felt it, too, trapped at the center of the earth, chased by uncertain dangers. Languishing. That was the worst part, the wheel of time turning without measure, the obsessive maps filled with circles. Even that made sense to her. Even suicide made sense.

But why had they separated from one another? When they most needed each other's company, these men had made themselves desolate and estranged. They had retreated to distant lonely hideouts, the sniper to his perch, Luke to his bamboo lair, this gunner to a noose.

There was no evidence of an enemy finding them here. Had the men taken to hunting one another, then? Or imagined themselves being hunted? Why not? The monkey meat could have passed on a brain fever. Had they been killed by their own ghosts?

She looked up, into the ever present smile of God. Where was the joke? In their suffering and confusion? No matter where you turned, the city seemed to mock you. She tucked her head down, containing her anger. Every which way, the place made you mad.

The tower seemed to drift toward her. Duncan would have led them there. It was more wish than calculation. She had no time for the rest of the labyrinth.

She came to the bas-relief crowding the base of the tower. She looked again and the carvings really were in motion. One of the stone children—a little girl—turned and looked right at her. Molly cupped one hand against her eyes and hurried past, to the stairs.

Duncan had come this way. His red and white scarf lay in a heap on the stairs. The rain must have washed it clean. For all his blood last night, there wasn't a drop on the scarf. She draped it around her neck and gathered her courage, step by step.

Higher and higher she wound. She battled her dizziness as she kept to the precarious outer edges. The doorways whispered to her, tempting her to come in and stay awhile. She resisted their havens. She forced herself to climb on.

As she neared the top, a motion in the grass far below made her melt against the stairs.

There was no mist to hide them this time, and the green light was as good as it got. And yet they still evaded a complete inspection. They appeared in pieces from the mouth of one of the great avenues.

A man's shoulder and arm surfaced, then sank into the grass. A head appeared, scouting right and left before ducking behind a pillar. A man's hunched back appeared. Some were bearded and naked. Others wore rotted fatigues stolen from the graveyard. Some went barefoot. Rifles and rucksacks parted the grass. They were a procession of weapons and gear. Their skin and bones were little more than vehicles for the war relics.

All carried the jungle on them. She thought the vines and weeds must be part of their camouflage. But then she spotted the small animals moving on them, lizards, and a snake, and even a monkey riding majestically on one's shoulder. The forest inhabited them. They had lost their souls to this place.

They were not ghosts.

Molly refused to call them that. She clung to her powers of reason. Call them supernatural and she would lose all control over her rational world. It was not that she rejected the idea of ghosts. Her mother was a ghost. But you possessed them, not the other way around. Ghosts were data. They were pieces of your past. They allowed you a dialogue with yourself, and they had no reality except the reality you granted them.

She granted them nothing. She had conjured up none of these hide-and-seek scavengers creeping through the grass below. As eerie as he was, Luke had appeared well before she had any inkling of him, or them. There could be no Blackhorse ghosts because Blackhorse did not belong to her past. She had no connection with the Eleventh Cavalry.

And so, while these men might haunt the ruins and mimic the dead, they were real in some way. If only she could focus her mind. There had been no way to directly confront their whispering and silhouettes on her tent and their slouching through the mist, but she could dispute their unreality. They were hunting her. She was hiding from them, whoever they were. And Duncan had probably sacrificed himself to shield her. All for nothing. They were bound to find her.

The real contest was not with them anyway, but with herself. She had no hope of defeating them. There were too many of them, and this was their territory, and she was fading fast. She couldn't beat them, but she could make sure they didn't beat her. Just holding on to her sanity would be a triumph.

The line of men—looters, lunatics, or manhunters caught in a Vietnam loop—worked diagonally across the overgrown square. They moved like a patrol, spaced in a line, taking their time. They had nearly reached the far trees when the ambush caught them.

At first, Molly couldn't understand what was going on. It looked more like a squall striking the grasses than an attack. Some havoc burst from the trees. Limbs bent, leaves parted. Birds sprang from their perches and filled the air with their colors and cries. From three sides, furrows sliced through the green surface of grass.

Peeking down from the edge of the tower, Molly saw shapes, degraded shapes, pieces of creatures that were even less than these pieces of men. They were human in theory. Human in outline. But in fact she couldn't be sure she was seeing anything at all.

They seemed to be part animal, part glass—or water—as they streamed out from the trees. They cast shadows like the shadows of fish, amorphous and distorted, muscling in the green light. She saw their weapons better than she did them, not bits and pieces of the Blackhorse arsenal, but ancient things, swords and axes scything through the grass, and they appeared to almost move of their own will, racing for the kill. The forest shapes converged on the patrol.

The battle had no real form. It was over in seconds. The grass thrashed in a furious centrifuge of shapes. It bent and whipped and pressed flat. She heard a howl crowded with men shouting. Then the whole aspect of the violence lifted. It was as if the wind had touched down and gone on. The men, the suggestions of them, vanished.

She didn't move for another minute. Something had happened down there, something elemental, a microburst or a dervish. The grass lay torn and flattened in a whorl, and that howl echoed another few seconds from the forest as if a battle of spirits was swirling within the fortress walls. Then the shadows went still again. The birds returned to the trees.

She could have descended at that point. Her pursuers were gone, or seemed to be. But where would she go? Her legs were going on her. Even if she made it back to the terminus, there was nothing left but ashes.

On her hands and knees, Molly resumed her climb. She was terrified of losing the last of her strength out here in the open. She wanted enclosure. She wanted sanctuary. A fairy-tale tower where the bad men could not find her.

She had to whisper her way to the top: "A little more." She had never before felt burdened by her flesh like this.

She reached the summit deck and peered over. The city wheeled in circles down there, a mandala of ruins and emerald grass.

Even as she looked, her hunters reappeared. The patrol emerged from the mouth of one of the great avenues. A man's shoulder and arm surfaced, then sank into the grass. A head appeared, scouting right and left before ducking behind a pillar. A man's hunched back appeared.

They were repeating themselves. Endlessly recycling. Ghosts, she thought, after all.

43.

The infection had spread into her wing muscles. The walls of her chest and shoulder and back were burning with strep. And yet she managed to stand and face the door.

The blood rushed from her head. She was patient. The spinning stopped.

The stone Amazon that had toppled from her niche was now restored to her place. Molly couldn't even tell which of the twins had been broken. Even the doorway looked restored. The sagging lintel stood level. The red columns seemed brighter, the moss scrubbed away.

"Duncan?" she whispered into the room. Not a whisper back.

She stepped inside. The statue women let her pass, and the room was just as she had left it. Where she and Duncan and Kleat had peeled back the carpet of leaves, the floor still broadcast its black SOS. Brass shells littered the stones. The aperture in the roof was pouring green light onto the far wall. She was alone with the remains of the Buddhas.

Their desecration didn't shock her this morning. She understood now. The soldiers had seen through the cosmic smiles. The city's tranquility was a lie. Beneath its facade, the fortress sanctuary was a deadly trap. In chewing off the Buddha faces with their gunfire, the men had been erasing a terrible deceit.

"Duncan?" Sweat seeped down her spine. It was cold.

Her grip slipped on the doorway. She caught her balance. She asserted it. Once down, there would be no getting up.

She scanned the room for a friendly patch of ground. The monkey hands reached out from the fire pit. The gutted radio set stood along one wall. War junk and dank shadows crowded the corners. Animal dung plastered the boxes and cans.

This was important stuff, the choice of her bed. It was her Kodak moment: Someday, a hundred years from now, another expedition would ascend this tower. And while they weren't going to find any Sleeping Beauty, she could at least compose her mortal remains without monkey hands and garbage for her backdrop.

Her eyes went to the chopped, riddled Buddhas. In and out of focus, they seemed to float in the green light, luminous and detached from the world, separate from one another, even separate from the wall. For all the savagery that had been heaped upon them, for all the bloodshed they had presided over in this spirit city, they still promised peace. Now if only some of their karma would rub off, maybe she could come back as a complete human being next go-round.

She set off across the hall, shuffling through the bullet shells and beetles. The Buddhas retreated into their niches. Ravaged by bullets, they looked more like lepers than deities, like victims, not masters of the universe.

Molly glanced up at the canopy. No sun, not even a single beam? It would have been so sweet to curl up on a spot of heated stone.

She arrived at the knife in the wall.

The knife was all wrong, a spiteful thing. Would they think she had stabbed the Buddhas? Kleat had grappled with it, and she knew the blade was jammed, but she gripped the handle anyway.

The blade slid free.

The wind must have moved the canopy, which had moved the trees, which had moved the stones. The joints had opened. The knife practically fell from the seam. The weight of it, all eight ounces, yanked her arm down. It dropped from her fingers.

She stared dumbly at the thing lying at her feet. The blade was scratched and mottled, a name engraved above the blood gutter. With the next storm, the stones would have shifted again and bound the knife. She'd happened along at the right moment, that was all.

A string of saliva dangled from her mouth. Lovely. In a stupor, she lifted her eyes.

"God," she whispered, and lurched backward.

The statues were changing.

Their pox of bullet holes was smoothing over. The Buddhas were regaining their stone flesh.

It had to be a trick of the light. Clouds were crossing above the canopy. Whales passing through the deep.

She closed her eyes and staggered, fetching up against the wall. Now was not the time to be seeing things. Her mother had died from hallucinations. And yet she could feel the wall against her palms and cheek, and the cool, gutted surface really was mending itself.

She pushed away from the wall.

Molly had spent a lifetime learning the rules. They allowed for yetis and unicorns, so long as you winked. They allowed for lost cities to float out like dust bunnies. You could hold heaven as a hope. But the rules did not allow for this.

The wall—the entire length of stone and statues—was healing. The bullet tracks dissolved. Thirteen smiles glimmered into being, so many Cheshire cats paying a visit. Faces formed around the smiles.

A vine tripped her. She might have blacked out. She smiled up at the fever dream. The metamorphosis streamed on.

At the far end of the wall, where the facade had been blasted, rubble began to reassemble. Lying there, Molly could not find words to describe it. Pieces of stone did not fly through the air and into place. Somehow the wall drew the destruction back into time.

She went with it, a pleasant delirium. As fissures sealed and lead slugs pattered to the floor like hailstones and the leprous figures became beautiful again, she forgot her pain and exhaustion. She all but vanished from her own mind.

Consciousness came and went.

Perhaps the wall had never been destroyed. Perhaps she had imagined it. Or again, that wondrous thought, maybe the ruins had imagined her. If the stones could command a people to shape them into a city, if the city were nothing more than an instrument for monsoon songs, why couldn't she be that little girl carved among all the other stories? What else was humankind—all life—but a figment of a stone spinning through time?

Her eyes opened. The wall was whole again. The war was gone. It had never been. How righteous, she thought. How stoned-out cosmic cool.

She rolled onto her back, a change of view. Parrots flickered overhead like bits of flame. A gecko eased in along the skylight. A few monkeys perched along the rim. Like this, in unconditional surrender, her mother must have watched the snow descend.

44.

The afternoon thunder arrived. It came up from the earth, not down from the sky. It was still too far away to hear. The vibrations buzzed against her skull. She remembered sitting in a restaurant along a river long ago and how the sunset had trembled. *Let it rain,* she thought. *Come what may.* She was finding her happy zone.

But then she saw the soldier. He was sitting at the far end of the wall where the rubble had cleared itself away. Thirty years ago someone had buried him violently, with plastic explosives. Now he was bared to the world.

His legs and boots were crushed flat. The rest of his skeleton rested precariously upright. It must have been hot the day he died. He had no shirt. But like Kleat, expecting trouble, he wore a flak jacket.

She knew him, or at least of him, not his name or his face, but his legend. The fragments of the journal had spoken of him. He was their commander. Here was the man who had gotten them lost and found them sanctuary, and doomed them by preserving them among the ruins. This was the tower of his tomb.

She dragged herself closer, a creature of her curiosity.

Their discoverers would link them, a man and a woman, a soldier and a civilian, two Americans caught in a faraway land. Never mind that she was as old as he was dead. Details. The story was too good. They were as good as married, a Romeo and Juliet for the ages.

The rubble had flattened his left hand in his lap. It looked like some complicated fossil. He wore a wedding band.

His skull leaned on his chest as if he were in mid-siesta. His sole wound, it seemed, was a crease along the temporal bone. The bullet had not pierced his skull. It might only have stunned him, in which case he'd been buried alive.

Molly touched nothing. The skeleton looked like a house of cards ready to fall. She lay beside him, resting her head, hunting for clues.

This was not another of their suicides. For one thing, there were more certain ways to put a bullet into yourself, and the bone was not scorched or powder burned. Also there was no weapon lying close at hand. And again, the bullet did not seem to have been a killing shot. Someone had shot him, and then buried him. Her eyes wandered higher. All in front of the Buddhas.

How had it gone?

He had caught them in the act of savaging the statues and gotten between their weapons and the wall. The journal fragments whispered to her. *It's not true he loved the city more than us. He was only trying to preserve us all.* They had looted the city, or part of it, planting that terra-cotta head on their exhaust pipe. Had he tried to protect the Buddhas? Had someone kept on firing?

There was just one wound that she could see. She couldn't find any bullet holes or bloodstains on the flattened fatigues or the flak jacket. Just the single shot along his head. Just one shooter.

Had it been an accident or an execution? Had they tried to revive him, or panicked and given him up for dead? No matter. They had blasted this section of the wall and hidden their deed under a ton of debris. That much was no accident. Someone had deliberately tried to conceal the evidence. The body, living or dead, damned them. And so they had shut it from sight.

The journal spoke of one man whipping up the mutiny. But once the commander was killed, the rebels had realized their fall from grace. At least the journal writer had expressed repentance.

The story took shape, a murder. The soldiers had driven the shooter from their midst . . . like Cain, the killer of his brother. He was the same man who had led them in mutiny. Molly knew it. The murder had shocked the rebels from their rebellion. They had scattered after the killing. The mutiny had dispersed.

The shooter had set off on foot, *west of Eden.* Did that mean he'd fled toward Phnom Penh or gone out the western entry, or was it simply the writer carrying through his biblical strand? No matter. Somewhere out there the killer had met his end. The rest of the Blackhorse men had stayed in the city, languishing, divided, hungry and diseased, drifting into madness, and, like her, too weak to leave, dying in animal niches among the ruins.

End of story. Everyone, it seemed, had paid for the sin. In a way, the commander was lucky. Of all the bones she'd seen in the city, his had come the closest to a permanent burial.

But the knife still bothered her. It could have been their way of marking the grave, but why mark a grave you wanted no one to find? No, she thought. Someone had added it to the wall as a finishing touch, after the shooting, after the killing, probably after the blast, a final piece of rage.

It was the shooter's knife. Molly knew it instinctively. He had stabbed the wall.

Thunder rippled far away. A breeze stirred the canopy.

She clutched her cold, fiery self.

"Now what?" she whispered to the bones.

It didn't seem right. They'd brought her here. *Her.* Luke had said so. But all this way for what? This was just another dead soldier from a dead war. Vietnam had nothing to do with her. She had a life. For a little while longer.

The trees moved. The floor shivered, or she did. It was like a dock that seems to move because the water is moving. The big river was waiting.

"Not yet," she said. *Where's my circle?* She deserved that much. A bit more beta. Some raw connect. Her missing link.

The tremors upset the careful construct of his bones. With the clatter of sticks and empty spools, the soldier spilled to pieces. The skull landed facing her, mouth parted, his jaw still wired in place with tendons. Weighted with vertebrae and ribs, the flak jacket tumbled into her hands. It was a simple matter to pluck the dog tag from inside.

The name was perfectly legible.

She should have known.

" 'O'Brian,' " she read aloud to him, " 'Duncan A.' "

The jaw stayed frozen, half open, caught in the act.

There was his date of birth. She made the calculation. He'd been shot on his birthday, or shortly after, twenty-one years old. She'd fallen for a younger man.

Molly cocked her head to see the skull.

His features emerged clearly now. It was almost like lying with him in her tent, watching his young face while he slept. There was his thick brow and his thin cheekbones, and the white teeth he'd brushed so religiously. She purged from her mind the poor creature dwindling in the rain last night, losing his long hair in her fingers, that phantom crumbling beneath her doubts. She closed her eyes and saw Duncan at dawn in the blue-green light.

Had he suspected his flesh encased a ghost? She recalled his briefcase full of tidbits and his confusion when she'd confronted him. And his odd reluctance to follow Luke to these ruins.

It wasn't that he'd tried to fool anyone. Duncan had been as truthful as he could remember, in fragments, with an Ace comb in his pocket, just a spirit borrowing himself together, the same as Luke and all the rest.

When had he escaped from the ruins? Obviously, Luke had been sent to fetch his restless brother back to the source, back to the underworld. But why bring her?

She had daydreamed about taking Duncan home with her. Over these last few days, that seemed to be what she was meant to do, to usher him back into America. But he'd turned the tables on her, not knowing himself. He'd brought her home with him.

More chills, more salty sweat. Her eyes rolled back in her head. Darkness threatened. Molly fought back to consciousness.

What were the laws of this place? The rain would purify them. Her bones would mingle with his. But then?

"Duncan?" she called to his spirit. Had he joined that never-ending patrol around the tower? Or flung himself up into the canopy? "Where are you?"

Suddenly she was afraid. She wanted reassurance. She had no answers, only more questions. Would she go out into the world with him now, or would they stay to wander through the ruins? How did it work? Would they take on disguises? Enter cities? Cross the oceans? Haunt the future? They could live a thousand lives. But in giving birth to themselves, would they forget their anchoring bones? Would they come to forget each other?

They had voices. Where was his voice? "Duncan?"

The flak jacket had fallen open. There was something in the pocket, an edge of plastic. She tugged and it was a sandwich bag containing a snapshot.

The photo was dog-eared and harshly faded. Even without the "Dec. '69" penned on the back, Molly knew the era by its chemicals and paper. She could have guessed the basic image. It was straight out of a war movie, the girlfriend picture.

Wife, she amended, glancing at Duncan's wedding band. The young woman had one, too. She was flashing it proudly, with bravura, grinning at their in-joke. Six or seven months pregnant, she was dressed—barely—in a polka-dot bikini. She'd snagged her man in the nick of time.

Molly laid her head on the flak jacket and studied the photo, sliding into its story. Duncan had taken it. They were on a beach. It was Hawaii, in the middle of his deployment to Vietnam. She wore a flower lei. Molly liked her. She was audacious, ripe to bursting, and wildly in love with the photographer. A real firecracker.

She did the math. Duncan had been twenty. A few months later, he had become a dad. A few months after that, he had faced his killer in this city of the dead.

Her face eluded Molly. The girl's hair cast a shadow, and that bulging tummy drew the eye. But that wasn't the difficulty. The face made no sense to her.

The girl had a hundred-watt smile and a sloe-eyed green gaze. A pair of rose-colored sunglasses perched on top of her bushy black hair. The humidity had blown her pixie cut to chaos. Molly could relate. Atomic hair, she called it. That's why she'd chopped hers short with surgical scissors. Black Irish did not go well with the tropics.

Molly stopped. The air leaked from her.

She was looking at herself.

She refused it. She had to be projecting. The fever was scrambling her mind. The ruins were stealing into her the way she had stolen into them, in darkness and fog. One step deeper, it seemed, and she might disintegrate.

The picture blurred, then sharpened. She struggled against it, then with it, finding her way into the impossible image. How could something so familiar feel so alien? The eyes, their shape, the nose, the smile, the hair . . . there was no denying it. That was her face in the photo.

Molly glanced at Duncan's silent bones, trying to fathom it. What did it mean? Had she died and wandered and finally been led to her lover? Could she be her own orphan?

A drop of rain fell from the trees. Not yet, she commanded the sky. There were facts. She recalled them, an obituary in the *Denver Post* dated 1971, a coroner's report, a grave marker among the wildflowers.

She fumbled at the belt holding her passport wallet and ripped open the Velcro and drew out her relic, a driver's license issued in 1967 in Bay City, Texas, to one Jane Drake, age eighteen. The black hair was long and ironed straight, Cher style. The eyes were green and full of blue sky, as if all her life lay ahead of her. It was the same face Molly saw in her mirror, though younger and sweeter and smooth. But it was also the face in a photo buried next to the heart of a dead soldier. How could that be?

Rain began leaking from the canopy. A drop splashed across the photo. Molly raced on.

Once upon a time, she tried desperately. Once upon a time, a war bride lost her one true love. When he went missing, she went missing, too. She wandered off into madness, into the midst of mountain gypsies, and finally, into the mouth of a blizzard. That much was true. Jane Drake had died in a roofless miner's shack in a blizzard on Boreas Pass.

Had she returned from the dead then, one ghost hunting another?

She searched her memory for Hawaii and young Duncan and the diamond on that finger, and the miner's cabin and the blizzard. She tried to feel them as memories of her own, but none of it came to her.

The raindrops splattered across the photo. The image was melting before her eyes.

Hurry, she thought. Today was for keeps. Darkness was her last call. The forest would render her to bones. She would join the wandering spirits and never know more than her name.

Molly blinked away the rain. Put away the ghosts. She was too full of ghosts. *Trust your eyes.* What was she missing?

She brought the snapshot closer. She looked at the tipped skull.

Here stood a young woman in her glory.

Here lay the bones that had broken her heart.

And—it was suddenly so obvious—in that womb slept their daughter, Molly.

The muscles in her face relaxed. The labyrinth unraveled around her. No longer a stranger to herself, she let the city take her over. Its canals became her arteries. Its stone told her story. Her tangled threads were simply paths among the ruins.

Had her mother sent her, Molly wondered, or had her father drawn her? Did it matter? They had never meant to lose her. They'd done the best they could, but the world had taken them away, the soldier in war, his bride in sorrow. She only needed to forgive them for their love. She leaned the photo among the bones. The rain ran from her eyes.

45.

Molly took turns. She traded bodies with the gecko clinging to the wall, and prowled a Buddha's palm. She hitchhiked on a parrot perching in the branches. She became a butterfly hiding from the rain. She spied on herself down there.

She looked like one of *MacBeth*'s witches haunting the edges of a battlefield, knife in hand. Her bloodshot eyes burned too bright in that mask of ash and smoke.

The thunder was majestic. She'd crawled to the knife. It looked like an Iron Age thing in her fist.

She knew the Blackhorse missing now. Even the bones still hidden in the forest had recited their names to her. They were all present and accounted for, even their ninth man, the rebel leader who had shot her father. His name was on the blade, "John Kleat."

There was no telling where Kleat had traveled after they'd banished him from the city. She understood his hatred of the Khmer Rouge better than he did now. His bones remembered what he did not, the enemy who had slit his throat. Maybe someday he would rise up from the black water in the *barays,* and escape these walls, and resume the search for his own remains. Maybe someday he would find the nonexistent brother who was himself buried in the hills or in a paddy or thrown down a well. More likely he would forget and join the creatures in the mud.

They were driven by urges, these unburied dead. Where memory began and ended, she couldn't say. They clung to their names, that much was certain, speaking them over and over. Also, no matter what they had become, they could not escape who they had been. She had been right to believe in Duncan's goodness. Wherever he was.

"Duncan," she called out.

She drifted in and out of delirium. The rain fell in slow strings. Now she was the gecko, now a butterfly, now a woman.

"Molly," she heard. *Let me sleep.*

They kept calling her name from the forest, the birds and monkeys and ghost warriors, enunciating all the varieties she might answer to, Molly, Maw-li, Moll-lee. They were helping her remember her name in the next life. That was her hope, that they would be kind and welcoming. On the other hand, they had summoned her to carry home her father and them, and she had failed. There was no reason to believe in their mercy.

She caught herself whispering a Hail Mary to the Buddhas.

"Molly." The voice was just outside the door, and it wasn't Duncan's.

She lay still. Her heart galloped. If only Duncan would come.

The doorway darkened. He was an emaciated thing made of rags. Part man, part bone, he entered.

She closed her eyes. The tip of bone ticked closer.

"Molly," he commanded.

He'd come for her eyes, not to take, but to give. She belonged to the city now. Would he use a spoon? What shade of green would her jade eyes be?

Please, she thought.

He heard her whisper, or maybe smelled it. "You're alive," he said.

She opened her eyes. His leg was a stick, not bone, lashed to his thigh with vines.

She thrust with the knife. It was a feeble act, and he stepped on her wrist and took the knife away. She knew better than to fight. Lie still. Let him do it.

"Lie still," the ghost said.

He stood overhead like a butcher sizing up meat. She searched for his eyes to connect with, but the rain smeared her vision.

She wanted to let go, to cast herself into the animals and scamper and fly and slither away. But suddenly she was anchored in her flesh. She couldn't leave her body. She struggled, a small motion, a whimper.

He tugged at a pouch. A dozen or more round jade balls spilled onto the floor. The eyes rolled against her cheek, and she moaned and looked away. The city was preparing her, last rites, its funeral mask. But she was still alive, or had she passed to the other side? How to tell?

"Don't fight," he said. "You're having a dream. Can you hear me?"

He lifted her shirt and looked underneath. She squeezed her eyes shut and the rain wept down her face. Would the eyes hurt as much going in as coming out? How loud would she scream? Where were her gecko and butterfly?

"Drink." He held a leaf to her mouth as a funnel. The rain trickled onto her tongue. A kindness before the maiming.

"You're leaving," said the voice. "Take the others with you. They no longer belong. Do you understand?"

"No." They were dead. How could they not belong? Limbo had borders?

"They were lost and the city took them in." The voice chased like water through her mind. "It gave them shelter from the storm. Why them, barbarians? Compassion, perhaps, or God's curiosity, I can't say. The city took them in as children. It gave them sight. It showed them the path. But they refused to see. Do you know how many great warriors came and laid aside their armor here? Not these men. All except Duncan. He saw something, I think."

"They were only boys," she whispered to the rain.

"Blind they came"—the words were strict—"now blind they go. I've gone to each of them and taken back the dream."

On one knee, he worked Kleat's knife. She felt the steel blade worm along her breastbone. With a tug, he split the shirt and peeled it away like skin. One leg at a time, he sawed away her pants.

She was so afraid. But, oh, the rain felt glorious. It bathed her burning flesh. It warmed her like a blanket. Her lips opened to the water.

His hands began moving over her, working away. She didn't dare look. For all she knew, he had opened her and was squatting to one side devouring her organs. Were the monkeys gathering for their share?

He pried open her eyelids and rain crashed into her brain. *My eyes,* she thought. The windows of her soul. "Please don't," she said.

"A little while longer," the ghost soothed her, plucking away leeches. "Everything will be clear."

Then he propped twigs under a large leaf to make a lean-to over her face and draped big banana leaves over her body and limbs. She was sinking.

"You're free. You freed them." He held up one of the jade balls. "But these stay. Take nothing but the bones. Forget the city. Remember the dream."

Blackness rose up.

She returned to consciousness just as he was leaving. The stick leg sounded like a clock walking away. Then she smelled the rich fragrance. Under another leaf, he had planted a handful of incense sticks. Slow smoke leaked up to the Buddhas. Only then did she recognize him.

"Samnang?" she whispered.

But he was gone, into the ruins.

46.

When she woke again, the rain was clattering on her shield of leaves and the incense sticks were ash. Her bloodstained clothes lay in a heap. She was naked and encased in black mud. Night was falling.

They were shouting her name again. They were everywhere out there. Their voices were climbing the stairs. *Duncan,* she prayed. *Save me.*

A light flashed in the doorway. Dark forms clustered behind it. More lights appeared. They wore sheets like Halloween ghosts. Ponchos, she realized.

"Molly?" The voice boomed through the room.

She watched from under her chrysalis of leaves, perfectly invisible to them.

"She's not up here," one said.

"But he told us a tower."

"It's empty. We got the wrong tower."

"We should have gotten him to draw a map of the place."

"Too late now. It's a miracle he lasted as long as he did. You saw what he looked like when they brought him in. Gut shot, bleeding out. The fuckers even took his leg."

"What the hell did she get mixed up with?"

"Bad company, man."

One had a cough. Others were winded. Their voices thundered, as if her last few days had passed in whispers.

The room lit green with distant lightning, then went dark. The sky rumbled.

"We don't belong here," a voice complained. "The captain gave us two hours. Night's coming. You could get lost in this place."

"Sam said she'd be here. Here's the city. Here's the tower."

"That was yesterday. She could have gone anywhere since then. We'll try again in the morning. It will look different in the morning."

It was like swimming up from a deep recess. Sam? The captain? She knew these voices. RE-1 had come for her.

And now they were leaving. Molly tried to speak. But her tongue had turned to leather. There wasn't enough breath in her lungs for even one word.

Their lights twitched away. It was over. She would never last the night.

But then the bones sighed beside her. "Boys," they whispered. *Duncan.* His wisp of a spirit.

Somehow they heard through the thunder. It caught them. Their lights swung around. One splashed on the skull.

"Christ, there's another one. And a flak jacket, look."

They came across the room in a siege of boots and the *whip-whip* of wet plastic and the one man coughing. One stumbled against her leg.

"There's something here."

They converged in a circle and stripped away the leaves, staring down at her from the caverns of their ponchos, faceless, awed. Even in the rain, she could smell them. That struck her, too, the smell of living men.

"Is she still alive?"

"What did she do to herself?"

One bent to her. "Molly? Can you hear me? It's us."

"What's she staring at?"

"We've got you now, Molly."

Voices like thunder. They filled the room. "Get a litter. Bring ropes. Tell the captain."

Shedding their ponchos to hold as a roof over her, they took on familiar faces, the hunters of the dead. As they pulled off their shirts, they made themselves half naked to warm her.

They couldn't seem to hear the hymn of the city. She looked into the rain, listening as it faded. It was harder and harder to hear for the clatter of gear and the thud of feet and the creaking of pack straps. Men were shouting down from the tower's ledge, calling out the good news.

So faithful, she thought, these warriors sent to harrow the underworld and unshackle every last American soldier's soul. Year after year they hunted the bones, even as the fragments drifted deeper, towed under by insects, roots, and the shifting earth. In the end their quest would falter. The worm would win.

But for the moment it was like a great battle had been fought, and they had carried the day. In finding one alive, even if she did not belong to them, the soldiers could put death aside. They could dream of themselves tonight, free to believe they were more than a dream of the ruins.

ACKNOWLEDGMENTS

The Reckoning takes history for its haunted house. In order to construct and inhabit it credibly, I sought out men and women who have lived various aspects of that history. They will be the first to notice my poetic license with procedures, details, and events. Any and all inaccuracies are mine alone.

I wish to thank army lieutenant colonel Gerald O'Hara, army chief warrant officer Tom Monroe, and retired marine master sergeant Joe Patterson of Joint POW/MIA Accounting Command (JPAC). They patiently detailed the grueling search and recovery process that seeks a full accounting of American soldiers who went missing in foreign wars, particularly in Vietnam, Làos, and Cambodia. Because my story takes place in 2000, three years before JPAC was formed, I refer to its two earlier sister entities, Joint Task Force-Full Accounting (JTF-FA) and the Central Identification Lab in Hawaii (CILHI).

I am indebted to Earl Swift, a staff writer for *The Virginian-Pilot*. Though he was writing his own book about the military's forensic quest (*Where They Lay*, a superb nonfiction account), this generous man did not hesitate to give me several hours of civilian perspective drawn from his trips with JPAC.

Many thanks to retired army colonel Charles L. Schmidt for enduring my questions and offering his advice about the 11th Armored Cavalry in Vietnam. Thanks as well to Geof Childs, whom

I peppered with spontaneous phone calls about the military and Vietnam.

I am especially grateful to Sophea Chum Satterwhite for helping guide me through Cambodian customs, language, and history. My other guide through Cambodia was Melissa Ward, the bravest person I know, who led me through the devastation and recovery during her assignment with UNTAC in 1993. Wherever in the world you are, Tiger Lady, thank you. And keep your head down.

I owe deep thanks to my editors Emily Bestler and Mitchell Ivers, who refused to leave me lost among my ruins. And with humble appreciation, my thanks to Sloan Harris, my agent and literary sensei.

Finally, Barbara and Helena, you are the blessings I count each day.